THE RUSSIAN HILL MURDERS

**Center Point
Large Print**

**This Large Print Book carries the
Seal of Approval of N.A.V.H.**

THE RUSSIAN HILL MURDERS

SHIRLEY TALLMAN

Center Point Publishing
Thorndike, Maine

This Center Point Large Print edition
is published in the year 2006 by arrangement with
St. Martin's Press.

Copyright © 2005 by Shirley Tallman.

The text of this Large Print edition is unabridged. In other
aspects, this book may vary from the original edition. Printed in
Thailand. Set in 16-point Times New Roman type.

ISBN 1-58547-694-3

Library of Congress Cataloging-in-Publication Data

Tallman, Shirley.
   The Russian Hill murders / Shirley Tallman.--Center Point large print ed.
      p. cm.
   ISBN 1-58547-694-3 (lib. bdg. : alk. paper)
   1. Women lawyers--Fiction. 2. Russian Hill (San Francisco, Calif.)--Fiction. 3. San
Francisco (Calif.)--Fiction. 4. Attorney and client--Fiction. 5. Chinese Americans--Fiction.
6. Large type books. I. Title.

PS3620.A54R87 2005b
813'.6--dc22

                                                                            2005019035

To Karen,
with love, respect, and admiration.
And to my husband, Bob, and my good friend H. P.
for all their love and support.

ACKNOWLEDGMENTS

To my writing buddies, Joanne Wendt and Nancy Hersage, for critiquing this manuscript before it went off to New York. I can't thank you both enough for your patience and dedication to Sarah, and to me.

As always, my gratitude to the California State Bar Association for putting up with a barrage of questions, and to the California Historical Society for helping me to envision and re-create Sarah's world.

Also, many thanks to Tami Suzuki, of the San Francisco Public Library, for her valuable help in gathering research material for this novel.

CHAPTER ONE

I t was not my idea to attend the charity dinner. True, it was a worthy cause, but the past weeks at the law firm I'd been so elated to join just months earlier had been mind-numbing. In truth, I was becoming more disillusioned with Shepard, Shepard, McNaughton and Hall with each passing day. Frankly I was in no mood to socialize.

My mother, Elizabeth Woolson, however, is nothing if not persistent. Eventually she wore down my resolve until I agreed to accompany my parents, my brother Charles and his wife, Celia, to the dinner. Mama also prevailed on the matter of my costume, insisting I wear the violet gown she'd had made for my brother Frederick's entrée into the world of politics—a gown I still considered too décolleté for my taste. Moreover, I couldn't look at the frock without remembering the murder that had occurred the night I'd worn it, a crime that had catapulted me into the grisly Nob Hill killings. Believe me, if I'd had any inkling that the occasion of its second wearing would have an equally chilling impact on my life, I would have burned the wretched thing on the spot!

On the matter of an escort I drew a firm line. Nothing could persuade me to accept the company of the latest bachelor to catch Mama's desperate eye. Her current prospect was a widowed dentist, the father of six children, five of whom still lived at home. I considered my life complicated enough without adding an elderly husband and a horde of motherless offspring to the mix.

In the end I found myself—blessedly unencumbered by the aforementioned dentist—in one of the most unusual houses on Russian Hill. I had never met our hosts, Caroline and Leonard Godfrey, but I knew them to be prominent members of San Francisco Society. Mrs. Godfrey was noted for her work on behalf of the city's poor and disadvantaged. Her husband, Leonard, was one of the city's most shrewd entrepreneurs. It was an open secret that he was the guiding, if often hidden, force behind many of the city's major corporations.

The Godfreys' home was the subject of much gossip. Three years earlier, it had joined a small group of exclusive mansions gracing the top of the summit. Russian Hill—said to have been named after Russian sailors who had been buried there before the California gold rush—was slowly beginning to compete with Nob Hill, its pompous neighbor to the south. The Godfrey residence, with its sharp angles and numerous windows, was considered by many to be too avant-garde. Indeed, some people went so far as to brand it "Godfrey's Folly." Personally, I found the home a refreshing change from the pretentious bastions constructed by other wealthy San Franciscans. But then my own architectural tastes are also viewed as unorthodox.

I had not circulated long among the glittering guests before I began to regret giving in to Mama's pressure to attend tonight's soiree. When I'd had all I could take of Paris fashions, society romances and social indiscretions, I sought refuge in an alcove featuring a large bay window. Peering through a strategically placed spyglass, I was able to make out much of the city below—including Portsmouth Square, the site of Joseph Shepard's law firm. As one of the first female attorneys in California, I'd been accepted as a junior associate in this establishment with the greatest reluctance. Since then, the entire cadre of senior partners had banded together in an effort to drive me out of their firm, as well as their lives!

Not only had I obtained my job through what they termed "female subterfuge," but I'd had the gall to "steal" (their word, not mine) one of the firm's prized clients. Adding insult to injury, I'd solved a series of gruesome murders, resulting in a glut of unwelcome publicity for my employers.

Ironically, it was this very newspaper exposure that made it impossible for the partners to come right out and fire me. On the other hand, if I could be "persuaded" to leave of my own accord, they'd be spared public reproach. This misplaced strategy, of course, merely caused me to dig in my heels and fight to hold on to my position. Still, I'd begun to wonder how long I'd be able to put up with their childish machinations.

"It's a beautiful city, isn't it?"

I was startled out of my thoughts to find a man in his mid thirties standing behind me. He stood an inch or two over six feet, and despite my bleak mood, part of my brain registered that this was possibly the most handsome man I'd ever seen. He wore a perfectly tailored black tuxedo, which couldn't conceal impressively broad shoulders and a narrow waist. His hair was thick and nearly shoulder length, an ebony mane that waved back from a tanned face.

As if amused by my frank appraisal, he smiled, and I was startled to feel my pulse leap. Good Lord, I thought, amazed he'd been able to elicit such an absurd reaction from me, an avowed spinster. With effort, I composed my face into what I hoped was a disapproving frown, only to be rewarded with an even broader smile.

"I apologize for my poor manners, Miss Woolson," he said in a voice that was deep and—forgive me for the romantic if fitting analogy—smooth as aged brandy. "I'm Pierce Godfrey. Leonard Godfrey is my brother."

I accepted his proffered hand and was surprised to find the skin rougher than I'd expected. His careful appearance suggested he might be something of a dandy.

"You have me at a disadvantage, Mr. Godfrey," I said more sharply than was civil. "How is it that you know my name?"

His eyes gleamed, but I couldn't decide if it was amusement or mockery. My temper flared; I had no patience for flirting or playing silly games, even with a man as attractive as Pierce Godfrey.

"You haven't answered my question," I said pointedly.

To my annoyance, he laughed out loud. "You are a woman who speaks her mind, Sarah Woolson. I'll be equally candid. I quizzed my sister-in-law when you arrived." He regarded me speculatively. "She tells me you're an attorney."

"Yes, I am." I studied him closely, on the lookout for sarcasm or veiled disdain for my vocation, a not uncommon reaction from men. I was surprised and, yes, I admit it, disconcerted when I could detect none. The man struck me as too smooth, too in control. I suppose I was searching for some imperfection to mar that faultless demeanor.

"I remember now," he said. "I saw your name in the newspapers a few months back. Something to do with a murder? Actually, several murders, as I recall."

"The press is prone to exaggeration, Mr. Godfrey. You mustn't believe everything you read."

"No." He drew out the word in a velvet voice, a tone at odds with the dark blue eyes searching my face with rude curiosity. "Now that I've met you, though, I rather think there was more truth than fiction to the newspaper articles."

I started to chastise him for this unwarranted assumption, when our hostess walked toward us. An attractive woman in her early forties, Caroline Godfrey had a full, sensuous mouth and smoky gray eyes that looked out upon the world with an unmistakable air of superiority. The low-cut bodice and tightly cinched waist of her scarlet gown set off her striking figure to excellent advantage.

Perhaps it was because of her stunning beauty that I was taken aback by the look of raw hostility she directed at my companion. Focused solely on him, she hadn't yet seen me, so I quickly stepped out from behind his tall figure.

"Miss Woolson," she said, looking surprised and not altogether pleased by my sudden appearance. "I'm delighted you could come." After a perfunctory smile, she turned to her brother-in-law. "Leonard requires your assistance in the parlor, Pierce. Everyone is gathering there now."

He gave her a measured look, then offered me his arm. "Will you permit me to escort you, Miss Woolson?"

Mrs. Godfrey's smile turned sour as she watched me accept her brother-in-law's arm. I felt her eyes following us as he silently led me from the alcove.

When we reached the parlor, Pierce excused himself and went to stand with his brother. A moment later, Caroline Godfrey joined them, her smile cordial and welcoming now, as she looked out over her distinguished guests. She spoke for several minutes, describing the new Women and Children's Hospital we were here to support. When she announced with perfect calm that tonight's goal was to raise one hundred thousand dollars for the project, I felt certain she was joking. To my surprise, the rest of the company took this startling pronouncement in stride. It was as if Mrs. Godfrey had laid down a challenge to their largesse, or perhaps, I thought a bit cynically, to their egos.

Pledging began. One after the other, huge amounts of money were called out, each pledge more munificent than the one that preceded it. Everyone seemed swept up in the excitement, including Mama and Papa. I even found myself calling out a sum larger than I could comfortably afford. Still, when it was finally over and Mrs. Godfrey announced we were very near our goal, I was proud to have played my own small part in the effort.

As guests broke off into small groups and footmen circulated, offering champagne, I went in search of my parents. I found them talking with Papa's closest friend and fellow jurist, Judge Tobias Barlow, a slightly over-weight, pleasant man ten years my father's junior. With Judge Barlow was his wife, Margaret—an attractive woman who worked with my mother on charitable projects—and Margaret's mother, Adelina French. I was startled by the remarkable resemblance between mother and daughter: both tall and slender with gold-brown hair and sparkling green eyes. Indeed, the two women might well have been sisters. I knew Adelina had made her home with her daughter and son-in-law since the death of her husband, Nigel French, and was a keen worker for the new hospital.

Also with the group were two men I'd never met. Mrs. Barlow introduced the more striking of the two as the Reverend Nicholas Prescott, a friend visiting from back east. Prescott, who appeared to be in his early fifties, was tall and muscularly slender beneath his dark suit and starched clerical collar. His full head of dark brown hair was sprinkled with just the right amount of gray to appear distinguished. He possessed an easy, unassuming manner, and I noted a gleam of intelligence and good humor in his clear brown eyes. With a wide smile, Reverend Prescott shook my hand, his attention so riveted on me that I might have been the only person in the room.

Mrs. Barlow introduced the second stranger as Lucius Arlen, the accountant who had been hired by the board to handle the new hospital's finances. Arlen was a heavy-set, stolid man in his late fifties, with a fidgety manner and a disconcerting habit of not quite looking you in the eye when he spoke.

The accountant acknowledged me with a stiff bow. "How do you do, Miss Woolson?"

Before I could reply, Mrs. French said, "Mrs. Godfrey thinks tonight's pledges will be enough to make a final offer on the Battery Street warehouse."

"Do you really think that's possible, Mr. Arlen?" Margaret Barlow asked the accountant.

Lucius Arlen looked pleased to be consulted. He cleared his throat a bit self-importantly and said, "I agree it looks promising. We've already met our goal tonight, and additional pledges are coming in. That will provide us with enough money to complete our negotiations with the owners of the property, and—"

He was interrupted by a loud commotion in the foyer. Conversation abruptly ceased as everyone strained to hear the cause of the disturbance.

"But, sir, you cannot go in," the Godfreys' butler called out. "Sir, please!"

A thin man in his forties strode defiantly into the parlor. He was dressed entirely in black, from his wrinkled flannel trousers and morning coat to his slightly dented stovepipe hat. His fierce eyes were also black, as were the hair and beard that flew riotously about his grim face. People instinctively pressed away from him as he marched to the center of the room. My father started forward as if to intercept the man, but Mama took Papa's arm and pulled him back.

"Brothers and sisters," the intruder boomed. "Ministering to the Jezebels of this city is an abomination!" He raised a worn leather Bible above his head. "Those who have sold their immortal souls to the devil do not deserve to be succored."

"Mr. Halsey!" an authoritative voice interrupted. "I will thank you to leave this house at once."

All eyes went to Caroline Godfrey, who stood framed in the doorway. Her gray eyes flashed with icy fury as she glared at the interloper.

"*Reverend* Josiah Halsey, if you please, madam," the man corrected, tipping his hat and making an ironic bow.

"Nothing about your presence here pleases me," Mrs. Godfrey snapped. "We intend to offer medical care to the impoverished women and children of this

17

city. *Respectable* women, Mr. Halsey. If you are insinuating that we plan to care for women who have no one but themselves to blame for their unfortunate circumstances, you are mistaken."

There was no need for Mrs. Godfrey to explain what she meant by a woman of "unfortunate circumstances." Everyone knew the term referred to an unwed mother, a prejudice I found galling. It was unjust that the child's father got off scot-free, while the poor mother was left to suffer the shame and consequences.

I looked across the room where my brother Charles and his wife, Celia, stood staring at the trespasser. Charles, a physician of unquestionable talent and limited income, was slated to lead the roster of physicians who had agreed to volunteer at the new hospital. From his sheepish expression, I realized this was exactly what he planned to do. Charles was far too kindhearted to turn even a penniless patient away, much less a woman who would otherwise be forced to deliver her child on the street. Apparently, he had failed to mention this to Mrs. Godfrey. I met my father's eyes, and we both suppressed a smile.

"Lies! All lies!" Halsey ranted, his malevolent black eyes fixed on our hostess. "I warn you, until the Jezebels acknowledge their sins and prostrate themselves before their lord and savior, food and shelter will but support their debauchery."

Mrs. Godfrey's patrician face had turned red, and her voice shook with rage. "How dare you! Leave this house at once or I will notify the police."

"You do so at your soul's peril." Again Halsey held up his Bible. "You may close your ears to the voice of truth, but be sure that in the end your sins will find you out!"

Mrs. Godfrey opened her mouth to speak, but no words came out. Clutching a hand to her breast, she gasped as if struggling for air. "Leonard," she choked. "Leonard—"

She swayed and would have fallen if my brother Charles and Reverend Prescott hadn't rushed forward and supported her to the nearest settee. Hurriedly, I reached for several cushions and placed them beneath the woman's head.

"Someone get her husband," I directed, and a frightened footman ran to do my bidding. At the same time, Mama handed me a damp cloth appropriated from one of the servants. I placed it across Mrs. Godfrey's forehead.

"Give her air," Charles ordered, as people pressed around the stricken woman. He pointed at the intruder. "And for God's sake, get that man out of here!"

There was a murmur of assent, and several men grabbed the black-clad Halsey. Despite his sputtered threats, they managed to physically eject him from the room.

My brother was taking Mrs. Godfrey's pulse when Leonard Godfrey, closely followed by his brother Pierce, entered the room.

"What happened?" Leonard demanded, kneeling

down by Caroline, who lay with her eyes closed, her face ghastly white.

"She's had an attack," Charles told him quietly. "Tell me, does she have a heart condition?"

"She suffers from angina. Her physician has prescribed medicine—" Leonard stopped as his head seemed to clear.

"Pierce," he told his brother. "Get Caroline's pills. They're on the night table in her room. And hurry, man!"

Without a word, Pierce Godfrey sped from the parlor, leaving behind him a room so quiet you could have heard a feather drop. Mrs. Godfrey stirred and a low murmur swept through the assembled guests. She looked around with glazed eyes, then, becoming aware of her husband's face, made an effort to sit up.

"Caroline, don't move," Leonard said, easing her back onto the cushions. "Pierce has gone for your pills."

For the first time, Mrs. Godfrey seemed to notice the sea of worried faces surrounding the settee. "Don't be ridiculous, Leonard." Her voice was still weak, but she forced a smile. "Dinner will be—"

"Don't try to talk," her husband admonished.

"But I don't—" She could go no further. Squeezing her husband's hand, she closed her eyes and gulped for air. To my horror, I noticed her skin was turning blue.

"You're a doctor, Woolson," Leonard begged Charles. "For God's sake, do something!"

"I'm doing all I can, Mr. Godfrey." My brother's

kind eyes were reassuring. "The medicine should relieve the pain and ease her breathing."

After what seemed an eternity but was probably no more than a few moments, Pierce returned with a small apothecary box. Leonard extracted a tiny white pill and placed it beneath his wife's tongue. We all watched in anxious silence as color gradually returned to her face and her breathing became less arduous. As the pain slowly receded, she again tried to sit up.

"Lie back, Caroline," Leonard told her. "You must give the medicine time to work."

"But dinner," she protested.

I was close enough to hear her husband's soft curse as he reluctantly turned to his guests. "Will you all please go into the dining room? I'll join you in a moment."

There was an awkward pause, as if, despite God-frey's admonition, no one was quite sure what to do. Clearing his throat, Reverend Prescott said, "We can best help Mrs. Godfrey by honoring her wishes." Taking Mrs. Adelina French's arm, he left the parlor. With anxious glances at their hostess, guests began fol-lowing the minister into the dining room. Charles and the two Godfrey brothers remained hovering by the stricken woman's side.

"Who was that man waving his Bible at us?" I asked my father as our party joined the general exodus.

"He's some sort of religious fanatic," Papa said grimly. "Evidently this isn't the first time he's bad-gered Mrs. Godfrey about the new hospital. He belongs to a Los Angeles sect that believes poverty and destitution are the result of God's punishment, especially when it comes to unwed mothers."

I was speechless. I trust I'm a faithful Christian, but I have no patience for those who use the Bible to promote their own bigoted ideology. My indignation must have been obvious, because Reverend Prescott quickly said:

"Let us pray that Mrs. Godfrey soon recovers, Miss Woolson. At the moment, that is our primary concern."

"Amen," Mama and Celia heartily agreed.

Papa and I seconded the prayer, although privately I felt nothing but contempt toward the hypocrite who had triggered the poor woman's attack.

Most of the other guests had taken their seats by the time we entered the dining room, and I was shown to my place by one of the footmen. The long refectory table was easily large enough to accommodate the thirty or so diners and was laid with ornate china, wine glasses and heavily carved silver. Floral arrangements and dozens of flickering candles completed the elaborate setting. The soup course had already been served, and I sensed the butler's growing distress as he watched it grow cold.

Those of us seated at the table were hardly less edgy than the servants. A sober-looking Lucius Arlen sat to my right. Next to him, my mother was talking to Judge Barlow. Catty-corner across the table, Margaret Barlow and her mother chatted with Reverend Prescott, who sat between them. There were two unoccupied seats at the table, presumably for my brother Charles and Pierce Godfrey, as well as our hosts' places at either end of the table.

I'm sure I wasn't the only one who felt like an unwilling witness to what surely should have been a family matter. I couldn't understand why we hadn't simply been sent home. Sitting here with our hostess lying ill only a few rooms away seemed tasteless in the extreme.

The footmen had begun pouring wine when conversation abruptly ceased, and I glanced up to see an unhappy Leonard Godfrey lead his wife into the dining room. Mrs. Godfrey looked drawn and pale, but overall she seemed much improved. She smiled gamely as her husband escorted her to the head of the table. But when he continued to hover behind her chair, she waved an impatient hand, indicating that he should take his own place.

"I want to apologize," she said in a surprisingly steady voice. "Not only for that appalling man who forced his way into our home, but for my brief indisposition. As you can see, I am quite recovered." As if to demonstrate this, she picked up her spoon and began eating her soup.

I watched my fellow diners react to her words with a mixture of relief and lingering concern. I doubt anyone was foolish enough to believe her attack hadn't been a good deal more serious than she claimed. Yet we could do little else but follow her example and try to behave as if nothing distressful had occurred.

I had just taken a sip of wine when Charles and Pierce Godfrey slipped into their seats, the latter opposite me.

"How is she?" I asked him as quietly as I could over the hum of dinner conversation.

"Probably not as well as she'd have us believe. My brother urged her to rest in bed until she could be seen by her own doctor." His expression grew grim. "But Caroline is a stubborn woman. She rarely allows anyone to tell her what to do."

His tone made me wonder if this statement had something to do with the tension I'd sensed between Pierce and his sister-in-law in the alcove.

"Mr. Godfrey's advice is sound," I said, "but I can sympathize with his wife. She's worked so hard for the new hospital, I'm sure she feels a responsibility to see the evening through."

"It's a poor reason to risk another, perhaps more serious, attack." He glanced at Caroline, his handsome face set in lines I couldn't read. Was it anger, frustration, incredulity? Or again part of that strange drama I'd witnessed before dinner? When he turned back to me, his face had softened into a smile. "I'm certain everything will be fine. Caroline has a way of coming out on top. Or perhaps she's just blessed with incredibly good luck."

Having no idea how to respond to this curious statement, I bent my head to my dinner. I'm sure the food was superb, but I tasted little of it.

"—I would be pleased if you would accept."

"I'm sorry, what did you say?" I looked up to find Pierce Godfrey regarding me with an odd expression. Perhaps it was the way the candlelight cast his face into sharp contrasts of light and shadow, but I had the bizarre impression of a buccaneer standing at the helm of his frigate.

"I asked if you would do me the honor of dining with me tomorrow evening," he repeated.

I didn't immediately reply to this unexpected invitation. Over the past few months I'd had to deal with far too many assertive men at the law firm to add yet another example of the species to my social life.

"I fear I'm busy tomorrow night," I said, buttering a roll. "But thank you for asking."

"That's unfortunate." Pierce's dark blue eyes studied my face, leaving me with the irrational feeling that he easily read my lie. "Perhaps some other night, then?"

"I'm sorry," I said. "I'll be busy all week."

"Ah, I'd forgotten. Your work must be demanding. Perhaps you're involved in another intriguing case?"

Inadvertently, he'd touched on a sensitive nerve and I stiffened. What I wouldn't have given to be involved in *any* case right now, much less an intriguing one. Unfortunately, Joseph Shepard, the senior partner at the firm, considered women attorneys incapable of performing any task more mentally stimulating than washing the dishes.

"I find all legal work interesting, Mr. Godfrey." That part, at least, was true. This was hardly the time in which—and Pierce Godfrey was certainly not the person in whom—to confide the anger and frustration I felt toward my employer and his male cronies. "It takes up a great deal of my—"

I broke off as a chair suddenly crashed to the floor. All eyes flew to Mrs. Godfrey, who half-stood at the end of the table. Her face was flushed, and her fingers were pressed to her temples as if she was in terrible pain.

"My head!" she cried hoarsely.

Her husband and Charles rushed to her side, easing her back into the chair, which someone had righted. Leonard pulled the apothecary box from his pocket and spilled out pills. The poor woman was trembling so violently, it was several moments before he could place one beneath her tongue. Obviously in mortal distress, she clutched helplessly at her bodice as she struggled for air.

"Do something!" Leonard shouted at Charles.

My brother was already doing everything he could, aided by Reverend Prescott, who had rushed forward to help. In an effort to ease her breathing, they'd begun to loosen the tiny pearl buttons at the back of her gown. Before they'd managed more than one or two, she bent double and began to vomit. Someone grabbed a serviette to dab at her face, but the gesture only spread the mess down her gown.

"Caroline," Leonard cried helplessly. "For God's sake, help her!"

Caroline's lips were moving, but no sound issued from her throat. The flush drained from her face as her

26

body was struck by another spasm, and her skin once again turned a ghastly blue. Then, as she drew in a rattling breath, her irises rolled up into her head until they showed only white, and she sank limply onto the floor.

Charles knelt and cradled her head, at the same time attempting to place another pill beneath her tongue. It was no use; Caroline Godfrey was beyond help. Nicholas Prescott dropped down beside Charles, bowing his head in silent prayer.

Someone cried out behind me, and several women began to weep hysterically. Leonard stared at his wife, his face white with shock and disbelief. Charles raised the woman's limp arm and felt her wrist for what seemed like an eon. Then, with a sigh, he gently closed her eyes.

"Is she—?" Leonard stammered. "That is, she can't be—"

Charles gave the distraught husband a regretful nod. "I'm truly sorry, Mr. Godfrey, but I'm afraid your wife is dead."

CHAPTER TWO

I did not sleep well that night and arrived at the law firm later than usual the next morning. Going directly to my office—if one could dignify a space hardly larger than a broom closet with this appellation—I removed my hat and coat and gathered up the stack of research papers I'd completed the previous Friday. With any luck, perhaps I'd be able to deliver the files before I was seen by one of the partners and banished to the firm's library or, infinitely worse, forced to face the odious machine that had, over the past few weeks, become my nemesis.

It was called the Caligraph, or typebar typewriter, an insidious device clearly invented by a fiend. The contraption had just come onto the market the previous year, the second machine of its kind to be let loose upon an unsuspecting public. For reasons that defy comprehension, Joseph Shepard had purchased one.

For the past three months it had sat upon my desk, an ungainly tribute to man's inhumanity to man. I had poked, prodded, coaxed and even shed tears in a mostly futile attempt to get the accursed thing to do my bidding. As far as I could see, the Caligraph had not been designed to accommodate any fingers designed by God. Mine certainly refused to cooperate. Every time I placed them on the keyboard they seemed to balloon to twice their normal size, usually striking two keys instead of the one I'd intended.

Covering this instrument of torture, I embarked on my appointed rounds. Thankfully, I was able to complete them without incident. The last file was promised to Robert Campbell who, like myself, was an associate attorney at the firm. I found him surrounded by books and a blizzard of papers. How he could think, much less accomplish any real work, in such disarray never failed to amaze me.

"So, there you are," he said, as usual not bothering with social niceties. "I expected this file an hour ago."

This morning, Robert wore a dull brown morning coat with a starched white wing collar and tan flannel trousers. The customary pencil perched behind his ear, and his orange hair flew about his craggy face as if he'd been caught in a windstorm. At six feet, four inches tall, and with muscles no suit could contain, he resembled a grizzly bear who had somehow landed himself inside a fishbowl.

"Where have you been all morning?" he went on, his Scottish *r*s rolling along in good form.

I ignored his poor manners. Criticizing Robert's rudeness would be like trying to stop a terrier from burying a bone.

"You have a nerve complaining. Especially as you weren't the one forced to plow through dozens of legal tomes to unearth this information."

"Ah, yes," he said, his tone almost, but not quite, apologetic. "I, er—it was good of you."

"Don't mention it," I retorted dryly. "I'll try to get to that probate case you're working on this afternoon."

He looked sheepish, and I saw that my earlier barb had found its mark. "No need to do that, Sarah. I'll, ah, try to find time myself this afternoon."

"That's up to you. From what I've gleaned so far, the case seems pretty straightforward."

As I turned to leave, he waved a newspaper at me. "Have you read this morning's *Examiner*?"

"No. Why?"

"You're in it. Or, rather, your family is. Your brother Charles is quoted on the front page."

I remembered the newspaper reporter who'd cornered Charles for a statement as we'd left the Godfrey house. My brother Samuel—who, unknown to our family, has published a number of newspaper articles under the nom de plume Ian Fearless—is fond of saying reporters will go to any lengths for a story. Including, it seems, standing for hours in the fog on the off chance of obtaining an interview.

I removed a stack of books from the room's only other chair, sat down and started to read. The headline announced the untimely death of one of San Francisco's foremost society matrons, then went on to list her charitable works, including her recent establishment of the Women and Children's Hospital. The last paragraph named some of her dinner guests, including Judge Horace Woolson and his family, then concluded with an interview with Mrs. Godfrey's attending physician, namely my brother Charles.

"It says she died of a heart attack," commented Robert.

I looked up from the paper. "Yes, she suffered from angina. Charles suggested the Godfreys' regular physician order an autopsy, though."

"Whatever for?"

"He seems to feel that Mrs. Godfrey's symptoms weren't entirely compatible with coronary artery disease. He thought an autopsy would lay to rest any lingering doubts about the cause of death."

30

Robert snorted. "Unbelievable. Absolutely unbeliev-able. It must run in the family."

"What's that supposed to mean?"

"It means you're not the only Woolson cursed with an overactive imagination. First you, then your brother Samuel, and now Charles. You just said the woman suffered from angina. Why look for mystery where none exists?"

"Unless you've suddenly become an expert on heart disease," I said acerbically, "I suggest you keep your opinions to yourself."

With that I stood and left his cubicle. As I crossed the clerks' antechamber, a nervous-looking woman with three small children in tow entered the office. She wore a worn but neatly pressed day dress and a straw hat decorated with faded ribbons. Her hair was light brown, and several errant strands flew about her wan face. The two youngest children clung to her skirts, while the oldest child, a girl of about six, held tightly to her mother's hand. From the bulge beneath the woman's dress, it appeared another child was on the way.

Hubert Perkins, the head clerk, gave the woman and her brood a disapproving look. "Do you have an appointment, madam?" he asked, not bothering to stand.

"I would—" the woman's eyes darted around the room. "That is, I'd like to speak to—"

She faltered, the clerk's surliness adding to her discomfort. I empathized with the poor soul. Hubert

Perkins had treated me much the same the first day I'd entered these rooms. I knew all too well what it felt like to be judged and summarily dismissed as being of no consequence.

I was about to walk over and rescue the poor woman when she looked up and saw me. Color flooded her pale face and her expression turned guardedly hopeful.

"Are you Miss Woolson?" she asked.

I was taken aback. To the best of my knowledge, I'd never met the woman. "I'm Sarah Woolson," I said with a smile. "Is there something I can do for you?"

"Rebecca Carpenter's my friend," she said. "You helped her get some money—when she was hit by a carriage?"

Ah, yes, Mrs. Carpenter. It was the first brief I'd drawn up for my new employer. "I remember the case very well, Mrs. . . . ?"

"Mankin, miss, Lily Mankin." She twisted the strap on her reticule. "My husband, Jack, was killed two weeks ago—in a fire at the contract shop where he worked." She hesitated, and tears filled her eyes. "Three people got out. My Jack and four other poor souls didn't. Only one door was open. The back door—" She swallowed with difficulty. "The back door was nailed shut."

"Nailed shut!" I exclaimed. Most sweatshops were little more than tinderboxes; they were always going up in flames, sometimes taking out whole blocks of similar buildings with them. When faced with such a common danger, why would anyone block off one of only two means of escape?

Deciding the clerks' chamber was not the place to discuss the matter, I suggested we go to my office. The woman gathered her children and followed me along the corridor to my office. There, I settled the widow in a chair and indicated another chair for the children. The two eldest, the six-year-old girl and her younger brother, obediently shared the seat, while I took the last chair behind my desk.

"Please," I asked. "Tell me what happened."

"Thieves broke the back door during a robbery," she told me, settling the youngest child on her lap. "Instead of fixin' the door, they nailed it shut."

Incensed at such callous disregard for the safety of one's employees, I realized this sort of thing happened far too often in a world where the poor and disadvantaged were considered dispensable. When one sweatshop worker died, dozens more were waiting to take his place.

"What is it you'd like me to do for you, Mrs. Mankin?"

"I was hopin' you could help me, like you did Mrs. Carpenter. I take in laundry and mendin', but it's not enough to pay my bills." She rubbed a hand over her extended belly. "Soon I won't even be able to do that."

"Have you spoken to your husband's employer?"

Two spots of color appeared on either cheek. "Jack never knew who owned the shop. Paddy McGuire ran things. In fact, I think he was the one who nailed the door shut. Another man came in every couple of weeks to check up on things. Jack never knew his name, neither, but thought maybe he was the owner."

"Have you spoken to Mr. McGuire?"

"Just once. Claims he don't know who owns the shop. He says the fire did him out of a job, too."

"Did your husband ever describe this man he thought might be the owner?"

She considered a moment. "He said he was big and always smokin' a cigar. Oh, and he wore a bowler hat too small for his head. Jack used to laugh at that." This simple memory brought fresh tears to her eyes.

Not much to go on, I thought. The description fit half of San Francisco's male population. If the story about the back door being nailed shut was true, we might have grounds to sue the sweatshop for criminal negligence. First I'd have to search for legal precedents, then we'd have to locate the owner of the shop, which might not prove easy. The men who held title to these places were reluctant to have their names known.

"When is your baby due, Mrs. Mankin?"

"In three months."

"How much money do you have left to support your family?"

"I can pay my rent for another week—and buy bread and milk. After that, we'll be out on the street."

"I trust it won't come to that," I said, giving her what I hoped was a supportive smile. "I can't promise anything, but I give you my word I'll do everything possible to ensure that you and your children are taken care of."

The smile she gave me in return warmed my heart and at the same time chilled the part of my brain that recognized the difficulties I'd be facing. She was frightened enough without my explaining how hard assigning liability in this sort of case would be.

Mrs. Mankin supplied her address, along with a description of Paddy McGuire, after which I saw her to the front door. I had just started back to my office when I was intercepted by an irate Joseph Shepard, a pile of file folders tucked under his arm.

"Who was that woman?" he demanded suspiciously. "Did she ask to see an attorney?"

I saw by Hubert Perkins's smug expression that he'd wasted no time reporting my interview with Mrs. Mankin.

"*I'm* an attorney, Mr. Shepard," I reminded him evenly. "As a matter of fact, she asked to speak to me."

"Don't talk rubbish. What possible business could she have with you?"

Oh well, I thought, I might as well be in for a dollar as for a penny. I described Mrs. Mankin's problem, then, hoping to touch some nerve of kindness buried beneath my employer's layers of greed, explained about the new baby expected in the spring.

I could have saved my breath. He instantly fastened on the legal ramifications of the case, ignoring any humanitarian issues that might be involved.

"You realize, of course, such a case is impossible to

win." He glared at me over his pince-nez. "I trust you didn't promise this woman our representation?"

"Of course not. I would never commit the firm to a case without speaking to you first. I pledged only my own efforts on her behalf."

"You did what?"

I should have seen it coming, but I was taken off guard when he started that awful sound at the back of his nose, the one he invariably makes when someone has the audacity to thwart him.

I had long since grown weary of these tantrums. "So, you see, Mr. Shepard, you need not trouble yourself," I continued, doing my best to ignore this outbreak. "Mrs. Mankin will be my responsibility."

"She will be no such thing! Under no circumstances are you to take that woman's case. Do you understand me?"

I was dismayed to feel my own temper rising; above all, I was determined to maintain my composure. "As you are fond of pointing out, Mr. Shepard, I am a mere woman. Nevertheless, you have made yourself perfectly clear." I didn't think it expedient to add that, despite its clarity, I had no intention of obeying his edict.

He wasn't quite sure how to take this. "Well, ah, that's good." He seemed to remember something. "I just passed the tea closet and noticed a number of dishes waiting to be washed. What if a client required coffee or tea? This sort of laxity is unacceptable."

Fixing him with a sharp look, I turned and started

toward the room set aside for refreshments—strictly reserved for clients, of course.

"Miss Woolson," he called out behind me. "I am not finished with you." With a sigh, I turned around to be handed the folders he'd been carrying beneath his arm. "Add these cases to your other files. Pages bearing my initials are to be typed." His eyes narrowed. "Which reminds me, the work you've turned in so far is appalling. I'm surprised you're experiencing so much difficulty with the Caligraph. My clerks could master the device in no time at all."

I held out the folders he'd just given me. "If they're so proficient, then perhaps they should type these."

All six clerks looked up from their work, fixing me with baleful eyes. They needn't have worried. Joseph Shepard had no intention of letting me off so easily.

"Since you insist on pursuing a—*livelihood* at my firm, Miss Woolson," he said through clenched teeth, "it behooves me to find something for you to do. My clerks are occupied with important business (at this, the above-mentioned clerks instantly bent back to their work). You, on the other hand, appear incapable of performing the most rudimentary tasks, much less those of a legal nature. As I informed you on the day you deceived your way into this office: a woman's place is in the home. It is God's plan, and no good can come from flaunting His will."

A dozen angry replies leapt to mind, any one of them more than sufficient to ensure my instant dismissal. *That's just what he wants,* I thought. *Tact,*

Sarah, you must use tact. Do not allow him to win in this manner!

Sure enough, the infuriating little man looked visibly disappointed when I refused to rise to his bait.

"I promise," I replied meekly, "to marshal my feminine frailties and do my best with these files."

His small eyes squinted until they resembled two shiny marbles; no doubt he feared I was mocking him. But reaching a conclusion on this point seemed beyond his limited ability.

"See that you do," he snapped, retaining a glint of suspicion. "When you've finished typing, you may research the remainder of the files. Since I require everything to be on my desk first thing tomorrow morning, I expect you to stay here until the work is completed."

His polished patent-leather shoes squeaked as he pivoted and strode toward his office.

The dreaded typewriting took even longer than I feared. Through trial and error, I'd become slightly more proficient at erasing my errors, although some pages came out looking as if they'd been rubbed in the dirt.

I never thought to say it, but when I at last covered the Caligraph machine for the day, it was a relief to move to the law library, even if the room was so dusty it made me sneeze. I was determined to get through Shepard's work quickly, so that I'd have time to look into Mrs. Mankin's situation. Unfortunately, when I finally got to the widow's case, the information I found was not encouraging.

For one thing, negligence in the law of torts—a civil, noncriminal wrong from which one might sue for damages—had only recently come into being and was rarely used. Even when it was employed it usually failed, since the courts almost always favored business, not the employee. To complicate matters, a doctrine called the "fellow servant" rule stated that one employee could not sue his employer for injuries caused by the negligence of another employee. In Mrs. Mankin's case, that meant before we could sue, we would first have to establish who actually nailed the sweatshop door shut and if it had been done on the owner's order.

It was after six when Robert poked his head in the door.

"Don't tell me you've been in here all day," he said, eyeing the stacks of books and notes piled in front of me.

"Just the last three hours. I haven't gotten to your probate case yet, if that's what you're after."

He came in and pulled out the chair opposite me. "I told you I'd take care of it myself." He looked around the gloomy room. "You should light the lamps. It's too dark in here to read."

I was surprised to see he was right. I'd been so intent on my tort work, I hadn't noticed the fading light.

Without waiting for me to agree, he stood, struck a match and lit several gas lamps. Holding one over his head, he perused a bookcase dedicated to probate.

"I've got the ones you're looking for right here." I pushed a stack of books across the table. "I thought I might get to them this afternoon, but I got side-tracked."

He glanced at my open tort book. "You aren't planning to take that widow's case, are you? She has my sympathy, but you have about as much chance of getting money from that sweatshop as you do of convincing old man Shepard to let you plead a case before the Supreme Court."

I started to ask how he knew the purpose of Mrs. Mankin's visit, then remembered the head clerk. "I see Hubert Perkins has been busy gossiping again."

"Perkins's daily news, more reliable than any newspaper in town." He frowned. "I suppose you're going to ignore Shepard and help the widow anyway. And probably lose your job in the process."

"How much of a loss would that really be, Robert? Any fool can see I'll never be assigned any worthwhile cases."

"Hmm. I think you're taking this too personally."

"Oh, really. When I joined this firm I knew it wouldn't be easy. I had no illusions that I'd immediately walk into a courtroom and argue a case. I expected to do my share of research and writing briefs. On the other hand, I hardly expected to be placed in charge of the typewriting machine from hell or to spend my days washing dishes and digging through law books for the benefit of the entire office, including those who are junior to me. Martin Long has been employed here for one month, yet he hasn't cleaned a single teacup. And he certainly hasn't had to do battle with the cursed Caligraph."

"He's also Judge Long's son," Robert pointed out.

"And I'm Judge Woolson's daughter. If you tell me that's different, I'll never speak to you again."

Robert sighed and opened the first probate book. "Far be it for me to say anything to you, Sarah. It may not be fair, but it is reality. Most people would agree that women have no business practicing law."

"And you, Robert?" I asked, looking him directly in the eye. "What do you say?"

He met my gaze, then looked down at his book.

"I say it's getting late. If we don't want to be here all night, we'd better get on with our work."

The next two weeks brought more of the same—as far as Shepard's firm was concerned. I was relieved when weekends arrived, not because they promised two days of leisure, but because they provided me with the only free time I had to pursue Mrs. Mankin's case. Of course I had initiated steps to relieve her financial situation. Thanks to Mama's resources, we'd been able to supply food, clothing and even a midwife to monitor the widow's pregnancy. We had also sent a good deal of light laundry and mending Lily Mankin's way, which would help to pay her rent.

The one thing I had not been able to provide was the

most important: I couldn't assure the widow there was any hope of suing the sweatshop.

Naturally, I'd endeavored to learn the name of the individual who owned the contract shop, or sweatshop, as they were coming to be called. Combing through records at the Registry of Deeds, I'd finally found the building registered to McKenzie Properties, listing an address on Sansone Street.

When I visited the business, though, I was disappointed to find a disreputable secondhand store on the ground floor, with two unoccupied rooms upstairs. The proprietor of the shop was not helpful. He claimed that on the first of every month he placed his rent money in an envelope and left it on a table in one of the upstairs rooms. Any mail addressed to McKenzie Properties was similarly handled. He never saw anyone collect either the rent money or the mail, but the table was always empty when he opened his store in the morning.

When I shared my findings with my newspaperman brother Samuel, he told me hiding behind sham companies was standard practice for owners who wished to remain anonymous. Legally, McKenzie Properties held title to the sweatshop, as well as to the building on Sansone Street, but the company might as well be ghosts for all the trail they left.

My only real hope of finding the owner of either building, it seemed, was to locate Paddy McGuire, the employee suspected of nailing the sweatshop door shut. If boarding it up had been Paddy's idea, then all was lost. On the other hand, if he'd been following the owner's orders, I would at last be able to file suit.

I'd enlisted Samuel's help to find McGuire, as well as his friend George Lewis, who had recently been promoted to sergeant on the San Francisco police force. So far we'd come up with nothing—a frustrating state of affairs, to say the least.

That weekend, I decided on a more direct approach: I would visit the site of the fire myself. Hopefully, someone in the neighborhood would be able to lead me to Mr. McGuire or perhaps to one of the other two survivors who made it out of the sweatshop. There was, of course, no guarantee I would succeed in my quest. On the other hand, I was weary of depending on others to do what I could do just as well, if not better, for myself.

I arrived home that evening to find everyone out. Pleased to have some time to myself before dinner, I'd just started up the stairs to my room when I heard loud shrieks issuing from the floor above. Taking the stairs two at a time, I reached the nursery to find Charles and Celia's children, six-year-old Tom and three-year-old Amanda, tied together on the floor by a length of rope. My brother Frederick's son, Freddie, a badly behaved boy of eight, was arrayed in feathers and armed with a small hatchet as he pranced around his cousins in some kind of Indian war dance. In one hand he held Mandy's porcelain bride doll, veil missing, only a few sparse hairs left on her bald pate. In the other hand, he clasped the hatchet and a cascade of curly blond doll hair, which he proudly waved about with every whoop.

"Good heavens, Freddie!" I shouted, collaring the little hellion. "Put down that hatchet this instant."

"We were playing the Battle of Little Bighorn," Freddie protested. "Tom is General Custer. I'm Chief Sitting Bull."

At that moment, Nanny Douglas arrived at the nursery door, carrying milk and cookies for the children. Hearing the wails of her charges—by now Freddie's offended cries were drowning out little Mandy—she nearly dropped her tray.

"Blessed Mary and Joseph!" She looked wide-eyed from me to Freddie's small captives. "I was only gone to the kitchen for a few moments. Master Freddie said he was hungry."

"I'm sure he did," I said, eyeing Frederick Jr.'s ample girth. "He also wanted you out of the room so he could scalp his cousins. Here," I said, handing her the hatchet. "Get rid of this, then please give the children their snacks. And I wouldn't leave the room again, if I were you. No matter what Freddie claims to want."

Mercifully, peace prevailed in the nursery until Freddie's mother arrived to claim her only offspring. So far, Frederick is the only one of my parents' children to leave home. He and his wife Henrietta moved out two years earlier, when city government set about destroying Rincon Hill by bisecting it at Second Street. Unable to get Papa to budge from his home of twenty-five years, Frederick erected his own house on the fringe of the Nob Hill swells.

Charles is a different story. Since my physician brother cannot turn anyone away from his surgery, he, Celia and their two children continue to live at home due to financial necessity. And Samuel? Suffice it to say that my youngest brother prizes his personal comforts far too much to go to the bother of moving into new quarters. A decision that suits me admirably. From childhood, Samuel has been my best friend and co-conspirator in mischief and mayhem. If I must remain at home—the edict of an outdated and biased society—at least I had one ally close at hand. Actually, this arrangement was not unusual; many families boasted three and even four generations residing beneath the same roof.

Mama and Celia came in shortly after Henrietta and Freddie's departure. As it happened, they had attended a board meeting to discuss who should take over leadership of the new Women and Children's Hospital now that Caroline Godfrey was gone. I was interested to hear they'd chosen Margaret Barlow for the job.

"She lacks Caroline's imagination and drive," my mother said as we went upstairs to dress for dinner. "But Caroline had completed the initial planning. What's needed now is organization and commitment, two of Margaret's finest qualities. I think she will do very well."

"I'm relieved to hear you say so," I said, reaching the door to my room. "I was afraid Mrs. Godfrey's death might delay the new hospital. Heaven knows the city needs it."

"That awful man who upset Mrs. Godfrey the night she died was loitering outside the Barlows' house," Celia said with a little shudder. "He kept waving his Bible and threatening dire consequences to fallen women who did not repent of their sins."

Mama clucked with disapproval. "This so-called Reverend Halsey has been turning up all over town, trying to marshal support for his outlandish cause."

"Mrs. French told me he accosted Mayor Kalloch outside the Metropolitan Temple last Sunday and harangued him about the Chinese issue," Celia put in. "Reverend Halsey seems to consider the Chinese an even greater threat to Christianity than women."

The note of asperity in my normally gentle sister-in-law's voice surprised me. Call it fancy, but I was visited by an awful premonition. If the odious Reverend Halsey was able to provoke even docile Celia, how might a more volatile person react to his ravings?

B efore I could set out on my adventure the following afternoon, Charles returned from his Saturday morning surgery. Motioning me into the library, he told me he had just learned the results of Mrs. Godfrey's autopsy.

"Death was caused by an overdose of nitroglycerin," he said, looking vaguely disturbed.

"Nitroglycerin! Isn't that an explosive?"

"When used with ethylene glycol nitrate it makes

dynamite. Medical nitroglycerin, on the other hand, is used to dilate coronary vessels and reduce blood pressure. It's an effective drug for the treatment of angina."

"That was what was in those little pills you and Mr. Godfrey put under Caroline's tongue?"

"Exactly."

"I don't understand. How could she die from a drug that was supposed to help her?"

"Too much of a good thing can be dangerous, Sarah. And there was a great deal of nitroglycerine in Mrs. Godfrey's system." He shook his head. "It just doesn't add up, and I mean that literally. Godfrey said his wife hadn't had a spell in weeks, which means there was no nitroglycerin in her system that evening. I administered four pills before we went in to dinner, a normal dose for a patient suffering an angina attack. During her second spell, she ingested only one pill. I've never heard of five nitroglycerine tablets being anywhere near enough to cause an overdose."

"Then how do you explain the autopsy finding?"

"That's just it, I can't explain it. There's a theory that if alcohol is consumed with nitroglycerine, it can result in a severe drop in blood pressure. But I don't remember Mrs. Godfrey drinking more than a glass or two of wine. Do you?"

I thought back, trying to recall the details of that fatal dinner. "I don't think she had time to drink much. As I recall, they'd just started serving the third course when she stood up, complaining of a headache."

"That's a common side effect of too much nitro-glycerine. In fact, she exhibited several symptoms of overdose—headache, vomiting, respiratory paralysis, cyanosis—"

"Cyanosis? You mean when her skin turned blue?"

He nodded.

"So that's why you were so keen on ordering an autopsy."

"Her symptoms point more to an overdose than an angina attack. Yet I don't see how that's possible given the small dosage she received. The Godfreys' doctor agreed that an autopsy was in order."

"Is the coroner troubled by the postmortem results?"

"Apparently not. He's ruled it death by natural causes." He sighed. "So, I suppose that's that."

"Yes, I suppose it is." Charles was a cautious man, a vigilant doctor. He would never suggest foul play without serious provocation. Yet if the coroner was satisfied with the postmortem results, what recourse did he have?

"I've done everything I can," Charles said, as if reading my thoughts. "No sense dwelling on it now." He turned to open the library door. "It was a terrible way to go, though."

CHAPTER THREE

Shortly after my talk with Charles, I received a surprise visitor. When our butler, Edis, announced that a Mr. Pierce Godfrey wished to see me, I thought I'd misheard. What on earth could he be doing here?

As fate would have it, Mama crossed the hall to see Pierce waiting for our butler's return. Naturally, nothing would do but that she show him in herself. I could tell by her expression she was already planning the wedding. Her only daughter, having reached the ripe old age of twenty-seven, finally had a living, breathing prospect. And, glory be, a dashing one at that!

After my mother withdrew—parlor door left discreetly ajar—I offered Pierce refreshments. He requested coffee and I sent our maid, Ina Corks, to fetch a fresh pot from the kitchen. While we waited, I expressed my sympathy at his sister-in-law's premature death.

He seemed unusually somber. I suspected the relationship between Pierce and Caroline had been strained, but I sensed that on some level he mourned her passing.

"My brother is taking it very hard," he said. "He wanders about the house like a lost soul."

"He's fortunate to have you."

Pierce's gaze grew thoughtful. "What do you say to a man who has just lost his wife? And so young. Caroline was only forty-one, you know."

Ina came in at that moment with the coffee. I knew it was Mama's doing that the tray contained our best silver set. Cook had included some small cakes and freshly baked cookies, as well as several of her delicious fruit tarts.

"I'm sure your presence is very consoling, Mr. Godfrey," I said, pouring the coffee. "Do you have family on the West Coast?"

"No. Just an uncle who lives in Australia and several distant cousins back east. Our parents died years ago."

"I'm sorry. But that's even more reason not to discount your importance to your brother during this trying time."

He smiled, and again I was taken aback by the man's charisma. Few women, I imagined, would be able to resist such appeal. I was happy to count myself a member of this select group.

"You're a study in contradictions, Miss Woolson." He eyed me candidly. "You portray yourself as a self-assured woman, in control of her life. But I suspect beneath that no-nonsense exterior, you possess a compassionate and gentle heart."

"Mr. Godfrey," I protested. "You hardly know me. It's presumptuous of you to venture such a personal, and unsolicited, observation."

"I apologize if I've offended you," he said, although I was irked to notice the smile hadn't left his eyes.

"Most women would consider compassion a virtue."

"The nature of compassion has nothing to do with it." I shifted in my chair until I was facing him. "See here, Mr. Godfrey, I'm sure you haven't called this afternoon to exchange platitudes. At the risk of appearing inhospitable, why are you here?"

The man had the impertinence to laugh. "San Francisco society must consider you a real poser, if you always speak your mind so freely."

"I have little time for society, so their opinion of me is of no consequence. Now, kindly tell me the purpose of your visit."

I'd made my words deliberately harsh, trying to get a rise out of this annoyingly self-possessed man. To my irritation, he seemed unperturbed as he finished his coffee, placed the cup and saucer on the table, then crossed his long legs in their perfectly creased trousers.

"I've come to see you on business, Miss Woolson."

I stared at him in surprise. "On business?"

"Yes. You see, I own a shipping line—or rather Leonard and I own Godfrey Shipping in partnership. We run routes to the Orient, as well as to Sacramento and up and down the Pacific Coast. As part of a planned expansion, we're placing a substantial order with a local shipbuilding firm. We've met to draft the preliminary papers, but I'd like you to act as our legal representative to draw up the final contracts."

"I see." Stalling for time, I refilled his coffee cup and decided upon a direct approach.

"Forgive my bluntness but why me? Why not consult

with one of the senior partners at my law firm? Any one of them would be delighted to represent you."

Taking up his coffee, he regarded me with equal candor. "Time is money, Miss Woolson, and I don't believe in wasting either. Why bother interviewing someone else when I've made up my mind to hire you?"

"Mr. Godfrey, as much as I appreciate the honor, it's only fair to tell you that I've been working as an associate attorney for less than six months. There are many lawyers in San Francisco with far more experience, especially with business and partnership law."

Again, that wicked little smile. "I'm sure there are. Nevertheless, I trust you, Miss Woolson. You don't play games, a trait I find refreshing and rare. What you lack in experience, you more than make up in intelligence and fortitude." The smile widened. "And, shall we say, the ability to take people's measure?"

I studied his face, wondering what really lay behind this remarkable offer. I admit I was flattered by the opportunity to represent one of the leading shipping companies on the West Coast. On the other hand, I was realistic enough to know that, in all probability, Pierce Godfrey had ulterior motives.

"Well, Miss Woolson?" he prodded. "I can promise you a generous fee for your services."

"What does your brother think of this?"

If I hadn't been watching him so closely, I might have missed the way his fingers tightened on the coffee cup. The move was reflexive, relaxing as quickly as it appeared. But it added one small piece to the puzzle: Leonard Godfrey knew nothing of his brother's offer to me. It was interesting to note that Pierce's expression never altered. He must be an amazing poker player, I thought.

"Leonard leaves day-to-day operation of the company to me," he explained smoothly. "In fact, you might call him a silent partner. He has numerous other business ventures, as you probably know. As long as Godfrey Shipping shows a profit, he's content to play a passive role."

"I see," I replied. I would have preferred Leonard Godfrey's approval of his brother's offer.

At that moment, Edis entered the parlor to announce yet another visitor. "Mr. Robert Campbell to see you, miss," he said in his usual, sonorous tone.

Robert! What in the world was he doing here? I started to tell Edis that this was not a convenient time, when the annoying Scot burst into the room.

"Hello, Robert," I said, not bothering to hide my irritation. "This is an unexpected visit."

As he was about to stare a hole through Pierce's head, I performed the introductions. Robert nodded a curt acknowledgment then, without being asked, took a seat.

"I'm not here alone," he announced without preamble.

I looked around, bewildered. "Unless your companion is invisible, you certainly appear to be alone."

"She's waiting outside."

"She? Who do you—?"

"For the love of heaven, be quiet and listen. I was catching up on some work at the office, when a Mrs. Mankin came pounding on the door declaring she had to see you."

"Mankin?" I said. "You mean Lily Mankin?"

"Of course I mean Lily Mankin. She's standing outside on the street. Seems to be afraid of disturbing you, the silly woman."

"What does she want?"

Before Robert could answer, Pierce stood up and reached for his hat. "Miss Woolson, please think over what we discussed. It could be a satisfactory arrangement for both of us." He turned to Robert. "Glad to have met you, Campbell. No, don't get up, Miss Woolson. I can see myself out. I look forward to hearing from you soon."

"What was that all about?" Robert asked after Godfrey left the room.

"He wants me to act as legal counsel for his company," I said, as if this sort of thing happened to me every day.

"He what?" Robert's eyebrows flew up so high they nearly got lost in his riotous hair. "But you're a—"

"Don't you dare say it! I get more than enough bigotry at work. The last thing I need is to be insulted in my own home." I took myself in hand, then asked more calmly, "Why didn't you ask Mrs. Mankin to come inside?"

"Don't be thickheaded. Of course I asked her to

54

come in. She refused. What am I supposed to do, drag her in?"

"Oh, for heaven's sake."

Ignoring Robert's sputters, I went out to the foyer and opened the door. Sure enough, Mrs. Mankin stood diffidently on the street, looking like a frightened rabbit.

"Mrs. Mankin, how nice to see you. Please, come in. I was just having a cup of coffee. Won't you join me?"

"I, ah—I'm not sure I should."

"Of course you should." I took her by the arm, and gently but firmly led her inside. "I don't see your children. I trust they're all right?"

"They're fine, thank you, ma'am. A neighbor friend is watching them."

"Mr. Campbell says you were looking for me at the office," I said, leading her into the parlor. Ringing for Ina, I requested fresh coffee and two additional cups.

Lily Mankin sank timidly into her seat, perching on the edge as if she might bolt at the slightest provocation. She stared about the room, her wide eyes taking in the furniture, Mama's bric-a-brac, as well as the prized silver tea service. Poor Lily, I thought. I'd had no idea my simple invitation would make her so uncomfortable.

"Relax, Lily, please," I said, after I'd served the coffee and offered Cook's excellent tarts. "Tell me what this is all about."

Lily reached a hesitant hand toward the dainty china cup I'd set before her, then pulled it back, as if afraid it might bite. "I got to be out of my rooms by the end of the month," she blurted.

"What?" I asked in surprise. "You've paid your rent, haven't you?"

"Yes. Thanks to you I paid two weeks in advance."

"Then why—?"

"A man came askin' my landlady about me. Said I was causin' trouble for his master. He told her if she knew what was good for her, she'd get rid of me. He wanted me out that day, but my landlady said I paid for two more weeks and I had a right to stay 'til then."

"That's preposterous! Who was this man? And who is his master?"

"My landlady was too scared to ask. But I think it's gotta have something to do with the fire—and the lawsuit."

"I wonder," I said thoughtfully.

"You can't blame my landlady, Miss Woolson. Things happen—you know, things no one can explain. She's worried, is all. I'd be, too, if I was in her place."

Robert broke in before I could reply. "Now you see where all your confounded meddling has led, Sarah? I warned you to let things be."

Robert knew I'd been trying to locate Paddy McGuire. In fact, I'd tried to elicit his help, but he'd flatly refused to participate in what he termed a "lost cause."

Ignoring him, I turned back to Mrs. Mankin. Already I had the glimmering of an idea how I might at least be able to solve her immediate problem.

"My dear," I told her, "I think I know a place where you can stay, at least for the time being. One where you'll be safe from this man and whoever he's working for."

"There you go again," Robert interrupted. "Don't build up her hopes making promises you can't keep."

Mrs. Mankin looked hesitantly between Robert and me. Her frightened face showed cautious optimism. "You really know a place like that? Where that man won't find me?"

"I promise you'll be perfectly safe," I said, darting Robert a warning look. "I must, however, understand your intentions about the lawsuit. Under the circumstances, do you still wish to pursue it?"

I waited while she thought about this, pleased she was giving it the serious consideration it deserved. Robert started to say something, but at a slight shake of my head, he reluctantly kept his opinions to himself. At length, she seemed to make up her mind.

"Yes, ma'am," she said firmly. "I want to go through with it. You and your mother have been real kind, but getting money from the man who caused my Jack's death is all I got to give my children. I know the chance of winning isn't good, but I want to at least try."

"Good," I said before Robert could lecture me yet again on the futility of little Sarah Woolson taking on Goliath. "If you've finished your coffee, let's be off. There's no time like the present to begin."

• • •

Pacific and Kearney streets presented an intriguing contrast: a seedy, if exotic, Chinatown, and the notorious Barbary Coast, populated by sailors, cutthroats, crimps—who supplied ship crews by whatever means necessary—bars, prostitution and gambling houses. The one quality both areas shared was a general villainy and squalor that was becoming famous, or infamous, around the world.

With so many Chinese and other immigrants competing for jobs, a number of San Francisco's sweatshops were located in or around this area. Samuel had penned several stories about these districts for local newspapers, and I knew many of the establishments were run by the Chinese. If that was the case, it might be next to impossible to locate the owner of the building where Jack Mankin died.

Not long ago, I'd shared an adventure with Margaret Culbertson, the dedicated and fearless woman who ran the Presbyterian Mission on Sacramento Street. While trying to rescue a young Chinese girl from white slavery, I'd met Li Ying, the most powerful of all the Chinatown tong leaders.

Through Li Ying, I'd learned much about the secret way of life that existed within Tangrenbu, or Port of the People of China. The Chinese, largely to defend themselves against increasing anti-Chinese attitudes, had banded together to form tongs, groups organized along the general lines of kinship and geographical origins. The result was a unique and intensely private subculture that protected its own. If the owner of the sweatshop where Jack Mankin died was indeed Chinese—and he wished to disappear—there was hardly a better place to accomplish that purpose than the dense ten-block-square area of Chinatown.

The same situation, of course, would not apply to Paddy McGuire. As a poor Irish laborer with no tong to protect him, he'd be forced to find a new job as soon as possible, probably in another sweatshop. Which was why I'd decided to start my search around Pacific and Kearney. If anyone knew Paddy's whereabouts, it would likely be people he had seen on a regular basis.

Robert and I dropped Mrs. Mankin off at her lodgings before going on to the scene of the fire. Not surprisingly, my colleague grumbled incessantly as our hansom cab plodded along, protesting he'd been tricked into accompanying me on yet another wild goose chase. Thankfully, I'd perfected the ability to block out his complaints, and I occupied myself by wondering what we would find.

To my surprise, instead of the mess of soggy, charred debris I'd expected, most of the rubble from the fire had been cleared away and men were already at work erecting a new building. Robert noted that the materials they were using probably wouldn't pass the city's new building codes, but I doubted that would matter. It was no secret that construction regulations were not as closely monitored in some San Francisco districts as they were in others.

"I suggest we separate," I told him. "You take that

side of the street. I'll start with the tobacco store on this corner."

"And just what am I supposed to ask?" he said testily.

"Oh, for goodness sake! Describe Paddy McGuire and the other man who periodically inspected the shop. Surely someone should remember them."

With an irritable grunt, my crotchety companion duly crossed the street. There, after a moment's hesitation, he entered the nearest saloon.

I tugged at the long cuirass bodice of my dark burgundy dress and brushed at the horizontal pleating that made up the matching skirt. Then, straightening my velvet hat, I marched purposefully to the tobacconist's shop and boldly entered. The clerk, who was waiting on a man wearing an odd assortment of work clothes, looked astonished to find a lady in his establishment. He finished with his customer, then, wiping his hands on his apron, turned to me in a fluster.

"Yes, ma'am, what can I do for you then? Some cigars for yer husband, maybe? I have some top-notch smokes over here."

"Yes, I see." Examining his merchandise, I spotted the Havana cigars favored by my father. "I'll take half a dozen of these, please."

The clerk beamed; these were probably his most expensive brand. "Snappin' good choice, ma'am. Yer husband will be sure to like these."

I didn't bother to correct him, since I'd only made the purchase to obtain information. While he wrapped the cigars in plain brown paper, I inquired if he knew either of the men we were seeking. He looked up when I mentioned McGuire.

"Everyone knows Paddy," he said, as if surprised I should ask. "He was the beatingest man on the street. Awful about the fire, wasn't it? For a while there I thought the whole block was a goner."

"Do you know where Paddy is working now?"

The clerk handed me the package. "I knew he was lookin' for a job, but I never heard if he found anythin'."

"What about the other man?" I said, briefly describing what little I knew about the stout man we hoped might be the owner.

"Don't know nothin' about him. Leastwise I don't remember seein' him in my shop." The clerk could not contain his curiosity. "If you don't mind my askin', ma'am, why are you so het up to find these fellows?"

Expecting this question, I'd prepared an answer. "I've heard that Mr. McGuire might be interested in doing a few odd jobs for us. I was told the other man might know where Paddy was employed."

The clerk scratched his head. "Sorry I can't help. I'm sure Paddy would be glad enough to make some extra cash."

Taking up the package of cigars, I thanked the man and left the shop. An hour later, burdened now with not only the cigars but a fresh fillet of salmon and a box of sweets for Celia's children, I met Robert, who was also carrying several parcels. I detected the smell of whiskey on his breath, a testament to the bars he'd visited on his side of the street.

"Nothing, absolutely nothing," he complained. "Everyone knows McGuire, but not where we can find him."

"What about the other man?"

He shook his head. "Not a thing. What about you? Any luck?"

"No." It was discouraging, but I was not yet ready to give up. "Let's try another street."

"Why? We've already wasted half the afternoon."

"Come on, Robert, just one more block?" I smiled, deciding a dose of honey might get me further than vinegar.

It didn't fool him for a moment. "I like it better when you're biting off my head than trying to butter me up." He grinned. "You're no good at it, you know."

Laughing, I crossed Kearney Street. Robert reshuffled his packages and set off in the opposite direction.

I was coming out of a shop midway down the block when it happened. A tall, heavy-set man stopped directly in front of me, his face so close I could see tufts of hair protruding from his beefy nose. His eyes resembled small black olives that had been poked into a plate of fat.

"Excuse me, sir," I said, endeavoring to move past him. It was like trying to push aside an oak tree. "Please, you're blocking my way." I was annoyed to hear fear in my voice. Surely he wouldn't dare harm me in broad daylight, in front of so many people. Then, looking around, I realized no one was paying us the least attention.

"Whatcha after, missy?" he asked, nearly bowling me over with his foul breath. "Why all the questions about Paddy?"

"I, ah, was told he's an able repairman," I said, wishing I sounded more convincing.

He seemed to find this uproariously funny. "Oh, you was, was ya?" The amusement was suddenly gone. He leaned in even closer. I caught a glimpse of rotting teeth, and again his fetid breath nearly caused me to choke. I tried to move away, but I'd backed up against the shop wall and there was no place else to go.

"And what about Killy, huh, missy? I ain't never heard anyone call him able—unless you got a different sort of work in mind. I hear he knows how to make the ladies happy, if you take my meanin'." His leering wink left little doubt about Killy's special talents.

Despite my fear, at least I'd just learned the name of the second man we were after.

"Yes, Killy." I forced a smile. "I'd be grateful if you could tell me where to find—"

"The only thing I'm tellin' you, lady, is to mind yer own bloody business. 'Cause if you don't, you just might find a hammer comin' at yer head instead of yer house." He wrapped huge, filthy fingers around the lapel of my bodice, ripping the fabric as he yanked me nearly off my feet. "It'd be a shame to spoil such a pretty face."

With a throaty laugh, he released me so suddenly I staggered into a fruit display, knocking down a crate of apples. The man didn't hurry but sauntered off as if he had nothing to fear. Which was probably true. Several people averted their faces as he passed, then turned and almost ran in the opposite direction.

It was several moments before I could move. My limbs felt as if they'd turned to mush and, to my horror, I'd begun to shake.

A small hand suddenly touched my arm and I nearly jumped out of my boots. "Don't mean to alarm ya, ma'am," a voice said. "I saw you talkin' to Bert Corrigan. You want to stay as far away from that hooligan as you can."

The woman who stood beside me was so tiny she barely reached my shoulder. She looked about forty but might have been much younger. A life of grueling work often aged these poor souls beyond their years. She wasn't an attractive creature, I thought, yet there was a quality about her that set her apart. Pride, I decided, and an unmistakable air of defiance.

"Are you all right, ma'am?" she asked when I didn't immediately answer.

"Yes, I'm fine now," I replied. "I admit Bert Corrigan gave me a bit of a fright."

"Hah! He could scare the devil himself, could our Bert." She looked up and down the street. "I know who yer looking for. I was in the fishmongers and heard you ask."

"You mean you know where I can find Paddy

McGuire or Killy? I'm sorry, but I don't know Killy's last name."

"It's Doyle, but that's all I know about him. He only shows his face around here when he has to. I know Paddy well enough, though. Got himself a job in a sweatshop on Washington Street. It's run by a Johnny—you know, a Chinaman. I think its called Wing Yo's. Seems our Paddy's doin' all right for himself." This last was said in a bitter tone, and her thin lips turned down at the corners.

"Why are you telling me all this, Mrs. . . . . ?"

"Never mind who I am. It's enough for you to know that my husband was killed in that fire, along with four other souls. And I know well enough it was Paddy McGuire who nailed that door shut." Her eyes burned so fiercely they seemed to gleam with orange sparks. "I don't know why you're lookin' for him, but I can guess it's to do with what happened. Somebody's gotta pay for those five lives!"

The fiery emotion in her eyes went out as suddenly as it had ignited, replaced by pools of tears. I realized the courage it had taken for her to approach me. If Bert Corrigan was an example of the retribution she might expect for talking to me, she was a very brave woman indeed.

"I'll do everything I can to see the responsible parties brought to justice," I said, placing my hand on her arm. "I'm sorry for your loss."

As if she could no longer hold them back, tears coursed down her face. Unwilling or unable to speak, she nodded her head and walked away.

I watched until she was absorbed into the crowd. Behind me, I heard a loud cry as the grocer discovered his apples rolling about the street. Ignoring the man's curses, street urchins snatched them up and ran.

Feeling responsible for the melee, I handed the man some money, then crossed to Robert's side of the street. I found him arguing with a butcher over the price of pork.

"I've found Paddy McGuire," I said, tugging on his arm.

"This man is no better than a common thief," he cried. You wouldn't believe the price he's asking for—"

"Did you hear me, Robert? I've found Paddy McGuire."

Robert seemed disinclined to end his quarrel, then noticed my torn bodice. "What happened to you?"

As I pulled my colleague away from the shop, the butcher let loose a string of profanities and slapped the pork back into the brine barrel.

"Damn it all, Sarah, who did this to you?"

As we walked on, I described my encounter with Bert Corrigan. Although I downplayed it as much as possible, Robert's face darkened with fury.

"Why didn't you call me?" he demanded. "That ruffian could have done far worse than rip your dress. Damn it all, woman, one of these days you're going to push your luck too far."

"Calm down, Robert. The man was unpleasant, but

he didn't actually harm me. And he did let slip the name of the second man we're looking for."

"Humph. As if we're ever likely to find the fellow."

"Oh, do try to be less pessimistic. It gets tiresome."

We'd reached the corner of Washington and Kearney and I wasn't sure which way to turn. The street had taken on more of the flavor of Chinatown and less of the Barbary Coast. As I say, I'd visited Chinatown only once before—the night I'd joined Miss Culbertson to save the young slave girl—but that had been after midnight. I was struck by how different the district appeared in broad daylight. What had seemed exotic by night now looked shabby and depressing. Most people either averted their faces as we passed or darted looks of suspicion and outright dislike at us. I couldn't blame them; we were the outsiders, members of the race who persecuted them for taking our jobs and for often doing them better and at lower wages.

The streets were jammed with little shops, one upon the other. Tables blocked the sidewalks displaying fruits, nuts, vegetables, cigars, herbs, potions and twisted roots. From the lanes and alleys came clouds of smoke from open cooking fires.

"Why don't you go to the right and I'll take the left," I suggested. "We're looking for a place called Wing Yo's."

"Not on your life. I'm sticking to you like glue."

I started to argue, then thought better of it. In truth, I wasn't anxious for another encounter with Bert Corrigan—or with any other street thug, for that matter. I

67

nodded my agreement, and we made our way toward Dupont. Since most shop signs were written in Chinese characters, though, finding Wing Yo's was all but impossible. It was doubly frustrating when I could find no one who spoke English.

Soon, even I grew discouraged. Robert, who towered over the Chinese like Gulliver in the land of the Lilliputians, grumbled about all the time we'd wasted. Leaving him to grouse, I stopped a young Chinese boy carrying crates of produce from a delivery wagon into a grocery store.

"Excuse me," I said, hoping the lad understood at least some English. "Do you know a shop called Wing Yo's?"

The boy shifted his crate and subjected me to very grown-up scrutiny. "Why you want to know?" The boy directed his question to me, but he was craning his neck to stare curiously at Robert.

I understood the look; in the lad's culture, it was men who asked questions, not mere women. The fact that the man was as tall as a giant must add to his confusion. I fought down the urge to educate the child on the injustice of such discrimination and kept silent. Robert, too, seemed to appreciate the significance of the boy's attitude, because he said in an authoritative voice,

"Don't keep us standing here all day, lad." He held a coin out to the boy, who grabbed it with alacrity. "Another of these is yours if you can direct us to Wing Yo's."

The lad's eyes lit with excitement. "One minute," he said and he quickly carried his crate into the store.

He was back outside in less than a minute, motioning for us to follow him. His small size allowed him to weave through the crowd with ease. We found the going more difficult, especially Robert, who negotiated the congested street like an elephant trying to make its way through a glass shop.

After two blocks, the boy stopped before a building indistinguishable from its neighbors. "Wing's up there," he said, holding out his hand, palm up.

Robert pulled out another coin but didn't immediately hand it over. "I don't see any sign. How do I know Wing's shop is really here?"

The boy muttered something in Chinese, then flung open the door to the building and took the stairs two at a time. Robert followed, while I hurried behind them. The narrow stairwell was dimly lit and smelled vilely of urine, garbage and strange cooking odors.

"Here," the boy announced, pointing to the only door on the uppermost floor.

Attempting to catch my breath, I knocked. When no one answered, I slowly opened the door. Inside, a dozen men and women bent over sewing machine, ironing, cutting and fabric marking tables. I turned and nodded to Robert. He barely had the coin out of his pocket when the boy snatched it and bounded down the stairs with even more speed than he'd ascended.

"Let's hope this really is Wing Yo's," Robert said as

we entered the sweatshop.

The room we found ourselves in did not seem large enough to accommodate the workers, who were equally divided between Chinese and Occidental. Though the day outside was cool and the room's two windows were wide open, the shop felt hot and airless. The floor was piled with partially sewn garments, while completed articles filled two tables by the door, shirts on one side, trousers on the other.

With a little shock, I realized the room had but one door, and I could see no fire escapes. God help these poor workers if fire broke out in the stairwell; everything in this room would go up like a tinderbox. It was another disaster waiting to happen, one potentially more deadly than the fire that had killed Mrs. Mankin's husband.

Two women glanced up as we entered the room, but at a warning look from a Chinese man who was teaching a young boy to iron, they hastily resumed their work. The man's eyes narrowed, as if he was not accustomed to visitors.

"Good afternoon," I said, smiling pleasantly. His expression remained noncommunicative. "We're looking for a man called Paddy McGuire."

My eyes scanned the room to see if anyone reacted to the name. Sure enough, a worker toward the back stared at me with a wary expression. Beneath a brownish-red beard, his face was thin and angular, his eyes intelligent and a bit cocky. A bold tilt to his narrow chin announced him to be a man not adverse to downing a friendly pint or engaging in a not so friendly fight.

"I'm Paddy," he said almost defiantly, ignoring his overseer's cautionary glare.

Hoping this dour Chinese understood English, I said, "May we please speak privately to Mr. McGuire? It won't take long, I promise."

The man seemed to understand well enough, or perhaps he just wanted us out of his shop. He nodded curtly toward the door we'd just entered. Paddy rose from his machine and, hitching up his pants, swaggered out into the hall.

"So?" he said, the instant we were out of the room. "Who the devil are ya, and whatcha want with me?"

"I'm Sarah Woolson and this is Robert Campbell. We're attorneys working on behalf of Mrs. Lily Mankin, who lost her husband Jack in that sweatshop fire—"

"Sweet Jesus, a woman lawyer!" Paddy assessed me as if I belonged in a zoo. "Never seen one of them before."

Ignoring his rude stare, I kept my voice professional. "We're here for information, Mr. McGuire. I understand you used to work with Mr. Mankin?"

McGuire regarded me warily. "What if I did?"

"In order to help his widow, we need to know who nailed that sweatshop door closed." I held up a hand before Paddy could explode. "Mr. McGuire, we're not here to accuse you of wrongdoing. Please, just answer the question."

Paddy raised an eyebrow. "What if it was me who nailed the bloody door shut? How's that gonna help Jack's wife?"

"If you boarded it up it on your own, it won't," I explained. "On the other hand, if someone told you to do it—the owner, perhaps—it will help her a great deal."

"Hah!" he snorted. "That's a good one. No one knows who owns these pigsties. Don't give a damn if any of us live or die, long as we keep the money pourin' into their pockets. The worthless bastard who owned the shop what burned down sure as hell never dropped in for a visit."

My heart felt heavy with disappointment. "So, you took it upon yourself to nail the door closed."

"I never said that now, did I?" he bristled. At first I thought he was trying to deny responsibility for blocking the exit. Then I realized it was quite the opposite. The guilt I saw reflected in his eyes was imbedded with deep self-reproach. Whether deserved or not, Paddy McGuire held himself responsible for the deaths of his five coworkers.

"Killy's the one told me to do it," he admitted at last, his voice full of self-loathing.

"Killy?" I said excitedly. "You mean Killy Doyle?"

"One and the same. Claimed he'd get around to fixin' the lock when he had time, the lazy slob." He stopped, plainly fearing he'd revealed too much. "You tell Killy I said that, and I'll be callin' you liars," he warned.

"If you've told us the truth," Robert said, "there's no

need for your name to be mentioned."

"You say Killy didn't own the sweatshop?" I asked.

"Nah. Killy's the muscle to bully people around, but he ain't got the brains or gumption to be boss of anythin' besides his own prick." His face reddened. "Beggin' yer pardon, ma'am. No offense intended."

Robert, whose own face had flushed, started to protest, but I cut him off before he could erupt.

"Mr. McGuire, do you know where we can find Killy?"

"Nope, never seen him outside the shop." His eyes grew sharp. "I'm warnin' you, though. If you do find him, you'd best watch yer backsides. And mind you keep me out of it. I only told you what I did to help Jack's wife. He and the others shouldn't a been trapped in that hellhole." With that, he turned and slammed back into the sweatshop.

Robert and I didn't speak until we were once again on the street.

"Now I suppose you'll insist on finding this Doyle fellow," he muttered as we went in search of a cab.

I saw the ghost of a smile playing around that broad mouth. How like him, I thought. In spite of the brusque exterior he put on for public display, Robert would never turn his back on a woman in need, much less a widow with small children to care for and another on its way.

"Of course," I answered matter-of-factly, happy enough to help him save face. "Under the circumstances, we can hardly do less."

CHAPTER FOUR

ama was waiting for me when I arrived home. For the past hour I'd longed for a hot bath and a hot cup of tea. One look at my mother's face told me both comforts were going to be delayed.

"You have a message," she teased, eyes alight as she waved a piece of white notepaper at me.

"A message from whom?" I asked, knowing from her delighted expression that it could only be from a man.

"Here, see for yourself." She handed me the notepaper, then stood eagerly watching my reaction. It read:

Dear Miss Woolson,
I would be pleased if you would accompany me
to Woodward Gardens next Sunday, March the 7th.
I think I can promise an enjoyable afternoon.
                    Respectfully yours,
                    Pierce Godfrey, Esq.

I reread the short note then, without comment, placed it in my pocket and started upstairs.

"Well?" Mama called out. "What are you going to do?"

"I shall send Ina with my regrets. Right now I'm

tired and would like to go to my room and have a bath."

"Sarah, you're hopeless. I could understand your reticence with the dentist, but Mr. Godfrey is a most attractive young man."

"I agree. But I have no time right now for courting."

Mama sighed in exasperation. "I thought you might say that. Which is why I took the liberty of accepting the invitation on your behalf."

I stopped and stared down at her. "You did what?"

"You're not getting any younger, Sarah. There may come a day when you'll regret slamming the door in your suitors' faces—especially a man like Mr. Godfrey."

I started to argue, then realized it would serve no purpose. The damage was already done. I could hardly cancel the engagement now.

"All right, Mama, I'll go," I gave in ungracefully. "But in the future, I'll thank you not to read my private communications, much less take it upon yourself to accept or decline invitations on my behalf."

As I finally sank into my bath, I forced thoughts of Pierce Godfrey from my mind and concentrated instead on Lily Mankin's lawsuit. Granted, finding Paddy McGuire this afternoon was a vital first step, but without Doyle we had no case. And I feared he would not be easy to find.

If Paddy was right, and Doyle didn't own the sweatshop, who was Doyle taking his orders from? How far did the chain of underlings extend before it reached the man who was ultimately responsible for dooming five men to their graves? I thought about Bert Corrigan, the bully who threatened me outside the Kearney Street grocery store. Where did he fit into this? Who had sent him to warn me—and why? And what would he do when he learned I had no intention of giving in to his harassment?

Despite the hot water, I felt a sudden chill. I lay my head back and willed my body to relax, but it was no use. My lovely bath had lost its ability to calm my agitated mind.

Sunday dawned bright and clear. According to Mama, who'd gone out early to do some gardening, it was a perfect March morning, cool but not cold, and thankfully free of fog. Since I'd been hoping for rain, this news did not cheer me. I've been accused of possessing an overactive imagination, but Pierce Godfrey really did remind me of the buccaneers I'd read about as a child. In books, pirates were exciting and romantic. In real life, this particular brigand left me confused and unsure. He was a man I didn't wholly understand.

I'd been in some indecision as to what to wear. I've long held the opinion that women's clothes are designed to restrict natural movement. As far as I'm concerned, this is not only unhealthy but impractical. I've actually witnessed women playing tennis in dresses outfitted with a train! I may not meet the edicts of Paris couture—which is torture if I ever saw it!—

but whenever possible I make my costume choices in favor of comfort rather than style.

In the end I chose a pale lavender dress of soft brushed cotton, with very little bustle, a straight skirt—with no added flounces to get in my way—and sleeves that allowed my arms to move freely. It was one of the least fussy gowns in my wardrobe. Moreover, at the risk of appearing immodest, I consider lavender to be one of my more becoming colors, complementing my black hair and violet eyes. I added a simple straw boater decorated with a lavender ribbon, as well as a matching parasol to protect me from the sun, and my preparations were complete.

Pierce arrived precisely at one o'clock, impressing Mama with his punctuality—as if she required any further persuasion regarding his suitability!

"You look lovely," he said approvingly as we left the house. "That gown is perfect for the Gardens. I never understand women who dress up for an outing as if they're going to a formal ball."

"Thank you," I said, pleased that we shared similar views on this subject. "I couldn't agree with you more."

Woodward's Gardens were located on Mission near Fourteenth Street. Instead of taking his carriage, Pierce thought it might be fun to make the trip in one of Henry Casebolt's mule-drawn balloon cars. These odd-looking vehicles—commonly called "bandboxes on wheels"—were round, fatter than cable cars, and equipped with an overhanging oval roof. One of their main attractions was that they could change directions at the end of the line with a simple pull of a bolt, which turned the upper part of the car entirely around. Personally, I found the ride a bit jerky, wobbling as it did from side to side like a ship. But as a novelty it was amusing enough, and we joined the rest of the passengers in hearty laughter as we lumbered on our way.

While I waited for Pierce to purchase our admission tickets to the gardens, I noticed a crowd gathered to one side of the gate. You can imagine my surprise when I spied Reverend Josiah Halsey standing in the center of the throng, spouting his bizarre dogma to a mostly amused audience. Once again he was dressed entirely in black, and his fierce dark eyes blazed out from beneath flyaway brows. As he preached, he waved the same tattered brown Bible above his head.

"From all false doctrine, heresy and schism, good Lord, deliver us," he quoted loudly from the Book of Common Prayer. "Listen to me, my brothers and sisters, for I will give unto thee the keys of the kingdom of heaven."

This was met with scattered jeers and a few rude remarks, causing a raucous outbreak of laughter. Halsey's lean, craggy face bore a look of frenzied ecstasy, and he seemed not to notice his audience's mocking response.

"I tell you that the wicked shall be turned into the fiery depths of hell. Repent before it is too late!"

"Shut up, you crazy old coot!" a man's voice yelled.

Another man cried out, "I'd just as soon go to hell than to that heaven of yours. Sounds damned boring!"

The crowd began to scatter amid giggles and little screams, as garbage from a nearby bin began flying at the minister. As I moved back out of the fray, I felt a hand on my arm, and found that Pierce had moved up behind me.

"It's that so-called minister who broke into Leonard and Caroline's house," he said tightly. "What the blazes is he doing here?"

"At the moment, he seems to be inciting a riot."

Even as I said this, a rotten orange came flying by my head. Women screamed and tried to draw their children away from the fracas, while men flailed their fists, more or less indiscriminately, as far as I could see.

Pierce took my arm and drew me away from the fight. As he did, I noticed Reverend Halsey slinking away from the brawl, Bible clutched tightly to his chest. A few moments later, a police wagon pulled up and several uniformed men jumped out and started to break up the fight. I looked around, but Revered Halsey was no longer in sight.

"Just like the night Caroline died," Pierce said with quiet fury. "He sowed his seeds of hatred and bigotry, then when they bore fruit, he was gone. Someone should stop that bastard before he causes serious trouble."

I was surprised by this vulgarity, but I don't think Pierce was even aware he'd used it. He continued to look down Mission Street where Halsey had vanished, his expression so malevolent I felt a chill go down my spine.

My happy mood was shattered. "Perhaps we should leave," I said, breaking in upon his thoughts.

"No, that's exactly what we mustn't do. We're not going to let that charlatan ruin our day." He smiled and took my arm. "Shall we?"

I returned his smile with some of my earlier enthusiasm. Pierce was right; if we left, Halsey would have won. "Why not?"

Despite the poor beginning, the afternoon turned out to be perfect. Our first stop was the park's splendid museum, where we spent a pleasant hour admiring the old masters, as well as laughing at some of the more avant-garde exhibits. After that we wandered about the grounds, feeding peanuts to the deer and bears, then taking a somewhat bumpy ride in a carriage pulled by two white goats.

We spread a blanket on the grass to eat our picnic dinner and listened to a band performing on a flower-laden platform. I don't think fried chicken, Saratoga chips and apple dumpling ever tasted as good as they did that lovely afternoon, especially washed down with ice-cold lemonade bought from a nearby stand.

Remembering the rickety ride we'd endured earlier in the balloon car, Pierce hired a cab for the journey home. Sitting there in comfortable silence, I was surprised to realize I'd found the day thoroughly delightful.

"A penny for your thoughts." Pierce sat across from me, his long legs crossed at the ankles. In the light filtering through the carriage windows, I could see his mouth curved in an enigmatic smile.

"What's funny?" I asked, then was surprised when he said, "You didn't expect to have a good time today, did you? No, don't bother denying it. It was written all over your face when I picked you up at your house. In fact, if your mother hadn't accepted the invitation for you, you would have found some excuse not to go."

This was so close to the truth, I felt color creep into my cheeks and was grateful the light in the carriage was poor.

I made an effort to look affronted. "I don't know why you'd say a thing like that. Woodward's Gardens is a splendid way to spend a Sunday afternoon."

"Woodward's Gardens was never the question, though, was it? I'm the problem, although I doubt it's anything personal. You probably would behave the same toward any man who showed you any interest."

"Mr. Godfrey, really—" I started to object, but he cut me off.

"Unlike most of your sex, you aren't looking for a man to take care of you." He smiled at what must have been my shocked expression. "You're intelligent, independent and know what you want from life. Most extraordinary, you're not afraid to go after it. I've traveled the world, Sarah, yet I've never met another woman remotely like you."

I found myself at an uncharacteristic loss for words.

"I apologize if I've embarrassed you. It's just that I find you remarkably refreshing. I can't remember when I've had a more enjoyable time."

"I think—" I said hoarsely, annoyed when I had to stop to clear my throat. "I think most men would find the qualities you named intimidating rather than refreshing. At least that's been my experience."

"Then we must broaden your horizons, Miss Woolson," he said softly.

His words, though seemingly harmless, were spoken in a tone so laden with hidden meaning that I felt goose bumps rise on my arms. Evening was fast approaching, and Pierce sat cast in partial shadow, but enough light fell upon him to reflect his eyes gazing at me speculatively.

"So, have you decided whether or not to accept my business proposition?" he asked.

"Your what?" I said, caught off guard.

"Last week I asked if you would act as my attorney on some company business. You haven't given me your decision."

"Ah, yes. Actually, I think it would be best if you brought this up with Mr. Shepard," I said, remembering the senior partner's rage over Lily Mankin's case. That incident would be nothing compared to my agreeing to represent a company as large as Godfrey Shipping!

He regarded me for a moment, then nodded. "As you wish. I haven't had the pleasure of meeting your employer, but I'll call upon him first thing tomorrow morning."

"You realize it's highly unlikely he'll allow me to represent you."

"Of course; that's why I came to you first. Your employer's chauvinism is no less than I expected." Again, that unreadable smile. "Don't worry, Sarah, I'm confident he can be made to see reason."

I didn't return his smile. I knew Joseph Shepard and, by his own admission, Pierce did not.

That evening I attended a meeting of the hospital board at the Barlow home on the north slope of Russian Hill. This was an older, more established area than the summit—where the Godfreys' home was situated—but it, too, commanded a spectacular view of the city.

Mama and Celia, who were members of the board, were excited that the group had successfully leased the Battery Street warehouse. Now everyone was eager to finalize plans for the necessary renovations.

It surprised me when Mama and Celia grew tense as we approached the Barlow home shortly before eight.

"What is it?" I asked. "Is something wrong?"

"It's that fanatic, Reverend Halsey," Mama replied. "Every time we hold a board meeting, he's lying in wait outside, ranting and waving his Bible at us."

"Thank goodness he doesn't seem to be here tonight," Celia said with a little shudder. "He makes my skin crawl."

"Speaking of Halsey," I put in, "Mr. Godfrey and I saw him today preaching outside Woodward's Gardens. Actually, screaming fire and brimstone is more like it. He actually incited a riot and the police had to be called out."

"I just wish he'd go back to Los Angeles or wherever he comes from," Mama said. "I wonder if he realizes how many enemies he's making?"

And with those naively prophetic words, we went inside.

Everyone gathered in the Barlow front parlor. The room was large enough to accommodate two wine-colored velvet sofas, placed on either side of a bay window, as well as several gentlemen's chairs and a scattering of smaller ladies' chairs. A lush Oriental carpet lay on the floor, and a number of delicate Chinese and Japanese prints hung on the walls. A fire crackled in the oversized hearth, and silver coffee and tea services had been set out on low tables. My eyes were drawn to an intricately beautiful tapestry hanging at the end of the long room. Upon examining it more closely, I was astonished to see that it looked like a genuine Gobelin.

"Lovely, isn't it?" Mama said, coming up beside me. "I don't know how they do it."

The meeting began, and I had no time to question this remark. On the way over, Mama had explained that the hospital board comprised roughly a dozen people, including the new chairwoman, Margaret Barlow, her husband, Judge Tobias Barlow, Margaret's mother, Adelina French, Mama, Celia, my brother

Charles, one or two other doctors and a few civic-minded individuals from the community. Several members were missing tonight, including Charles, who'd been called out on a case, and Judge Barlow, who was attending a function with my father at their club.

Reverend Nicholas Prescott was also in attendance. Catching my gaze, my mother whispered that when Margaret assumed leadership of the board, she begged the minister to take on the role of the hospital's spiritual advisor. Eyes twinkling, Mama promised that I was in for a rare treat.

Everyone settled into a seat, and Mrs. Barlow called the meeting to order. She introduced Reverend Prescott to those who had not yet met him, then asked if he would lead us in a prayer. Smiling, he rose and bowed his head. I noticed that every eye in the room was fastened on the handsome cleric, as if drawn there by a magnet. Especially, I saw with amusement, the women.

As Prescott began his invocation, I closed my eyes and found myself falling beneath the spell of those warm, fluid tones, so comforting and soothingly intimate. The tension began to drain out of my body and I slowly relaxed. It seemed as if my body were floating in a world of perfect peace.

Then someone coughed and I came back to myself with a start. Opening my eyes, I saw that everyone around me was equally spellbound. Margaret Barlow had an otherworldly look on her face, while her mother, Mrs. French, seemed to be in some kind of trance. Even Mama and Celia were clearly enraptured by the man. Had he mesmerized us? I wondered. I'd heard of this practice, but I hadn't believed it possible. Now I wasn't so sure.

Mama flashed me a knowing smile in the silence following Reverend Prescott's prayer, pleased she'd been proven right. The quiet did not feel uncomfortable; rather, it seemed companionable and calm. I had the impression no one wished to shatter the serenity the tall minister had created in the room.

After several moments, Mrs. Barlow cleared her throat and asked Lucius Arlen to present his financial report. The accountant stood and, looking about the room as if to ensure he had everyone's attention, placed his spectacles atop his globular nose and opened a black ledger.

"Largely due to the one hundred twenty thousand dollars raised at Mr. and Mrs. Godfrey's charity dinner," he began, "we were able to reach an agreement with the owners of the Battery Street warehouse and have signed the lease papers. Renovations on the new hospital have already begun and, according to the survey we commissioned, will be less extensive than we originally feared. This will not only reduce our initial costs, but will allow the hospital to accept its first patients several weeks earlier than scheduled."

An excited murmur swept through the room. Celia clasped her hands together in delight as Mama whispered that women were already begging for admission to the hospital. Now, mercifully, they would not have to be turned away.

Mr. Arlen turned a page in his ledger, then removed his glasses and again regarded the room until it became quiet.

"Having said that, I must stress the need for fiscal restraint. For instance, I question the amount of money that has been allotted the kitchen staff, especially as the cook is Chinese." This last word was uttered with obvious disdain.

All eyes went to Margaret Barlow. "I assure you Mr. Chin is a Fine Chef and comes highly recommended." Her tone was a bit defensive. I knew from Mama that Mrs. Barlow had hired Chin Lee Fong away from an upscale hotel on Turk Street.

"The man is *Chinese,*" he repeated, as if Mrs. Barlow had missed the significance of the man's racial origin. "You are paying him a white man's wages."

Mrs. Barlow seemed unable to find a suitable retort. She looked helplessly at her mother, who said, "Mr. Chin has been offered a wage commensurate with his skills, Mr. Arlen. Are you suggesting that in good conscience we should offer him less than a fair living?"

"I'm saying we must not lose sight of our limited resourses, Mrs. French. As Chin will be cooking for a charity hospital, I consider it reasonable that we readjust his salary or hire someone who will do the job for less."

When this statement elicited loud opinions, both for and against the proposal, Mrs. French gave her daughter a sharp look, at which Margaret hastily recalled her duty as chairwoman. Thanking Arlen, she asked one of the doctors to report on the number of beds and the amount of medical equipment required to accommodate the first patients.

The accountant closed his ledger with a sharp snap and returned to his seat. Was he anti-Chinese? I wondered. Since I'd met the enigmatic tong lord, Li Ying, I'd begun to grasp the misunderstanding that existed between our two cultures. While it was true the average Chinese immigrant preferred to isolate himself from the *fan kwei* (foreign devils), it was because once he'd earned enough money, he planned to return to his homeland. The few brave souls like Chin Lee Fong who ventured outside Chinatown were usually regarded with distrust. Was this what was bothering Arlen, or were the hospital's finances really so dire?

On the whole, I considered the accountant's report favorable. The fact that at least some of the hospital's rooms could be put to immediate use was vital to the plan I had come here to propose.

When the general business of the evening had concluded, I asked permission to address the board. Standing, I explained Lily Mankin's situation, then proposed a practical solution to her predicament: we could allow the widow and her children to occupy one of the existing rooms in the hospital while the rest of the building was being renovated.

"Wait, please," I put in, when my suggestion produced a murmur of disapproval. "Mrs. Mankin is honest and hardworking. What's more, she's adept at sewing, ironing and cooking. I have no doubt she would make a fine nurse if properly trained. I believe it would be to the hospital's benefit if she lived in as a full-time staff member."

"What about her children?" asked a heavy-set matron, who sat ramrod straight on her lady's chair. "Who is going to care for them while Mrs. Mankin performs her duties?"

"We've made plans to establish a nursery for children confined to the hospital, as well as for the offspring of women who are giving birth," Mrs. French replied, giving me a conspiratorial smile. "Allowing Mrs. Mankin's children to use this room would not pose a problem."

When there were no further objections to my proposal, Margaret requested a vote, and it was unanimously decided to permit Mrs. Mankin and her children to move into the hospital as soon as a room could be made ready. Celia gave my arm a little squeeze, sharing my elation that the poor widow and her children would not be forced out into the street.

As Margaret saw us to the door after the meeting, she invited anyone interested to tour the new hospital the following afternoon. Mama and Celia accepted with alacrity. I thought about it a moment, then I, too, accepted her kind invitation.

I think everyone gave a collective sigh of relief when we exited the house to find no sign of the volatile Reverend Halsey lurking outside.

"Perhaps he finally realized the hospital isn't an instrument of the devil," Celia ventured.

"Perhaps," Mama said doubtfully. "Somehow I can't imagine Mr. Halsey giving up that easily, though."

I silently agreed, and on the walk down the hill found myself wondering what Halsey was up to.

As it happened, I did not have to wait long for an answer. Samuel and Charles were waiting for us when we arrived home, their somber faces declaring louder than words that something was wrong.

"What is it?" I asked.

"It's Reverend Halsey," Charles answered. "He was found dead tonight. One of my colleagues—who was also a guest at the Godfreys' charity dinner—was the first doctor called to the scene. He recognized the victim as Josiah Halsey."

"How did he die?" Celia asked, eyes wide with shock.

"It appears Mr. Halsey suffered a fatal heart attack."

It was past midnight when Mama and Papa retired for the night. The rest of us were equally fatigued, but Charles, Celia, Samuel and I decided on a nightcap before following our parents upstairs. Choosing to sit in the more informal—and to my mind cozier—back parlor, Samuel stoked the dying embers of the fire until the room glowed in flickering shades of amber and gold. After tonight's shocking news, it felt reassuring to be sitting here with my family. Leaning back in my favorite armchair, I allowed Papa's aged brandy to spread welcome heat throughout my body.

Charles and Celia sat on the settee. Samuel, who had replaced the fireplace poker, stood with his back to the hearth, thoughtfully rocking back and forth on his heels. Of the four of us, Celia alone seemed edgy and unable to relax.

"What's bothering you, Celia? Is it Halsey's death?"

She gave her husband a weak smile, as if embarrassed to admit that the minister's passing distressed her. "It's just so unnerving, Charles. Sarah said Reverend Halsey seemed fine when she saw him at Woodward's Gardens this afternoon. How could something like this happen so suddenly?"

"People die of heart attacks every day, my dear," Charles told his wife. "Often they occur with no warning."

I placed my brandy snifter on a small cherry wood table. "Caroline Godfrey suffered from angina for years, yet her attack was every bit as fatal as Halsey's. And she had medicine and a doctor on hand to save her."

Charles sighed. "Unfortunately, a physician and the right medicine don't always guarantee a patient's survival." He said this as if he were personally responsible for the shortcomings of modern medicine.

Belatedly, I realized how my words might be misconstrued. "I'm sorry, Charles, I wasn't blaming you. You did everything possible to save Mrs. Godfrey."

He gave me that wonderful, big brother smile I'd loved since childhood. Samuel was the sibling I could count on to help me fight my battles. But it was gentle, kind-hearted Charles who provided a sympathetic shoulder to cry on.

"I know you don't hold me personally responsible, Sarah," Charles said. "But it's difficult not to experience a sense of failure when you lose a patient."

We were all silent for a few minutes, then I asked, "By the way, where was Halsey found?"

"On Lombard Street. Not far from the Barlows' house."

"Hmm. Does anyone know where he was living?"

"I doubt anyone knew him well enough to ask. Your friend George Lewis was at the scene, by the way," Charles said looking at Samuel. "Evidently, he found no identification on the body."

Samuel spoke from where he stood by the fireplace. "Why did you ask where he was living, Sarah?"

"I was trying to understand what he was doing on Lombard Street tonight. If he had a room nearby, that would explain it. On the other hand, given his habit of appearing uninvited at hospital board meetings, he might have been on his way to the Barlows' home when he suffered—"

"A fatal . . . heart attack?" Samuel finished for me.

That slight hesitation, as well as the way he spoke the last two words, caught my attention. "You say that as if you question whether he died of natural causes."

Samuel swirled his brandy, then left his place by the hearth to take a seat in an armchair.

"I've never been a big believer in coincidence,

Sarah," he said. "It's been my experience that when something seems too improbable to be true, it usually is."

"Are you suggesting, Samuel, that Reverend Halsey caught something from Mrs. Godfrey the night of the dinner?" Celia looked to her husband. "I didn't think heart disease was contagious."

Charles's smile was rueful. "It isn't—at least, not as far as we know. But even if there was some truth to the notion, Halsey was never close enough to Mrs. Godfrey that evening to catch anything, not even a simple cold."

"Have they ordered an autopsy?" I asked Charles.

He nodded. "It's not an uncommon procedure when a victim dies suddenly, or if he hasn't been under a doctor's care." He cleared his throat. "I know it's tempting to imagine a connection between Mrs. Godfrey's and Reverend Halsey's deaths, but when I said people die of heart attacks every day, I was serious. Caroline Godfrey was being treated for a severe coronary condition. Josiah Halsey was a religious fanatic, not the sort of peaceful life one associates with good health and longevity. And don't forget, he was at an age when heart attacks among men are not unusual."

"All right, Charles," I put in. "But what about the excessive amount of nitroglycerin found in Mrs. Godfrey's system? How do you explain that?"

There was an instant outcry from Samuel and Celia, and Charles explained Mrs. Godfrey's autopsy results.

Celia shook her head, sending soft blond curls bobbing about her worried face. "I'm sorry, but I don't understand any of this."

Samuel drained what was left of his brandy, then placed the glass on the table and said, "I think what it means, my dear sister-in-law, is that, tempting as it is to jump to conclusions, we shall have to postpone further speculation until Reverend Halsey's postmortem is completed."

CHAPTER FIVE

I arrived at the office the next morning to find Hubert Perkins, the head clerk, waiting to pounce on me.

"Mr. Shepard wants to see you in his office," he said. He drew out his fob watch. "You are fifteen minutes late."

"If I am, Mr. Perkins," I retorted, weary and in no mood for verbal sparring, "it is hardly your concern."

The clerk's face flushed with anger. "Punctuality is always my concern, Miss Woolson. Mr. Shepard is waiting."

"I'm afraid he'll have to wait a few more minutes," I said, refusing to be rushed. "I must go to my office first."

Ignoring Perkins's high-pitched protests, I made for the former storage room set aside for my use. Frankly, I was still troubled by our late-night conversation the evening before. I wanted to believe Charles was right;

people died of heart attacks every day. Just because it happened to two people whose paths had so recently crossed did not mean their deaths were connected, much less suspicious. Why, then, couldn't I get Caroline Godfrey and Josiah Halsey out of my mind?

Realizing I couldn't put my employer off any longer, I removed my hat and coat and prepared to walk into the lion's den. Opening my employer's door, I found that he was not alone. Seated across from him was Pierce Godfrey.

Belatedly, I remembered the purpose of Godfrey's visit. So much had transpired since our talk in the carriage the day before, I'd forgotten his promise to speak to Joseph Shepard about my acting as his company's attorney.

"For heaven's sake, come in and close the door," Shepard barked, when I stood uncertainly in the doorway. One look at his face told me he was not pleased with his early morning visitor. In fact, his expression put me in mind of a sadly failed Yorkshire pudding. "You've met Mr. Godfrey." It was not a question so much as a criticism.

"Yes, we've met. Good morning, Mr. Godfrey."

Pierce, who stood as I entered the room, gave a small bow. "You're looking well this morning, Miss Woolson."

"Thank you. I'm feeling well."

Shepard, who had remained seated at my arrival, glared at me. "Let us get on with this, shall we?"

Pierce assisted me into a chair. As he did, I wished

I'd been a fly on the wall to witness my employer's reaction when Pierce announced that he wished to hire me as his attorney. The senior partner must have come close to apoplexy. Even now, the vein in his temple pulsated with suppressed anger.

"Mr. Godfrey has come on extraordinary business, Miss Woolson." Shepard's jowls quivered with indignation. "I'm astonished you led him to believe you'd be willing—much less qualified—to act as legal counsel for his firm."

"It is Mr. Godfrey's choice, Mr. Shepard," I replied.

"Then you should have spared no effort clarifying the situation. Such an arrangement is out of the question!"

"And why is that?" Pierce inquired politely.

Shepard clamped on his pince-nez and subjected the younger man to a squinting appraisal. "Why it—it's unheard of, that's why. Good Lord, man," he sputtered as if Pierce might be suffering from failing vision. "She's a woman!"

Pierce smiled. "So I've noticed. Still, I'm confident that her gender has not adversely affected her brain, which I've found to be first-rate. I'm sorry if this upsets you, Mr. Shepard, but I've made up my mind. I will settle for no one but Miss Woolson to represent my company."

"But she has no experience whatsoever in corporate law."

Pierce gave a dismissive wave of his hand. "Perhaps not, but I'm sure she'll learn quickly. After all, she passed her California Bar Examinations."

"Her father is a judge. She had help."

"I'd be surprised if she didn't," Pierce agreed. "On the other hand, I doubt if Judge Woolson was permitted to take the examination for her. She accomplished that on her own—and did exceedingly well, I might add."

I shot him a surprised look. "How do you know—"

He smiled. "Miss Woolson, much as I admire you, I would never consider hiring an attorney without assuring myself of his—or her—qualifications. You have nothing to be ashamed of, I assure you. Your scores were in the top percentile. I'm sure you agree, Mr. Shepard, that is impressive."

"I—I—"

Shepard's fleshy face had turned a shade of bright red, and I found myself tensing for the inevitable explosion. Sure enough, he began that dreadful sound at the back of his nose, building in tempo until it trumpeted forth in full volume. Out of the corner of my eye, I saw Pierce staring at him as if fearing the man had taken leave of his senses.

Ironically, Shepard's resistance to Pierce's request was the final incentive I needed to accept the position. "When would you like me to begin, Mr. Godfrey?" I asked, carrying on with the conversation as if my employer weren't sitting there braying like a donkey.

"Actually, I was hoping to go over some of the details today. Then, on Wednesday, I'd be pleased if you'd accompany me to Henry Finney's shipbuilding firm, where we'll sign the final contracts."

Shepard's annoying outbreak had gradually abated, but his pale eyes bulged with righteous ire. "No! Not under any circumstances. Not only is Miss Woolson unqualified for the position you're suggesting, but surely you must realize no company would enter into negotiation with a woman!"

"I have already apprised Mr. Finney of my decision to retain a woman as my legal representative. I realize, of course, that Miss Woolson is a recent associate, but given your firm's reputation, I'm sure you would never hire an attorney whose abilities were less than exceptional."

Finding no ready retort to this statement, Shepard had to content himself with casting another withering look in my direction. Since I had more or less relied on subterfuge to obtain my employment in his firm, I averted my eyes.

Pierce seemed to take my employer's silence as tacit agreement. Standing, he extended his hand across the desk. "Thank you, Mr. Shepard, it's been a pleasure. I look forward to working with Miss Woolson and with your firm."

Subjecting me to one last, furious glare, Shepard turned back to Pierce, his expression one of scornful misgiving.

"I fear you will regret this decision, Mr. Godfrey. Don't say I didn't warn you—"

There was a knock on the door. Before Shepard could respond, Robert entered, his sharp gaze going first to me, then to Pierce.

"Yes, Campbell," Shepard snapped. "What is it?"

"Mr. Wilton is waiting to see you in the outer office," Robert said. "Perkins says he doesn't have an appointment."

"Why didn't Perkins inform me of this himself?" the senior partner demanded, no doubt feeling the need to take his foul temper out on someone.

Again, Robert shot me a quick look. "I, ah, was on my way to Miss Woolson's office and offered to deliver the message for him."

"Oh, for the love of—" Shepard got up from his desk, pausing in front of Pierce. "I'll bid you good day, Mr. Godfrey. If your arrangement with Miss Woolson does not prove satisfactory, please inform me. Our firm employs a number of excellent attorneys who are at your disposal." With that, he turned and marched out the door.

The three of us stood awkwardly in Joseph Shepard's wake. When neither man spoke, I broke the silence.

"You remember Robert Campbell, don't you Mr. Godfrey?"

"Yes, of course," Pierce said, reaching out his hand. "Good to see you again, Campbell."

Robert returned his shake. "Godfrey," he responded a little stiffly.

I wanted to kick Robert in the shins. Surely he could show more civility than that. And why did his face look as if he'd just bitten into a sour lemon?

"You said you were on your way to my office, Robert?" I said, working to make my tone pleasant.

"I, ah, had a case I wanted to discuss with you." His eyes flickered to Pierce, then quickly back to me. It didn't require a mind reader to know he was dying to find out why Pierce had come to see Shepard. "I see that you're busy. We can do it later."

"I'd appreciate that, if you don't mind," Pierce told him amiably. "I am going out of town later this afternoon, and I'd like to familiarize Miss Woolson with some documents."

"Of course," Robert said, walking to the door. "I'll leave you to it, then."

Leading Pierce to my office, I partially closed the door behind us (yes, upon occasion even I find it expedient to obey the social proprieties) and slid the typewriting machine to the far corner of my desk. Taking out a sheaf of papers, Pierce spent the next hour explaining them to me at length. It was nearly noon when we'd finished.

"All this work has given me an appetite," he said. "I'd be pleased if you'd have lunch with me."

I was tempted to accept his invitation, then remembered the hospital tour scheduled for that afternoon. There was also the matter of his behavior. Even now that I'd been retained as his attorney, his manner toward me tended to be less than professional. No, if this business relationship were to succeed, firm lines must be drawn.

"I'm sorry, but that won't be possible, Mr. Godfrey. Perhaps another time."

His intense blue eyes remained on mine longer than

was necessary. "As you wish, Miss Woolson. I'll pick you up at your house at ten o'clock Wednesday morning."

"I shall be ready," I answered, matching his tone. "I hope you have a pleasant journey."

I stood watching him walk out with long, confident strides. As he disappeared into the hall, I wondered what in heaven's name I'd gotten myself into.

That afternoon, Margaret Barlow gave us an interesting tour of the new Women and Children's Hospital. Her mother, Adelina French, Reverend Nicholas Prescott, Mama, Celia and several other board members had also joined the group.

The old warehouse was a beehive of activity. On the main floor, workmen scurried about tearing down walls and erecting others to form a floor plan very different from the original structure erected thirty years earlier. The first ward had already been completed, and several of the dozen or more beds were occupied. Nurses bustled about tending the patients, all of them women who would soon be in labor.

"Babies have a way of ignoring construction schedules," Margaret told us with a smile, "so we completed this room first."

"That was a wise decision," Reverend Prescott put in, regarding the room with approval. "It's important that the new mothers have a clean bed and a roof over their heads."

Margaret gave the minister a grateful smile. "It's still

a bit chaotic, but we will soon put things to right." She led us around a pile of rubble. "Most of the initial renovations will take place on this level and will house the larger wards. Fortunately, there are rooms on the second and third floors functional enough for immediate occupancy. Eventually, of course, they'll be remodeled as funds become available."

She led us to a storage area that had been converted into a modern hospital kitchen. There were exclamations all around when our eyes lighted on a brand new Sterling Range, a huge cast-iron stove with nickel paneling and beautifully decorated tile. Equally impressive was the tall, cylindrical hot-water heater standing next to it. Considering the hours it took to heat water on a stove—even a stove as large as this—the water heater would be a marvelous labor-saving device for the staff. But how had the hospital managed to come up with the money to purchase two such costly appliances?

Adelina French must have noticed our astonishment. "Mr. Leonard Godfrey donated the stove and the water heater to the hospital in honor of his late wife. I can't count the times Caroline told me, 'Proper healing requires proper food.'" Adelina turned her head, but not before I saw tears brimming in her green eyes.

Reverend Prescott gently touched the woman's arm. "I was not well acquainted with Mrs. Godfrey, but I'm sure she would be pleased with your efforts," he said softly.

As he spoke, a small, wiry Chinese man entered carrying a sack of flour over one shoulder. He wore an interesting mix of East and West: the dark tunic and pants common among the city's Chinese but, instead of the usual slippers, heavy brown boots and a very Western-looking bowler hat. Unable to see his long hair queue, I assumed it was tucked beneath the hat. When he saw us, his face twisted into angry lines, as if resentful we had invaded his domain.

"This is our cook, Chin Lee Fong," Margaret said. Chin executed a stiff bow, hardly pausing as he walked to the pantry to dump the bag of flour against the wall. Behind him, a thin young woman of about nineteen came in carrying pots and pans. The girl had a pale complexion and large, impudent-looking hazel eyes. A riot of red curls popped out here and there from beneath a starched white cap. "And this is our kitchen maid, Dora Clemens."

The young woman stopped in her tracks, regarding us with bold interest. She paused when she came to Reverend Prescott, and her sharp face broke into a saucy grin. Ignoring the rest of us, Dora executed a suggestive little curtsy, plainly intended solely for the attractive minister.

Chin snapped impatiently at her in rapid Chinese, then in broken English. "Lazy good-for-nothing. Bring pots. Now!"

The girl turned sullen eyes on the cook, then, without hurrying, handed the pans to Chin. Muttering angrily beneath his breath, the cook stood on a stool and hung each pan carefully above the cast-iron stove.

"That stove is Chin's pride and joy," Mrs. French explained, in an obvious attempt to draw attention away from the kitchen maid, who continued to stare openly at the minister. "Woe be it if anyone else so much as touches it."

"He's a splendid cook, so you must forgive us if we humor him," Margaret said.

One woman in the group commented that she didn't blame the cook one bit. "If I had a stove like that, I'd protect it with my husband's pistol," she exclaimed, her expression indicating she was only half joking.

"Shall we proceed?" Margaret asked.

She led us up a flight of stairs to the second floor, where the original warehouse offices had been located. Eventually, she told us, they would house not only the hospital's administrative staff, but also a chapel and the promised playroom for hospitalized children and for the offspring of women who had given birth. The third, uppermost floor would be reserved for surgical operations, storage and a temporary morgue.

Not surprisingly, Reverend Prescott showed particular interest in the chapel, and he looked around the room approvingly. I admit I'd been keeping an eye on Prescott since the tour began, curious to see if I'd imagined his amazing charisma. My interest turned to embarrassment when I realized every female eye in our group was also fastened on him. Margaret Barlow deferred to him as if he were a visiting potentate, while Adelina French hung on his every word. Prescott appeared to be unaware of his appeal, but I suspected this was largely feigned. Behind those smiling eyes, I guessed he was conscious of every glance, every sigh, every whisper.

Our next stop was the room—actually two small rooms joined by a connecting door—that Lily Mankin and her children would soon occupy. I admit I'd been concerned about the arrangement, fearing the board's promise to house the Mankin family might have been forgotten in the excitement of opening the hospital. I'd even put off informing the widow of the planned accommodation in case it didn't materialize. I now realized that, far from breaking their word, Margaret and her mother had given the family's housing needs thoughtful consideration.

"We chose these rooms for Mrs. Mankin because they catch the morning sun," Adelina said, pleased by my delighted expression. "And they're located close to the children's playroom."

I was already picturing the rooms filled with Lily's homey touches. "She'll be so pleased, Mrs. French. And exceedingly relieved. I can't thank you enough for your efforts."

Several more rooms on the second floor were also ready for occupancy or were already being used by staff members. Margaret showed us her own office overlooking Pacific Street, which was large and tastefully furnished.

"This is only temporary," she explained. "We're in the process of hiring a hospital administrator, but it's proving more difficult than we anticipated. When we do hire someone, this will be his office."

We were startled by the sound of loud voices erupting from the next room. When they turned into full-scale shouts, Mrs. Barlow excused herself and went out into the hall.

"Kwei-chan!" I heard a male voice scream. "Villain! How you expect me cook without proper supplies?"

I followed Margaret out of the office to find Chin Lee Fong facing off against Lucius Arlen, the hospital's accountant. Although Arlen towered over him, Chin showed no fear. He glared up at Arlen as if he would have liked nothing better than to engage the accountant in physical combat.

"I'm not a fool, Chin," Arlen shouted. "I know well enough that a good portion of the money I've given you has ended up in your pocket."

"You call me thief?" the cook exploded, shaking his fist and exploding into a torrent of Chinese.

"I'm stating the facts as I see them," Arlen retorted. "This is a charity hospital, Chin, not the Palace Hotel."

Margaret bravely stepped between the two men. "Stop it, please! Mr. Arlen, you know I authorized Mr. Chin's expenses. I'm sure he hasn't taken any money for himself."

Arlen's look was pitying. After all, what could a poor, trusting woman know of such things? "With due respect, I've had a great deal of experience with this sort of pilfering. I have attempted to warn you, madam, but you seem loath to listen. Chinamen are not to be trusted!"

106

Chin bristled with rage. "You no better than boo how doy," he yelled, referring to the thugs in some of the more violent tongs. "You lie, try get me fired!"

"That's where I'd like to see you, all right, out on the street where you belong—where all you yellow devils be—"

Arlen stopped in mid-sentence as an authoritative voice boomed, "Arlen! Chin! You heard Mrs. Barlow. That is enough out of both of you."

The two men fell into startled silence as Judge Barlow's commanding figure strode down the hall. Chin's bravado changed to sulky deference, while Arlen's face flushed a blotchy red.

"I'll deal with you later, Chin," the accountant snapped, dismissing the cook with an angry gesture. "Now get back to the kitchen."

Chin started to speak, then took in Judge Barlow's stern face and seemed to think better of it. Spinning on his heels, he stalked in silent fury toward the stairs.

Mrs. Barlow looked mortally embarrassed. "I apologize for this outbreak. With all the confusion going on, I'm afraid our tempers have become a bit frayed."

"Don't make excuses for them, my dear," Barlow said, watching Chin's departing back. "They're grown men and should know better than to behave like squabbling children."

"Judge Barlow, I assure you—" the accountant's face darkened an even deeper red as he choked off the words, obviously deciding there were times when silence truly was golden. Turning to Margaret, he said, "Actually, I'm glad to see you, Mrs. Barlow. There's an urgent matter I must discuss with you before you leave for the day." He entered his office and picked up one of his black ledgers. His demeanor now seemed more agitated than angry, as if something were seriously amiss.

"Mr. Arlen," Margaret said, following him to his desk. "Can we postpone this until I've finished with my tour?"

"I would prefer to do it now, Mrs. Barlow," Arlen persisted. "It really can't wait."

"I'm afraid it's going to have to wait, Mr. Arlen," Judge Barlow interrupted. "If you recall, Margaret, we have an appointment with Mr. Peterson this afternoon."

"Oh, it slipped my mind." Margaret turned to our group. "I'm afraid we must meet with our architect," she explained. "We're building a home in Menlo Park, you see."

"Whatever the problem is, you can speak to my wife about it tomorrow," Barlow told Arlen and, without waiting for a reply, marched out of the accountant's office.

"I'm sorry, Mr. Arlen," Margaret said after her husband's abrupt departure. "Will tomorrow morning do?" She glanced at her mother. "Or perhaps you could speak to Mrs. French in my stead? She knows nearly as much about the hospital as I do."

The accountant hesitated, then shook his head. "No,

I'm sorry, I prefer to speak to you."

"Are you sure?" Mrs. French offered kindly. "If there is anything I can do—"

"Thank you, Mrs. French," he said, "but it's a matter best kept between myself and Mrs. Barlow."

"Mr. Arlen seemed upset," Mama said quietly as Margaret led us down the hallway. "I hope it's nothing serious. It would be awful if we had to stop work on the hospital now."

I had no time to reply, as Margaret had stopped in front of a storeroom where dozens of old, rusty paint cans were piled everywhere. As she went on about projected occupancy, I'm afraid my mind wandered. Mama was right; Arlen appeared unusually upset. Moreover, I was sure it had something to do with the books. Raising money for a project of this magnitude was always a challenge, but I'd heard that thus far donations had been generous. What could be wrong?

Mama gave me a little nudge, and I came out of my thoughts to find the group trooping up the stairs to the top story. As we climbed, I glanced out a dirty window, surprised to see how dark it had become outside. Clouds blotted out the sun, and streaks of fog billowed in from the Bay to grip the streets with long, ghostly fingers.

I shivered and realized it had nothing to do with the chill warehouse or the gathering fog. Whatever Lucius Arlen was so anxious to tell Mrs. Barlow, I had an ominous feeling it did not portend well for the new hospital.

I had not invited Robert to join me on my visit to Lily
Mankin the following afternoon. As a matter of fact,
I had actively opposed it. But of course the redoubtable
Scot was not easily discouraged. He'd discovered
where Lily Mankin lived, and he flatly refused to allow
me to travel alone to this—according to him—less
than reputable district. Ever since Joseph Shepard had
bribed him into dogging my steps during the Nob Hill
murders, he seemed to consider my safety his personal
concern. In all fairness, this attitude had, upon occasion, proved useful. At the moment, it was simply
annoying.

"What do you really know about Lily Mankin?" he
demanded. "You've spoken to her what, twice? Yet
here you go butting into her life. I can tell you who
they're going to blame if this little arrangement doesn't
work out."

"Oh, Robert, do be quiet."

"Blast it, woman, if I've said it once I've said it—"

"Far too many times. If you dare say it again, I'll
scream. I'm not interfering, Robert. I'm simply
bringing Mrs. Mankin and the hospital together for
their mutual benefit. And that is all I care to say on the
subject."

We drove the rest of the way in silence, contempla-
tive on my part, sulky on Robert's. Ever since I'd
toured the warehouse the day before, I'd been eager to
give the widow the good news. Adelina French said
Lily could move into her new rooms as soon as they'd

been given a fresh coat of paint. The timing was perfect, as Lily had less than a week before she'd have to vacate her current premises.

When our clarence—a brougham converted into an extension-front hack capable of carrying four instead of the usual two passengers—drew up before a frame house several blocks south of the Slot (that is, south of the Market Street cable car line), I was pleasantly surprised. The neighborhood, though poor and unpretentious, was hardly the disreputable district of Robert's imagination. In fact, San Francisco teemed with areas like this, where hardworking men and women eked out a modest livelihood in the fastest growing city on the West Coast.

Lily, appearing weary and somewhat disheveled as she tried to calm the child squirming in her arms, seemed genuinely delighted to see us. Turning the toddler over to her daughter, she led us into a room that evidently served as kitchen and parlor for the family. Through an open door, I spied a second, smaller room, furnished with a small bed and several cots. Toys were scattered about, but otherwise the room appeared spotlessly clean. The dingy walls were hung with prints—most of a religious nature—as well as several beautifully executed embroideries, which I assumed the widow had done herself. Beside the room's only overstuffed chair sat a basket of mending, most of it, I'm sure, sent over by Mama and her friends.

Lily insisted I take this chair, then bustled to the stove to fetch tea. She returned bearing a pretty, though slightly chipped, porcelain pot and several matching cups, along with a modest selection of cookies, which the children eyed eagerly. Despite the widow's objections, Robert and I professed not to be hungry and urged her offspring to help themselves to the unexpected treat.

While they munched happily in a corner, I informed Lily of the board's decision to allow her rooms in the new hospital. As I spoke, her eyes filled with tears and, to my embarrassment, she impulsively threw her arms about my neck.

"Oh, miss, I don't know how to thank you. You and your mother have been that good to us. And now this, when I thought for sure we'd be thrown out onto the street."

"Mrs. Mankin, there's no need to—" I stopped for air and to extract several strands of her hair from my mouth.

As if realizing from my choked voice that she was impeding my breath, she drew back a step. I was unnerved to see that her expression bordered on adulation.

"You're too modest, miss, and that's a fact. You've done more for us than you'll ever—"

"Then you're agreeable to the board's offer of a room at the hospital?" Robert broke in. His tone, although abrupt, was not unkind. I had to smile. Like most men, he was embarrassed by such an unabashed display of emotion.

"Yes, sir, I surely will. And I won't let the hospital

down, neither. I've heard of that woman with the lamp—I forget her name—what nursed them soldiers in the Crimean—"

"Florence Nightingale," I told her.

"Yes, ma'am, Miss Nightingale." Her face glowed. "Do you think—? I mean, is there a chance I could learn enough to be like her? You know, nurse sick people and all?"

I regarded this brave young mother. "Yes, Mrs. Mankin, I think you would make a fine nurse. I have no doubt that you're going to be a very valuable asset to the hospital."

When we'd finished our tea, we said our goodbyes and stepped outside to find our cab waiting for us as instructed. Frankly, I hadn't expected the visit to take so long, or we would have discharged the driver upon our arrival. Despite the added expense, I was secretly pleased to have the brougham at hand. Darkness was approaching, and the late afternoon air was unseasonably chilled.

Robert had just assisted me into the four-seat hack when, out of nowhere, something large and sharp came hurtling through the open door, hitting me in the face and throwing me onto the carriage floor.

"Sarah, are you all right?" Robert hovered above me, face white with concern. He tried to raise me up, while at the same time he felt about the floor for the object that had hit me. After a moment, he held up a large rock, a piece of paper attached to it with a string.

"What in the name of—"

I scrambled to my knees and leaned out of the open door. I was in time to see a tall, beefy figure run toward the corner. Before he turned onto the next street, I caught a glimpse of his face. Granted, the light was poor, but there was no disguising that face—it was one I would never forget.

"Follow that man!" I commanded our driver, who was perched in his seat at the front of the carriage. "He just turned right at the corner. There's a bonus for you if you keep him in sight."

"Right-oh, miss," the driver called out, and he clicked his dappled-gray horse into such violent acceleration that I barely had time to close the carriage door before we were off at breakneck speed. Our cabbie took the corner so fast I feared the carriage was going to veer over onto its side.

"Have you gone mad?" Robert yelled from where he'd been thrown to the floor. "You're going to get us killed!"

"I recognized the man who threw the rock," I said, keeping my eyes glued to the street. "It's Bert Corrigan, the thug who threatened me that day on Kearney Street."

Uttering a curse, Robert pulled himself onto the seat, then untangled the note from the rock. Holding it close to the window, he squinted to make out the writing.

"What does it say?" I called back over my shoulder.

"It says if you don't stop asking questions about the sweatshop fire, you'll live to regret it. I knew your infernal meddling would bring us nothing but—"

"There he is!" I called up to our driver. "He got into that cab. Whatever you do, don't lose him."

The driver's words were lost in the rattling of our cab's wheels as they negotiated bumps and fissures in the street. Face pressed to the window, I watched Corrigan's hack dart in and out of traffic, causing pedestrians to shake their fists and horses to rear with fright. We followed close behind, adding our own disorder to the general mayhem. Instead of slowing down, our driver clicked his horse into a fast trot as he endeavored to keep the other carriage in sight.

"This is insane!" Robert shouted above the clatter. "Whoever this fellow is, he must know we're after him. The only place he's going to lead us is on a wild goose chase."

I swallowed an angry retort. What Robert said made sense. Bert Corrigan wouldn't knowingly take us to his boss. But if he thought he'd given us the slip—

Once again I called to the cabbie, "Stay as far back as you can without losing sight of him."

I caught a brief glimpse of our driver's broad grin and realized he was just a boy—a boy having the time of his life. It was doubtful he owned the brougham himself; more likely he was one of a stable of drivers. The man who did own the cab was not going to be happy if we caused damage to his carriage. More important, I would never forgive myself if we injured an innocent pedestrian or precipitated a traffic accident.

"Please, slow down," I repeated, as the lad seemed disinclined to give up the chase. "I don't want our quarry to know he's being followed."

At this, our driver gave me a knowing wink and reined in his horse until we were traveling at a more sedate pace. Adroitly, he maneuvered the cab until we were partially hidden behind a delivery wagon. We could still see our prey, but Bert would find it difficult to spot us. Sure enough, after several blocks—and as many evasive twists and turns—Corrigan must have thought he'd lost us, because his hack slowed until it, too, blended into the flow of traffic.

Leaning back, I released my breath in a deep sigh. Only then did I notice a warm liquid flowing down my face.

"Good God, Sarah, you're bleeding." Robert fished a handkerchief out of his pocket and dabbed at my forehead. It came away dark and sticky. "That damn rock! We've got to get you to a doctor."

"Don't be silly, it's just a scratch. And I have a perfectly good doctor in my own home."

"Sarah, this isn't a game. You've managed to make someone very angry. As usual, you're in over your head."

"I don't plan to confront Bert Corrigan personally. I just want to find out who he's working for."

"And in the unlikely event you do find out? What then?"

Before I could answer, Corrigan's carriage pulled to a stop in front of a small redwood house on the corner

116

of California and Union streets. It was a solid, middle-class neighborhood of wood-framed houses, most boasting the ever-present bay window. Somewhat surprised that Corrigan would be paying a call on such a street, I instructed our driver to rein up midway down the block.

"The gent's gettin' out," the lad said.

"Shh," I called up to him, although I doubted Corrigan could hear our voices from where we were parked.

We watched Corrigan get out of the cab and walk to the house. He rang the bell, and after a moment the door was opened by a large, nattily attired man smoking a cigar. Despite the man's ample girth, he was not unattractive, although at the moment he appeared furious to see Bert Corrigan at his door. Stepping outside, he looked hastily up and down the street, then, with a curse, yanked Corrigan inside and slammed the door behind them.

"I think that's Killy Doyle," I said eagerly.

"Why? Because he was smoking a cigar?"

"No, of course not. But if the man was a friend of Corrigan's, why was he so upset to see him? Then there's the way he was dressed. Paddy said Killy Doyle considers himself a lady's man. Well, that fellow is a dandy if I ever saw one. Besides, Bert Corrigan's a street rough. I doubt he has social acquaintances living on a street like this. An employer, yes, but hardly a friend."

Without waiting for Robert to reply, I fished a pencil

and notebook out of my reticule and copied the address.

Robert still looked doubtful. "All right, assuming you're right—just *assuming*, mind you—what now?"

"I'm going to pay a little call," I said, allowing our young driver to help me out of the carriage.

"You ain't goin' up to that door by yerself, are you?" the lad asked, his brown eyes large with concern.

"No, of course not," Robert growled, coming to stand beside me. "God only knows what mischief she'd get into if left to her own devices."

"Want me to go with you?" the boy asked hopefully.

"Certainly not," Robert told him, rather more severely than I thought necessary.

I smiled at the lad. "You've done very well, er . . ."

"Eddie," he said, beaming. "Eddie Cooper."

"Well, Eddie, why don't you wait here? If for any reason we're not out of that house in half an hour, ride like the wind to the nearest police station for help."

Eddie's smile grew so wide I thought his face might split in two. "Yes, ma'am. I will. You can count on me."

"A little melodramatic, don't you think?" Robert said as we approached the redwood house.

I gave a low chuckle. "That boy is having a grand time. I see no reason to dampen his fun."

"Why not, indeed. Your forehead is still bleeding, Sarah. I don't think you begin to grasp the seriousness of this business."

118

Without replying, I rang the bell. A thin, middle-aged woman wearing an apron and cap answered the door.

"Yes?" she said. "What do you want?"

Robert shot me a look that said he wished nothing to do with the interview, then pointedly raised his face to stare at the carvings above the door.

I restrained my instinct to give him a good kick.

"We're here to see Mr. Corrigan." I tried to sound friendly, but it was difficult with blood trickling down my face. The woman stared at my wound, and I increased the pressure of the handkerchief on the laceration.

"I don't know any Corrigan," she said brusquely. "You have the wrong house."

"Perhaps you were unaware that Mr. Doyle let Mr. Corrigan into this house not five minutes ago," I persisted, letting slip Killy's name to see her reaction. When she said nothing to correct me, I stepped forward just far enough to peek inside the house.

"I told you Mr. Doyle doesn't know anyone by that name. You have to leave now. I have work to do."

Before I could draw breath to try another tack, the woman slammed the door with so much force that if I hadn't jumped backward, I'd have been hit squarely in the face.

"Good heavens," I cried, realizing that in my haste to retreat, several drops of blood had dropped onto my bodice.

"Well, you were right," Robert admitted. "It seems

we've found Killy Doyle. Here, you're making a mess of that." Taking the handkerchief, he dabbed more or less ineffectively at the stains on my dress, but their position just above my bosom made this task all but impossible for him to perform.

"Oh, for pity's sake, give me that." I took the cloth and started back to the carriage. "This gown is ruined at any rate. Let's get home and try to make sense of this."

Young Eddie looked almost disappointed to see us return to the carriage so quickly and with no new wounds to show for our efforts. I gave the lad my home address, then leaned back in the seat and resumed pressing Robert's now blood-soaked handkerchief against my wound.

"I hope your brother Charles is at home," Robert said. "That wound needs attention."

"If he's not, I'm sure a simple plaster will do. Head wounds always appear more serious than they actually are. For heaven's sake, Robert, stop fussing like an old woman."

This last comment managed to insult my companion sufficiently so that we passed the remainder of the journey to Rincon Hill in silence.

CHAPTER SIX

Naturally, Robert insisted on helping me inside the house and I, noting the time, invited him to join us for dinner. It was only when I heard laughter coming from the parlor that I realized my mistake—I'd completely forgotten my parents were hosting a dinner party that night to celebrate the opening of the new hospital.

Before I could explain this to Robert, Mama came hurrying toward us.

"Sarah, you're late," she said, then noticing the blood on my face, cried, "Good heavens, you're injured!"

"Mama, please, it's nothing," I protested. "Your guests will hear."

It was too late. My father was already advancing toward us, closely followed by Celia and Judge and Mrs. Barlow.

"Sarah, my girl, how did this happen?" Papa exclaimed, his shocked eyes taking in my battered head and blood-spattered dress.

I searched for an explanation that wouldn't reveal our true business that afternoon. Robert forestalled me.

"Some hoodlum threw a rock into our cab. I don't know if he meant to hit Sarah, but—"

"A rock?" Mama gasped, clasping a hand over her mouth. "Sarah, you might have been killed!"

Papa fixed hard eyes on my associate. "Mr. Campbell, do you know the identity of this hoodlum?"

"Yes, sir. Sarah thinks his name is Bert Corrigan." Robert caught the warning look on my face, but again it was too late. Papa's face had suffused with rage.

"And who is this Bert Corrigan?" he demanded.

"He's just a man we met when we were looking for Paddy McGuire," I said, playing down the affair. "He doesn't seem pleased we're investigating that sweat-shop fire I told you about, Papa."

"Doesn't seem pleased!" Robert exploded. "He threatened you with bodily harm if you didn't stop your confounded interference. And by God, you would have done well to heed his warning. Now look what's happened. An inch more to the right and there's no telling how much damage that rock might have done." Despite my glare, his square, stubborn chin jutted out defiantly, as if challenging me to deny the truth of this statement.

My mother placed shaking hands on my shoulders, scrutinizing the wound with horrified eyes. "Sarah, it's still bleeding." She turned to Papa. "Horace, hurry and send someone to find Charles. He went out on a call about an hour ago, but he must come home at once."

"That may not be necessary, Mrs. Woolson," Margaret Barlow said in a quiet voice. "I have some practice treating wounds of this sort. Let me have a look." She stepped forward and examined my laceration with a critical eye. "The cut is fairly deep, but I don't think it requires stitches. I'll need soap and a basin of hot water, then when the wound is clean, I'll apply one of my mother's herbal creams. It's soothing and will facilitate healing."

Mama hesitated. I knew she would prefer to have Charles care for my wound. On the other hand, who knew how long it would take to find him?

"Yes, all right," she said at last, giving Mrs. Barlow an uncertain smile. "I appreciate anything you can do for her, Margaret."

Torn between accompanying us and attending to her guests, Mama stood wringing her hands in the foyer. When Robert remained beside her, Papa motioned him to follow us upstairs.

"You might as well come, too, Campbell," he told my colleague. "With your help maybe I can make sense of what happened to my foolish daughter."

Robert reluctantly complied, standing awkwardly just inside my bedroom door as Papa fetched the items required to tend my head.

"As a child I used to assist a dear friend who was a chemist and who occasionally tended minor injuries," Margaret explained. "I was probably more of a nuisance than a help, but I learned a great deal from watching him." She searched through her reticule until she found a small vial of what looked like some sort of white ointment. "Ah, we're in luck," she said with a smile. "As it happens, I have some of my mother's excellent herbal salve with me tonight. I used some to nurse a small cut my husband suffered earlier this evening."

A quarter of an hour later I sat on the edge of my bed, skillfully swathed with Adelina French's herbal ointment, patched with plaster and sipping a cup of Cook's strong black tea. After receiving our profound thanks, Margaret returned downstairs, leaving Papa free to demand that Robert and I give him the full story of our afternoon's adventure. Realizing he wouldn't rest until I gave in, I grudgingly related all that had transpired, including our discovery of Killy Doyle.

"I don't think Doyle actually owns the shop," I ended, "but I'm hoping he'll lead us to the man who does."

"Us?" Robert broke in. "By us I assume you're including me in your nefarious plans?"

Papa made an exasperated sound that caused us both to fall silent. "You're dealing with dangerous people, Sarah. Tell the police what you've learned, and let them make of it what they can. Because of the 'fellow servant rule,' it will be next to impossible to file suit on behalf of the victims who lost their lives in that fire, anyway. You'd be much wiser to channel your efforts into changing the law, instead of placing yourself in harm's way."

He took hold of my shoulders, until I was forced to meet his eyes. "I want you to promise me you'll stay out of this, Sarah."

I met his stern gaze, but I was at a loss as to what to say. Much as I loved and respected my father, I'd given my word to a woman who had no place else to turn.

"Papa, I—"

At that moment, Mama appeared to announce dinner. With worried eyes, she inspected my forehead. Now that she realized I would live to see another day, her earlier fear had turned to angry exasperation. Proclaiming that I had frightened her half to death, she threatened a litany of dire consequences if I did not come to my senses and behave like a proper young lady.

"Wash your face, Sarah," she ordered. "And change that soiled gown before you come down to dinner."

After Mama went downstairs, my father gave me a final, appealing look. It pained me to let him down, yet I could not bring myself to make a promise I knew I couldn't keep.

"Please, Papa, don't worry," I told him. "I give you my word I'll be careful."

The expression that crossed Papa's face was enough to make me cry. All my life I'd sought to please him, to live up to the challenge of being his only daughter. It was, after all, due to his patient tutelage that I'd become an attorney. I owed him so much, yet I could not sacrifice my integrity.

"You should listen to your father, Sarah, and leave this business to the police," Robert said, after Papa was gone.

I sighed. "Don't be naive, Robert. You know as well as I do there's little the police can do. Even if they were inclined to step in, they haven't the manpower to investigate a fraction of these shops."

"Ah, but you do have the inclination." His voice was mocking. "Sarah Woolson, defender of the impoverished and destitute. Even if it kills her!"

Suddenly, I felt very weary. My head ached, not only from the rock, but from the hurt I had caused my father. The last thing I wanted right now was to engage in an argument I knew I couldn't win.

"I have to change for dinner, Robert," I told him, and closed the door behind him to attend to my toilette.

I came down to dinner to find that Robert had declined Mama's invitation to join us. He'd pleaded a previous engagement, one I knew he didn't have.

Also among the missing were Adelina French—who was suffering from painful arthritis—and Lucius Arlen, who'd sent Mama a message explaining he was too ill to attend. It crossed my mind to wonder if whatever had been bothering him at the hospital might have something to do with his absence. But, as Robert never tired of saying, perhaps I was just looking for trouble where none existed.

As Ina served the soup, I saw that most of the hospital board was in attendance, including Reverend Prescott, who appeared as handsome and charming as ever. No one was rude enough to comment on my tardy arrival, but the bandage on my forehead earned me a number of curious glances.

My brother Charles, obviously bursting with news, returned just as the last of our guests were departing. A short time later, he, Celia and I slipped into the library for a private talk.

"All right, Charles," I said, unable to contain my curiosity. "Did you get the results of the autopsy?"

"Yes, I did, and Halsey's postmortem results are certainly unusual. The coroner found high levels of an alkaloid called hyoscyamine in his system, along with other related toxins."

Celia and I looked at him blankly.

"Hyoscyamine is the main poison found in *Datura stramonium,* or jimsonweed, which is part of the nightshade family," he explained. "You may not know it by name, but you've probably seen it growing wild in the country or in forests along the shoreline."

"I don't understand," Celia said. "I thought Reverend Halsey died of a heart attack. What does this jimsonweed have to do with it? It doesn't sound like something you'd want to eat."

Charles gave a wry smile. "Actually, some people very willingly ingest it. The plant is famous for its mind-altering properties. It's mentioned in Homer's 'Odyssey' and in some of Shakespeare's plays. Closer to home, soldiers in colonial Virginia ate jimsonweed and behaved erratically before they died. Years ago, Italian women used it to dilate their pupils, which was considered beautiful at the time."

"I doubt Halsey cared about his looks," I said dryly. "And somehow I can't conceive of him trying to alter his mind. He was too sanctimonious and smug for that."

Charles sank onto the sofa next to his wife. "There can be little doubt, I'm afraid, that Reverend Halsey was deliberately poisoned."

"How long does this poison take to work?" I asked. "Remember, I saw Halsey the afternoon he died and he looked fine."

"That's hard to say," Charles replied. "Symptoms may occur four to six hours after ingesting the plant, sometimes even sooner. The coroner suspects it was placed in some coffee Halsey drank shortly before his death."

"A cup of coffee," Celia repeated. "I know people found the man annoying, but who would go so far as to poison him?"

"I'm sure that's a question Samuel's friend on the police force would like answered," Charles said. "Evidently George Lewis has been assigned to the case.

"I know what you're thinking, Sarah," Charles went on, watching me. "But there's no reason to believe Mrs. Godfrey and Halsey's deaths are connected. I admit I'm concerned about the high level of nitro-glycerin found in her system, but there may be a perfectly logical explanation for how it got there. Besides, Mrs. Godfrey and Reverend Halsey had nothing in common."

"Except the new hospital," I said thoughtfully.

"It's doubtful the police will agree with you," Charles said with a yawn. "At any rate, they've decided not to release the cause of Halsey's death. I suppose they hope it will somehow help them find the killer."

Stretching, he got up from the sofa. "Come on, Sarah, it's time you were in bed. I'll be surprised if you don't wake up in the morning with a black eye. Maybe you should take the day off tomorrow."

I sighed. In truth, my head ached worse than ever, and I didn't look forward to meeting Pierce the next day with a discolored eye.

"This is one time I'd be more than happy to take your advice, Charles. Unfortunately, it's not possible."

"Well, at least let me examine you in the morning to ensure the wound hasn't become infected. Although I must say Mrs. Barlow did a pretty good job of it."

"Thank you, Charles," I said, kissing him on the cheek. As I did, I thought back to the many times he'd "doctored" me since our childhood. I doubt if Frederick and Samuel together provided Charles with as much hands-on experience in his future vocation as did his little sister.

Regrettably, Charles's prediction proved only too correct. By morning, my headache had somewhat abated, but my right eye was a dreadful purple color. Charles duly replaced the plaster on my forehead, but even a slightly smaller bandage did nothing to improve my sad appearance.

Despite courteous efforts to behave as if nothing were wrong, Pierce could not entirely mask his surprise when he picked me up in his carriage promptly at ten o'clock. He insisted on hearing how I'd come by my injuries, and when I gave him an abbreviated version of what had happened, he astonished me by bursting out laughing.

"Sarah, you continue to amaze me. Yes, I know," he said, holding up a hand, "what happened to you was dangerous, and I'm more grateful than I can say the injury wasn't more serious. But I know of no other woman who'd have placed herself in such a situation in the first place. You're wonderful!"

I hardly knew how to respond to this surprising statement. "I did nothing more than enter a brougham cab, Pierce, something a great many San Franciscans do every day. The fact that some ruffian saw fit to hurl a rock is hardly a reason to—"

Once again his laughter stopped me. "Come on, Sarah, the very fact that you see nothing unusual about your life makes it all the more remarkable. No, don't shake your head. You're one of a kind, whether you're willing to admit it or not."

Enough was enough! These far too personal—and embarrassing—statements had to cease. Straightening my skirt into neat folds, I looked him in the eye. "Mr. Godfrey, are we or are we not about to attend a meeting involving matters of serious concern to your company?"

After a startled moment, he nodded. "Yes, but—"

"Then hadn't we best use what little time remains to us to settle upon a strategy?"

"Yes, of course, you're right." Taken aback by my candid remark—ironically, one of the very qualities he professed to admire—Pierce took a moment to order his thoughts. "As I explained earlier, most of the vessels constructed on the Pacific Coast are two- or three-masted schooners. They're not as grand as the downeasters built on the East Coast, but they're more than adequate for the coastal trade, which constitutes a fair portion of our company's business."

"Yes, I understand."

"In the past, we've purchased vessels from several local shipbuilders. Now, because of our planned expansion, we're placing a more substantial order. That's why we've approached Henry Finney, the largest shipbuilder in San Francisco."

"I gather you're not pleased with the prices Finney has quoted you."

"No, I'm not. Yet he's the only one who can fill our order in the specified time." He smiled. "Which is why you're here, Sarah."

My returned smile was ironic. "To work a miracle, Mr. Godfrey? You don't ask much of me."

"No, not a miracle. A strategy. Henry Finney came over from Ireland on a packet ship, pockets empty, head crammed with ideas. He pulled himself up by his bootstraps, learned the shipbuilding business from the ground up, and eventually opened his own yard. He's a 'man's man,' a rough sort of fellow who'll be taken off guard to find himself dealing with a woman attorney."

I raised an eyebrow. "But you told Mr. Shepard you'd informed Finney about me."

"Yes, that's true, I did. What I failed to mention is that Finney thinks it's a joke. He doesn't believe for one minute that I'd hire a woman as an attorney."

"I see," I said, not entirely pleased. It was one thing to enter the meeting believing I was expected and quite another to discover I was being used as a ploy to throw Finney off guard.

I considered my options until our carriage halted in front of a weathered brick building at the waterfront end of Bay Street. Behind the structure I saw a vast shipyard, where a number of wooden ships were at various stages of construction.

"Are you ready?" Pierce asked, helping me out of the carriage.

"Yes, as a matter of fact, I am," I replied, having just arrived at my decision. Regardless of Pierce's *strategy* in hiring me, the fact remained that I was a licensed attorney. The happenstance of my gender was neither here nor there. I would ignore Pierce Godfrey and Henry Finney's childish power plays and do the job for which I'd been trained, and for which I was now being paid.

I won't deny that I was frightened. I was, after all, a woman entering a wholly man's world. Nevertheless, I was determined to succeed. Paraphrasing a comment the tong leader, Li Ying, once made to me, it was sometimes necessary to make the opponent's rules work for you.

Pierce and I entered a small room containing a single desk, behind which sat a middle-aged man I instantly identified as something of a dandy. Not only was he meticulously dressed—far more elaborately than his surroundings warranted—but everything about him spoke of fussy attention to detail. Each item on his desk was in its place and arranged just so, from his freshly sharpened pencils to the neat stack of papers from which he'd been working. At our approach, he looked up, then instantly assumed an expression of sympathy at the sight of my companion.

"My dear Mr. Godfrey," he gushed, circling the desk to grasp Pierce's hand. "I was so sorry to hear of the loss of your sister-in-law. Such a tragedy."

"Thank you, Sloan," Pierce said, looking ill at ease.

Pierce had explained in the carriage that, although Henry Finney was the driving force behind the ship-building company, Octavius Sloan managed the everyday running of the business with zealous control. Finney often joked that Sloan had more information stored in his head than in the office file cabinets. Pierce thought that Henry Finney stood somewhat in awe of Sloan, since the latter had spent a year or two at a university back east, while he'd received little formal education. In many ways, the office manager was treated more as a silent partner than a mere employee.

"Miss Woolson, I'd like you to meet Octavius Sloan," Pierce said, introducing the thin, fidgety little man. "He's been with Finney's as far back as I can remember."

"Twenty-two years, Mr. Godfrey," Sloan put in

proudly. "Since the day Mr. Finney first opened for business." His face took on what I can only describe as a sly expression, as he turned the conversation back to Caroline's death. "I realize, of course, that the relationship between you and Mrs. Godfrey was, ah, somewhat strained. Nevertheless, I'm sure you must feel her loss very deeply."

Pierce's face turned dark. I realized Octavius Sloan had overstepped some invisible line.

The clerk quickly recognized his faux pas and hastened to add, "I apologize, Mr. Godfrey. I assure you I did not mean to be impertinent. Naturally, it's none of my concern."

"No, Sloan, it isn't," Pierce told him bluntly. "We have an appointment with Mr. Finney. Please be good enough to inform him we're here."

I considered this surprising exchange as we were quickly, and silently, led upstairs. Apparently I hadn't merely imagined the hostility I noted between Pierce and his sister-in-law the night of the charity dinner. Once again, I wondered what had occurred between them to cause such animosity.

We were led into a spacious office on the third, and highest, floor of the building. The room had several large windows, two of which afforded a splendid view of the Bay and a busy wharf with long finger-piers pushing out into the water. A third window looked out over a bustling shipyard, where construction workers scurried over the skeletal spines of ships like ants on a pile of sugar. The poor immigrant boy from the

Emerald Isles had done very well for himself, I thought.

Henry Finney was a short, genial man in his early fifties, with sandy-red hair beginning to fade with age. Twinkling blue eyes smiled out at us from a lined, weatherbeaten face. His speech was heavily flavored with a rich Irish brogue, his movements energetic and sure. He had the habit of waving his hands as he spoke, revealing thick ropes of muscles stretching in his neck and beneath his rolled-up sleeves.

"How are you, Mr. Godfrey?" Finney said, taking Pierce's hand in a firm grip. Without waiting for a reply, he turned to me, his craggy face expressing surprise, not only, I surmised, at finding his client accompanied by a woman, but one moreover with a badly bruised face. "And who is this fine lady you've brought with you?"

"Finney, this is Sarah Woolson, an attorney with Shepard, Shepard, McNaughton and Hall. I'm afraid Miss Woolson met with an accident yesterday," he added, as Finney continued to look curiously at my blackened eye.

Finney's bushy red eyebrows rose. "Well, now, I'm sorry to hear that, Miss Woolson. Be that as it may, Mr. Godfrey, you can't expect me to believe this young lass is a lawyer. Come now, lad, introduce us good and proper."

"I assure you it is nothing less than the truth, Mr. Finney," I said, impatient to end this wearisome game. "I have been employed by Mr. Godfrey to represent his company's interests in these negotiations."

"Negotiations?" The Irishman's eyes widened in what appeared to be genuine astonishment. "But we've already come to an agreement now, haven't we, Mr. Godfrey?" He motioned for us to be seated at a table overlooking the Bay. "You said you'd be wantin' four two-masted scows and two three-masted schooners, the last of the six to be delivered no later than fifteen months from signin' the contract." He grinned easily at Pierce. "Nothin' could be more straightforward than that now, could it? And we've already agreed on the rates, which are fairness itself."

Pierce started to speak, then caught my eye. "Miss Woolson has gone over your proposal, Finney. Perhaps she'd be good enough to give us her professional opinion."

Several expressions crossed Finney's face—skepticism that I could have an opinion worth listening to, impatience that his valuable time was to be so flagrantly wasted, then resignation that he had no choice but to humor his customer.

"Right then, Mr. Godfrey," he said with a sigh. "But I'm tellin' you flat out you won't find a better deal than mine anywhere on the West Coast, and that's a fact."

Now that the time had come for me to play my part in this little drama, I found myself curiously calm. So far, Finney had fairly dripped Celtic charm. Despite that, I was sure that beneath the jocularity he possessed a shrewd mind and probably a will of iron.

"Mr. Finney," I said in my most professional voice,

"the terms you outlined for the purchase of these six ships are not satisfactory."

Finney's face, which was already a ruddy color, turned a decidedly darker shade of red. "What do you mean, not satisfactory? I'd be losin' money if I set them any lower." He regarded me with narrowed eyes, as if wondering how far he could go without antagonizing his prospective buyer. "No disrespect intended, Miss Woolson, but I'd hardly expect a woman to understand matters of such a confusin' nature. And havin' to do with shipbuildin' in the bargain. Now, if you'll let Mr. Godfrey and me get back to—"

"I have not yet finished, Mr. Finney," I broke in, noticing Pierce trying to stifle a grin. "Surely you're aware the British have started building steel-hulled ships. Those companies that have switched to steel are receiving very favorable insurance rates from Lloyd's of London, far better, I might add, than the insurance rates charged to the wooden boats our country currently builds. It isn't difficult to see—even for a mere woman—where this will eventually lead. Already, the down-easters are being replaced by the new steel-hulled vessels. Which means, Mr. Finney, that there is a surplus of the down-easters to be had at greatly reduced costs."

Finney's face grew darker by the minute. A shadowy glint in his eyes told me he was only too aware of the changes in shipbuilding taking place abroad.

"But they wouldn't be new, nor would they be built to Mr. Godfrey's specifications," he argued. "They'd have to be completely refitted. And there's the cost of sailing them around the Horn."

"Yes, that's true. But I understand there are many years of service left in the down-easters. Even with refitting and sailing them to California, my client would still realize a substantial saving over buying new ships at the prices you've quoted." I gave the irate Irishman my sweetest smile. "Of course, we'd prefer to do business with a local merchant."

"Price isn't everything," Finney all but exploded. "Reputation must be taken into consideration. The quality of our ships can't be bested by anyone on the West Coast."

"That may be, Mr. Finney," I replied calmly. "The same cannot be said of the New England ships, which even you must agree are renowned as the cream of the American fleet. They are nearly as fast as the clipper ships, can be used for either local or international trade and, as I've pointed out, may be obtained for far less money than the price you quoted Mr. Godfrey."

Finney seemed incapable of speech. He turned his furious gaze to Pierce, as if hoping a member of the male sex would be more open to rational thought than this demented female who had somehow found her way into his office. Pierce pretended not to notice the shipbuilder's distress.

In a reasonable voice, Pierce said, "You've brought up some valid points, Miss Woolson. Certainly the possibility of purchasing some distressed down-easters must be taken into consideration."

"Wait, not so fast!" Looking as if he might choke on his words, Finney said, "Perhaps my man was too hasty drawin' up these figures. Give us a day or two to rethink matters. As you say," he added, throwing me a sour glare, "it's best to keep business close to home. Finney's looks after its own. We'll see that you come out ahead with this order, Mr. Godfrey, and with six of the finest ships to be found anywhere in the country in the bargain."

Pierce was laughing so hard by the time we entered our carriage, he could hardly give my address to the driver.

"If I didn't already have a luncheon engagement," he said, wiping his eyes, "I'd take you to the finest restaurant in town. The look on Finney's face when you trotted out all that business about the down-easters was priceless. By the way, how did you come to know all that?"

"One of my close friends is a newspaper reporter," I said, not mentioning Samuel's name. "You'd be surprised how quickly he can come up with even the most obscure facts. And this information was readily available."

"I've heard about the British building steel-hulled ships, but I had no idea they were being given special insurance rates by Lloyd's of London. You're right, you know. When the wooden-ship owners have to start paying higher rates, it's going to revolutionize the industry."

He stared at me. The expression on his face made me

acutely uncomfortable. "I know I've said it before, but you're absolutely amazing!"

"Mr. Godfrey," I objected.

"Pierce, please," he interjected.

"As you wish," I agreed somewhat reluctantly, preferring to keep matters on a more formal basis. "The point is, I did only what any good attorney would do—male *or* female. There's no need to rave on about it."

Looking out the window, I saw we weren't far from the new Women and Children's Hospital. "If you don't mind, I'd like to make a brief stop to check on Mr. Arlen before returning to my office. If you'll just drop me off, I can make my own way back to Shepard's."

He checked his fob watch. "I have an hour before my luncheon appointment. If your visit is brief, I'll be happy to wait."

As it turned out, my business took barely five minutes. Bad news, I've noticed, does not take long to deliver.

"It's terrible, it is, miss," a distraught young nurse said, fairly bursting with self-importance. "The whole hospital's in a state about it, I can tell you."

"What is it? What has happened?"

"It's that accountant, Mr. Arlen, miss," she said with wide eyes. "He went and died sometime during the night. Of course he'd been ill, but still his death was an awful shock. Mrs. Barlow was so upset she left the hospital in tears."

The young nurse looked suspiciously around the

ward as if to make sure no one was listening, then lowered her voice until it was barely above a whisper.

"There's been rumors that Mr. Arlen didn't die a natural death," she went on, drawing out these last words with great drama and a knowing wink. "Such a shocking thing to happen. Just dreadful!"

Dreadful indeed, I thought, as I walked somewhat dazedly to Pierce's waiting carriage. As far as I was concerned, there could no longer be any doubt. A vicious killer was on the loose—a villain who was methodically murdering people connected, in one way or another, to the new hospital.

Where would it end? I asked myself. How many more victims were on the killer's list?

CHAPTER SEVEN

My bruised and bandaged face caused a sensation when I entered the office half an hour later. For once, Hubert Perkins was too dumbstruck to comment on some imagined fault, while several clients waiting to see a partner stared at me as if I'd just stepped out of a boxing ring. Nodding a polite greeting to the group, I made my way with as much dignity as I could muster toward my office. Behind me, a dozen pairs of eyes bored into my back until I reached the door and went inside. I had just removed my coat and hat when Robert burst in without bothering to knock.

"You look like hell, Sarah. Why didn't you stay home today?"

"You always know just the right thing to say, Robert," I told him, sinking gratefully into the chair behind my desk. "And you know well and good why I couldn't stay home. Mr. Godfrey and I had an important meeting this morning."

"Oh, was that this morning? I'd forgotten." Naturally, he'd done no such thing. In fact, I suspected that was his real reason for barging into my office. "So, how did it go?" He made a poor attempt to appear casual as he turned a chair around and straddled it.

"The meeting went very well, thank you. Some points in the contract required clarification, but in the end I think Finney's will do nicely for my client."

I thought Robert looked a bit disappointed, although I wasn't sure why. I wondered if he were annoyed that my alliance with Pierce Godfrey was turning out to be a success.

"Oh, yes?" he said, feigning indifference. "I'm glad to hear it." He started to get up, but I stopped him.

"Actually, Robert, I just received some disturbing news." I explained what I'd heard at the hospital. "According to the nurse I spoke to, there seems to be a question of foul play."

Robert stared at me blankly, and I realized he'd never met the accountant. Even after I explained who Arlen was, he still looked vacant.

"Don't you see?" I said in exasperation. "Arlen is the

142

third person connected with the Women and Children's Hospital to die in less than two weeks. And I'm sure something was bothering him about its finances." I went on to describe our tour the previous Monday, including the accountant's apparent concern over the books.

"You think that has something to do with his death?"

"I don't know it for a fact. It just seems strange he should die so soon afterward. He really was upset that day."

"Which means absolutely nothing. Good lord, Sarah, not a day goes by that there aren't any number of things that disturb me. Only you could turn something so ordinary into a case for murder. Actually, three murders!"

The wretched man was impossible. "All right, then—how do you explain the high levels of hyoscyamine found in Josiah Halsey's system? And don't try to tell me he took it by accident, because there was far too much of the stuff in his system to have found its way there by mistake."

He stared at me in bewilderment. "What the devil is hyoscyamine?"

I described the alkaloid as best I could. "It's commonly called jimsonweed. Evidently it grows wild in the countryside, so anyone would have access to it."

"As long as they knew what to look for."

"Well, Halsey's killer did."

Finally, it seemed, I'd said something to make my colleague pause. It was easy to follow Robert's thoughts as they raced across his broad face.

"All right, I'll concede that miserable excuse for a minister was probably killed—God knows he must have had enough enemies. But," he said, raising his hand as I started to interrupt, "I see no reason to believe it has anything to do with this Arlen fellow. Anyway, you have nothing but rumor to back up your notion of foul play. I assume there'll be an autopsy. Until then, I suggest we keep our imaginations in check." He regarded me from beneath furrowed brows. "An exercise you would do well to practice more often, Sarah."

He was out of the room before I could come up with a suitable response. I sat for several minutes gazing despondently at the mountain of files piled on my desk. It was growing increasingly difficult to muster even a modicum of enthusiasm for the repetitive drudgery that had become my job. Still, the stack would only grow higher the longer I ignored it.

Resigned, I uncovered the Caligraph machine and got to work. Not surprisingly, my fingers seemed unusually clumsy today, and my thoughts kept wandering back to Octavius Sloan's thinly veiled comments about Pierce and Caroline Godfrey. He'd described their relationship as "strained." Well, I had the evidence of my own eyes to support the fact that they'd been anything but friendly. But why?

By midafternoon I could stand it no longer. Waiting until Perkins was absent from his desk by the door, I gathered up my coat and hat and slipped out of the office. Fortunately, I was able to catch a horsecar, and after only one transfer, I walked the few remaining blocks to the end of Bay Street. I hadn't given much thought to what excuse I'd give for returning to Finney's only hours after leaving, but something told me my story wouldn't have to be particularly convincing. From what Pierce had told me, Octavius Sloan was always amenable to a good gossip.

As it turned out, my feeble excuse about having lost a glove was hardly out of my mouth before the office manager, beaming from ear to ear, led me to a chair beside his desk. I was offered tea, which I accepted, and some rather stale-looking cookies, which I politely declined.

Rubbing his hands together, he said, "Now then, Miss Woolson, you must tell me everything. Whatever you said in that meeting this morning has Finney in a tailspin."

While it was unethical to divulge specifics of the meeting, I had, after all, come here in search of my own information. *Quid pro quo,* I thought, and wondered how best to satisfy his curiosity without overstepping professional boundaries.

"I fail to see why Mr. Finney should be upset," I said carefully. "Portions of the contract required clarification and, in one or two instances, financial recalculation."

Sloan slapped his knee in approval. "I knew it! You questioned his prices, didn't you? I've been after him for ages to be more competitive. His only reply is,

'Finney's builds the best and charges accordingly.' "
Sloan perfectly mimicked his employer's Irish brogue.
"Stubborn as a mule, that man. Now a woman has
proven me right. Who would have thought?"

He eyed me speculatively as he nibbled on a cookie.
"Now, why did you really come back here, Miss
Woolson? And, please, don't tell me again about a
missing glove. You weren't wearing gloves this
morning."

I smiled. No, I hadn't been wearing gloves. I rarely
did, as a matter of fact, for the very real reason that I
was always losing them.

"You've seen through my little ruse, Mr. Sloan.
Actually, I was curious about something you said this
morning—about Mr. Godfrey's relationship with his
sister-in-law. You seemed to imply that it was less than
friendly."

Sloan raised thin eyebrows and studied me speculatively. It was not difficult to deduce his thoughts; he
was torn between engaging in a good gossip and
speaking ill of a prized client.

I had anticipated this reluctance and had prepared a
response. "Mr. Sloan, I give you my word that anything you say about this matter will remain between us.
My interest is purely personal." At least for now, I
silently added.

This seemed to be the reassurance Sloan was looking
for. "That is good of you, Miss Woolson. It would
hardly do if it became known that I had told tales out
of school, now would it?" He settled back in his chair.

146

"So, you are interested in the infamous Godfrey affair."

"Excuse me?"

His eyes twinkled. "The affair was conducted most discreetly, Miss Woolson. Few people knew about it."

"Are you saying Mr. Godfrey and his sister-in-law were—that is, that they . . ."

"Oh, yes, Miss Woolson, that is exactly what I'm saying. Whether or not Mr. Leonard Godfrey was aware of the, er, close friendship between his brother and his wife, I cannot say. Since the two brothers appear to be on good terms, I suspect he did not."

"But you still haven't explained the reason for Mr. Godfrey and his sister-in-law's falling out."

He shrugged thin shoulders. "As to that, I cannot say. The maitre d' of the Palace Hotel, who is an acquaintance of mine, happened to see the two engaged in a heated, er, discussion, in one of the hotel's private dining alcoves. From what he overheard, he assumed the two were terminating their relationship on less than affable terms. In fact, Mrs. Godfrey actually slapped her brother-in-law before storming from the room. My friend said he would not soon forget the look on her face as she demanded that he summon her a cab."

"I see. When did your friend witness this exchange?"

He stopped to consider. "It must be close to a year now. Since then, well, I've heard rumors describing the polite, but icy, rapport between the two."

As I had seen at the charity dinner, I thought. Aloud, I said, "I appreciate your candor, Mr. Sloan."

Again, his eyes twinkled as he drained the last of his tea. "And I appreciate the clever way you got the best of Henry Finney, Miss Woolson. I shall have uncommon fun with him about it for weeks, I assure you."

Octavius Sloan was still chuckling as I left the shipyard office and started for Rincon Hill. It was after five o'clock, too late to return to the law firm, and frankly I had much to think about. An hour later, I was still mulling over Sloan's surprising revelations as I approached my home to find Eddie Cooper, the young cabbie who had done such a splendid job following Bert Corrigan to Killy Doyle's residence, parked out front.

"I've been waitin' for you, miss," he announced, jumping down from atop the brougham's driver's seat.

In the daylight, I could see the lad was no more than fourteen or fifteen, an inch or two shorter than myself and very slender. His long, thin face would have been quite pleasant-looking had it not been for a scattering of pock marks and a ragged two-inch scar along his left cheek. These defects hardly mattered, though, once you noticed the boy's eyes. A rich, chocolate brown, they were alert and curious, glinting with quick intelligence. His hair, unevenly cut and reaching to his shoulders, appeared surprisingly clean. As did his patched and oversized clothes. Although undoubtedly as poor as Job's turkey, the boy seemed to be no stranger to soap and water.

"I got news," he said, sounding very pleased with

himself. "I watched the house we followed that plug-ugly to last night, and he and the gent what owns the place pulled foot out of there before dawn this morning."

I stared at the boy. "Are you saying that Killy Doyle and Bert Corrigan went somewhere together?"

"Yes, ma'am. Took off with suitcases and one of them fancy cases lawyers and such carry. They ain't comin' back, neither. The gent, Mr. Doyle, was rippin' mad. He told that big ruffian it was all his fault they had to do a bunk."

"Eddie, this is important," I said urgently. "Did you hear them say where they were going?"

"I knew you'd want to know, miss, so I got close as I could without bein' seen. But they didn't say nothin' about where they was off to. Just took off in a hack like the devil himself was after 'em."

This was very bad news. I kicked myself for marching up to Doyle's door the night before. I'd foolishly tipped off our prey. Now they'd disappeared, and with them perhaps my last hope of putting together a case for Lily Mankin.

Hiding my disappointment, I praised Eddie for his initiative and, pressing a coin into his hand, asked if he could return the following morning. I explained we would be moving a woman and her family to the new hospital on Battery Street and that it might require several trips.

His eyes lit with pleasure, and I guessed it was not solely because of the extra fares he would earn.

"You name the time, miss, and I'll be here," he promised, then eagerly asked if I wanted him to keep watch on Doyle's house again that night.

Explaining that would be like watching the barn after the horse had been stolen, I declined his offer. With a tip of his cap, Eddie assured me I could count on him to perform any and all jobs, especially any that might result in capturing those "bad eggs."

As I watched the lad urge his horse into an easy trot, I somehow knew that I could.

I saw my friend George at the police station this afternoon, and he told me about the accountant's death," Samuel said as we drank coffee in the library after dinner. The house was blissfully quiet. The children were in bed, and everyone else had gone out for the evening.

"Yes, Lucius Arlen. Did George happen to mention why they're treating his death as a possible homicide?"

"Evidently, that's what Arlen himself told his landlady. The police have taken some of his vomit—apparently there was a good deal of that—to be analyzed. And of course an autopsy's been ordered."

"And still the police refuse to connect this latest murder to the others," I said in disbelief. "Well, George's superiors may be blind as bats, but that needn't stop him from finding the truth."

"I'm sure he'll do what he can, Sarah, but he can't launch an independent investigation. They'd have his badge."

I drew a breath to argue, but one look at my brother's face told me it was pointless. Even now that he'd been made sergeant, George was severely limited in how much he could take upon himself. On the other hand, no one could fault him for keeping his eyes open.

"Speaking of George, there's something I'd like him to do." I described my confrontation with Bert Corrigan the night before, as well as Eddie's claim that Corrigan and Doyle had skipped town. "George must have some underworld informants. Ask him to find out as much as he can about those two. Especially where they'd be likely to hide."

"I can ask," Samuel agreed somewhat dubiously. "I can't promise that he'll do it."

"Just try, please?" I stopped him as he started to get up. "There's something else, Samuel." Without mentioning the office manager's name, I related Octavius Sloan's account of Pierce and Caroline Godfrey's illicit relationship.

"My, my, you have been busy today," he said when I'd finished. "If your informant is right, the affair must have been damned discreet. I certainly never heard of it." He regarded me curiously. "Why does this interest you, Sarah? You were never one for idle gossip."

I hesitated, curiously reluctant to share my thoughts, even with Samuel. Realizing this was foolish, I blurted, "I thought if there were bad feelings between Pierce and Caroline, he might have—" I stopped as Samuel's expression went from an astonished grin to outright laughter.

"You thought he might have murdered her? That's quite a stretch, Sarah, even for you. Besides, wouldn't Leonard Godfrey have a better motive for doing in his wife than her lover? After all, he was the one being cuckolded."

"That's true. But the first thing we have to do is verify the story. That's where you come in."

"Don't tell me," he said with a resigned smile. "You want me to check newspaper files."

"Along with your regular sources, yes."

"All right, I'll see what I can find out. I'm sure you realize, though, that if either Pierce or Leonard Godfrey did kill Caroline, it shatters your theory of a single murderer. I can't see them killing Halsey, however much they disliked the man. And I doubt if they even knew Arlen."

"No, probably not. But someone killed three people."

I read sympathy in my brother's eyes, as well as concern and a deep love. Perhaps because we were the two youngest children, he and I had forged a special bond. We'd shared everything growing up: toys, secrets, hidden forts and endless mischief. Drawing courage from those years, I allowed my true emotions to show, something I had not done in a long time.

"I'm frightened, Samuel," I told him in a hoarse whisper. "Something tells me this isn't the end of it. Don't laugh, but I sense evil here; a very sick mind is behind these murders."

My mouth felt dry, yet my hands were damp as I

clenched my coffee cup. "I can't stop asking myself who is going to be next."

True to his word, Eddie Cooper was parked outside our house at eight o'clock the following morning, and we quickly drove to pick up Robert at his lodgings. I'd been pleasantly surprised when the Scot agreed to help move Lily Mankin into the hospital, for it would have been difficult for Eddie and me to accomplish the job on our own.

I'd arranged for a lorry to transport Lily's meager furniture to the hospital, but we drove the widow and her family to their new home in Eddie's brougham. Fortunately, the carriage was large enough to comfortably accommodate four adults instead of the coupe's customary two.

The three children seemed more interested in our mode of transportation than in where they would soon be living, and I deduced that this was their first ride in a hack. The eldest boy, a lad of about four years, kept darting from one side of the vehicle to the other, despite his mother's efforts to restrain him. The eldest girl and her youngest brother, who sat on Lily's lap, stared wide-eyed out the window as if they'd suddenly been transported into another world.

The four-year-old had taken a liking to Robert and regaled him with questions about the carriage, the neighborhoods we were passing through and, my favorite, why horses ate hay instead of meat as dogs and cats did. The expression on Robert's face was priceless, especially when the child ceased his fidgeting long enough to squirm his way onto the Scot's lap. I was amused to observe Robert's initial shock at this liberty soften into a smile, and the attorney actually began bouncing the boy on his knee.

We arrived at the hospital to find the police already there, questioning the staff about Lucius Arlen's movements the day before he died. We were greeted by a harassed-looking Reverend Prescott, who explained that Mrs. Barlow's mother, Adelina French, had taken a turn for the worse and that Margaret had stayed home to attend her. In her absence, she'd asked him to oversee the running of the hospital. He eyed my battered face with ill-concealed curiosity, but to my relief was too polite to inquire why I resembled a ruffian who had gotten the worst of it in a street brawl.

"Until Mrs. Barlow returns, you shall have to put up with me, I'm afraid." He gave an ironic little smile, and once again I was struck by the man's charisma. "I'm sorry you had to call when there's so much chaos, Miss Woolson. Mr. Arlen's death has been very unsettling."

"I'm sure it has," I agreed.

"Still, I don't understand why the police are involved. Surely there can be no doubt that Mr. Arlen died of influenza."

I had no wish to discuss my theory about Arlen's death with the minister. Noncommittally, I said, "I'm sure they merely wish to be thorough, Reverend

Prescott. Hopefully, they'll complete their work quickly and leave you in peace."

Robert and I showed Lily and her children up to the second floor. While they explored their new quarters—and Robert and Eddie helped the lorry drivers with the widow's furniture—I went in search of information. To my delight, I found George Lewis in the kitchen questioning the cook, Chin Lee Fong. Because both men were facing away from the door, I was able to overhear a good deal of the interview without being seen. I make no apologies for eavesdropping. I believe I've mentioned my conviction that one must occasionally bend conventional mores in order to achieve one's higher goals. I felt confident this was one of those times.

As usual, Chin was loud and defensive. "I know nothing about that cow *chung*," he spat. I knew enough Mandarin to realize Chin had just accused Arlen of being not only a lowly bovine but one with questionable parentage. "He cut my pay, try get me fired, filthy mongrel!"

"Is that what you fought about?" George asked.

"Fight?" Chin spat contemptuously. "Which fight you mean? We fight all time. Can't talk reason to man with no brain."

"I have witnesses who claim they saw Mr. Arlen entering this kitchen close to eight that evening."

Chin threw up his arms in obvious disgust. "Lies! All lies. I told you I not see him."

Just then, I heard approaching footsteps and quickly

ducked behind some packing cases. In a moment, two uniformed policemen passed my hiding place and entered the kitchen.

"Harlen, Dobbs, it's about time," I heard George say. "I want you to collect samples of all the food in this kitchen, especially the tea and coffee."

Chin's explosion at this invasion of his domain was immediate and loud. "No! You not touch anything. Missus not like. I not like. I have nothing to do with pig's death."

"Get him out of here," George told his men. "And see if you can find the kitchen maid, Dora Clemens."

From my hiding place, I watched the policemen half carry a struggling, vigorously protesting Chin Lee Fong out into the hall. As soon as they were gone, I entered the kitchen, anxious for a private word with George.

"Miss Sarah," he said, looking startled by my sudden entrance. "What are you doing here? And what's happened to your face?"

It was a natural enough inquiry, but I was growing weary of fabricating stories to explain my bandaged and bruised face. This time, I decided to tell the truth.

"I was hit with a rock, George. Thrown by a street hooligan. But that is not why I'm here. I trust you've had an opportunity to speak to Samuel?"

George Lewis, a personable young man with a pleasant, boyish-looking face, wore his police uniform—a single-breasted "mission-blue" frock coat, buttoned up to a rolling collar at the neck—with pride, especially now that it displayed his new rank of sergeant. For several years we had enjoyed a friendly, if slightly formal, relationship. I was surprised, therefore, when he didn't seem the least bit pleased to find me here today.

"I saw him," he replied, avoiding my eyes. "He told me about those two fellows you're looking for. I've never heard of Doyle, but Corrigan is well known at the station. Still, without an official complaint filed against them, I can't use department recourses to conduct a search."

"What about the owner of the sweatshop that burned down?"

I had to raise my voice in order to be heard over loud bumps and scrapes coming from the room above us. Since I knew this to be Lily Mankin's new quarters, I assumed Robert and the lorry drivers were busy moving in the widow's furniture—and making a very noisy job of it.

"There's virtually no way to find him, Miss Sarah," George answered. "Most owners make sure their paper trail is impossible to follow."

Since this response was no more than I'd expected, I moved on, anxious to make the most of our time alone. "Samuel tells me you suspect Lucius Arlen might have been poisoned."

"At this point we know nothing for sure. Of course there's the autopsy—"

"Yes, yes," I said, cutting him off impatiently. "But what is the official view of the three murders?"

He ran a finger along his starched white shirt collar as if it had suddenly grown too tight for his neck. "I know you think the three deaths have something to do with the hospital, Miss Sarah. I admit you were right about the Nob Hill murders, but this case is different. There's just no way to connect the victims."

I gave an exasperated sigh. "This is no time to prevaricate, George. What makes you think Chin killed Arlen?"

He seemed taken aback by my bluntness, but then his handsome face often bore a startled expression in my presence. I'm not sure why. (Samuel has some silly notion that the man is enamored of me.) Whatever the reason, I did not let it distract me from my purpose.

"Well, George? Has the cat got your tongue? Why have the police fixed on Chin Lee Fong?"

"Given the circumstances, Chin is the logical suspect. He and Arlen were always fighting, and half a dozen hospital employees have sworn the two hated each other."

"That's hardly a secret, George. But it's a leap to suppose Chin hated Arlen enough to kill him. Did anyone actually see the two together before Arlen left the hospital that day?"

"No," he said, then added, "That's why I want to interview Dora Clemens. By all accounts, she was one of the last people to go home that evening."

We were interrupted as Harlen and Dobbs returned to the kitchen.

"We can't find Dora Clemens," Harlen told George.

"Seems she hasn't come in today."

I looked at my lapel watch and saw it was nearly eleven. "What time does Miss Clemens normally report for work?" I asked Harlen, the taller of the two men. George gave me a quick look, but nodded for the man to answer.

"We was told she's supposed to be here by seven, miss." He glanced at George, then added, "She doesn't seem to be very popular with the rest of the staff, but she was punctual enough. And she's never missed a day's work without sending along a message."

George ordered Dobbs to find Miss Clemens's home address. Once she'd been located, he was to take another man, go to her residence and bring her to the hospital. After Dobbs was gone, he instructed Harlen to complete the search of the kitchen, then turned to me, his expression unusually impatient.

"I don't know what else I can tell you, Miss Sarah. Until I've spoken to the kitchen maid, or found someone who saw the two men together that evening, I have little to go on." He nodded toward Harlen, who was going through the cupboards in what appeared to be a methodical fashion. "Maybe we'll find something in all this."

I wasn't convinced that finding traces of poison in Chin's kitchen would constitute reliable proof of wrongdoing. It would be all too easy to plant incriminating evidence in a room as accessible as the hospital kitchen. On the other hand, such a find would be extremely damaging to the cook.

Since there seemed little more to be accomplished here, I was about to take my leave when Harlen came in, leading an agitated Dora Clemens. Remembering the girl's sullen expression the first time we'd met, I wasn't surprised to see her thin lips pursed into an unattractive pout nor to note the glare she directed at the policeman holding her arm.

"This here's Dora Clemens," Harlen said, giving the girl a little push. "One of the nurses saw her sneakin' in the back door and slipped me a nod."

George regarded the truculent young woman, then asked, "What do you have to say for yourself, my girl? Why are you so late getting to the hospital this morning?"

The maid drew herself up to her full height, which was barely to George's shoulder, and managed to appear as if she were staring down her thin, pointed nose at him. "What's it to you if I'm late?"

Harlen gave her a poke from behind. "Watch yer tongue, girl. And give the sergeant a civil answer."

Dora gave Harlen a withering look and grumbled, "I wasn't feelin' well, if you must know."

George's expression was skeptical as he motioned Dora to take a seat at the table. "I've got some questions for you. And I want honest answers, or it will go hard on you."

Crossly, the maid sank onto one of the straight-backed chairs and glowered up at George through hard, wily eyes. I noticed her face seemed pale, and she was perspiring more than the temperature in the kitchen warranted. I wondered if she really had been sick that morning. She certainly didn't look well now.

"If yer want to ask me about that daft accountant," Dora told George, "I don't know nothin'. I stayed as far away from him as I could."

"Why was that?" George asked.

"Threatened to give me and cook the sack," she retorted, as if George was an idiot for not knowing this. "Said all Chinamen was lying devils, that me and the cook was robbin' the hospital blind."

"Are you sure Mr. Arlen didn't have provocation to believe you might be helping yourselves to food or ready cash?" George persisted. "Maybe he caught you or Mr. Chin pocketing something from the kitchen."

Dora half rose from her seat, and her pale face blotched an ugly red. "I never did no such thing! And don't you be sayin' I did, 'cause it's a rotten lie."

As if to punctuate this outbreak, there was another series of loud bangs from above our heads. Good heavens, I thought, wondering if Robert and the lorry men were throwing Lily's furniture into the room.

George, too, glanced up at the ceiling before turning back to the kitchen maid. "I'm not accusing you of anything, Dora, so just calm down. By the way, what time did you leave the hospital the day before yesterday?"

"Just after supper. I saw to the cleanup, then got outta here sometime after seven."

"And where was Mr. Chin when you left for home?"

"How should I know? It's not up to me to keep track

of him, is it? He can go to hell for all I care."

"You don't care for Mr. Chin?" George inquired, raising sandy-colored eyebrows.

"Why should I?" she retorted defensively. "All he does is yell at me. He cooks good enough but acts all high and mighty, for a Chinaman and all."

"Dora," George said. "This is important. Was Mr. Chin in the kitchen when you left here on Monday evening?"

Dora squinted slyly up at him and once again ran a hand over her perspiring brow. Coyly, she said, "I don't remember. I might have heard him talkin' to someone."

The red patches on Dora's cheeks had grown so bright they looked as if they'd been painted on. Her sharp, glassy eyes darted from George to the other policemen, as if trying to gauge their reaction to this statement.

"Was it a man's or a woman's voice you heard?"

"Oh, it was a man, all right." She paused, then went on in a slightly lower voice, "I heard him swearin' at Chin and soundin' savage as a meat axe."

"No one swear at me!" Turning, I saw Chin Lee Fong standing in the doorway glaring at the maid. "Why you tell lies, worthless piece of sheep dung?"

"That's enough, Chin," George motioned for Dobbs to stop the cook's angry advance into the kitchen. "I told you to stay away until we were through."

"It late, I start lunch. You go, come back later."

George hesitated, then nodded to Dobbs, who reluctantly relinquished his grip on the agitated cook.

Turning his back to us, the chef began banging pots and pans. Dragging out a bag of flour, he dropped large handfuls into a bowl. When he saw we were still there, he said, "Go away! Talk later. Cook now." Addressing Dora, he snapped, "Take off coat. Time to work, lazy girl."

The kitchen maid rolled her eyes and shrugged out of her wrap. Tying a white apron around her slender waist, she went to fetch potatoes from a bin in the storage pantry.

I caught George's eye, and he shrugged in resignation. "Have you finished in here?" he asked Harlen, who had continued to collect samples during the maid's interview.

The tall policeman nodded and tied off the bag he'd used to deposit individual wrappings of marked food samples.

"You can get on with your duties for now," George told Chin. "But I want to talk to you again later." His gaze went to Dora, who'd begun to peel potatoes. "I want to speak to you, too, Dora. Perhaps you should think over your story and decide exactly what you saw that night."

Dora ignored him. Wearily, she rested her weight against the sink as she worked. The young woman really didn't look well, I thought. Or perhaps it was just the excitement of being questioned by the police. That and Lucius Arlen's death would be a disconcerting experience for anyone, much less an illiterate kitchen maid. The poor thing was probably terrified.

Following me out of the kitchen, George said, "You heard Chin and Arlen's fight on Monday afternoon, didn't you, Miss Sarah? What can you tell me about it?"

I explained what I'd seen and heard of the argument, then added, "What Dora said was true; Arlen came right out and accused Chin of being a thief. Mrs. Barlow, on the other hand, seems to think highly of the cook. She told Arlen she'd authorized his expenses and that she was confident he hadn't pocketed any of the money."

"Interesting," George said noncommittally. "We should know in a couple of days if Chin is keeping any poison in his kitchen. It's not unusual for people to lay in a supply of arsenic to kill rats, but the Chinaman insists Mrs. Barlow forbade anything of that kind in a hospital kitchen. Well, we'll soon see."

With that, George left to interview the nursing staff, and I started upstairs to check on all the banging I'd heard, as well as to reassure myself that Lily and her children were settling in comfortably. Before I reached the first landing, I heard a loud scream, which seemed to come from the direction of the kitchen.

There were heavy footsteps above me, and Robert suddenly appear on the second-floor landing. "What now?" he exclaimed, then, without waiting for a reply, brushed past me on his way downstairs. Whirling after him, I was forced to yank up my skirts to keep up with his long strides.

When we reached the kitchen, we found one of the older nurses sitting on the floor, Dora Clemens's head in her lap. As we made our way into the room, Dora doubled over and threw up all over the nurse's spotless apron.

A string of Chinese chatter came from the corner of the kitchen, and I looked up to find Chin watching Dora, a look of fear and repulsion on his face. I hurried over to the ghastly tableau on the floor, anxious to help if I could.

"I've sent someone for a doctor," the nurse told me, shifting Dora's head so that she wouldn't choke on her own spittle. "She seems to be in a great deal of abdominal pain, perhaps from some kind of gastric fever."

Dora's face was creased with pain and her pale skin had turned a sickly yellow. As I knelt down beside the girl, the little maid's teeth started to chatter, then her body began to shake violently. Giving a strangled scream, she once again became sick. This time, the vomit was mixed with blood.

I'd just removed my jacket to cover the shivering girl when one of the hospital physicians entered the kitchen and all but pushed me aside in his haste to bend down beside Dora.

"What's wrong, nurse?" he asked. Holding Dora's wrist, he gave her dilated pupils a rapid inspection. Reaching for his stethoscope, he endeavored to place it on the little maid's chest. But Dora appeared too agitated to lie still; with loud groans, she contorted her thin body in an effort to pull away.

Gently holding the girl still while the doctor examined her, the nurse listed the maid's symptoms. Evidently, Dora had suddenly doubled over in pain and collapsed onto the floor. The physician listened but kept his attention on the girl, who seemed to be growing weaker and more incoherent.

I turned to see George Lewis enter the kitchen, followed by Harlen and Dobbs. Taking in the scene, George went to squat by Dora. Over the doctor's protests, he bent close to her face.

"Dora, who did this to you?"

"This young woman is gravely ill," the doctor protested. "Please, allow me to tend her."

"How bad is she?" George asked, holding his position.

The doctor hesitated, but I could see the answer on his face. George must have seen it, too, for he clasped the maid's hand and tried to lift her head.

"Dora," he whispered urgently, "tell me what you saw Monday evening. You heard Chin speaking to some man. Do you know who it was?"

Dora's pale eyelids fluttered and opened. She turned her head toward the door. Following her gaze, I spied Reverend Prescott standing next to Robert, his dark eyes grave as he looked down at the suffering girl. He started to come forward, then seemed to change his mind and remained where he was.

Despite her agony, Dora managed to give the minister a weak smile, then her glazed eyes turned to the cook. "He—"

"What about him, Dora?" George pressed. "What did you see Chin do?"

"Took money—money for—" Again, she faltered, her eyes closing then opening with difficulty.

"Money?" George prompted. "Chin was stealing money?"

Dora managed a weak nod. Her watery eyes bore into George's face. "Cookies," she whispered. "In the cookie—"

"You mean the poison was in some cookies Arlen ate? Are you saying that's how he was killed?"

"No." Her face twisted in frustration. Struggling to raise her head, she managed to look directly at the cook. "Put it in coffee—"

"Who put the poison in Arlen's coffee?" George demanded. "Was it Chin?"

With renewed determination, the doctor positioned himself between Dora and the policeman. "I cannot allow you to ask any more questions. Can't you see that she's—"

He broke off as Dora's body was stricken with another, even more violent, convulsion. Hearing a gasp from the corner, I looked up to see that Chin's normally dour face wore a surprised, uncomprehending expression. He started sputtering in Chinese but was silenced by a poke from a nearby nurse.

There was a mumble of shocked whispers from people gathered by the door. My gaze went to Reverend Prescott, and I was startled to see his handsome face had taken on an otherworldly look. He was staring at the maid, but his eyes looked unfocused and miles away. Was he in some kind of trance? I wondered. Or had his minister's eyes seen something that had escaped the rest of us?

Beside him, Robert was also staring helplessly at the girl. Catching my eye, he seemed to be imploring me to do something. I sadly shook my head. With a horrible sense of déjà vu, I realized there was nothing I could do—perhaps that anyone could do—to save Dora Clemens's life.

The attack seemed to go on forever, then gradually Dora's shaking became less pronounced and her struggles to suck air into her lungs lessened. I watched in dismay as a stream of blood trickled out of the girl's mouth. Her eyes were still open, but they had lost their ability to see. Looking up from the crumpled body, I saw that, like Robert, Nicholas Prescott's trancelike face was as white as his starched collar.

Then the minister seemed to come out of his stupor. Kneeling by Dora, he took the maid's hands into his and I was again reminded of Caroline Godfrey's death scene. Mumbling what sounded like a blessing beneath his breath, Prescott bowed his head in prayer. Following his example, everyone in the kitchen lowered their heads and joined the minister in silent respect for the young woman.

When he finished praying, Prescott reached out and gently closed the girl's eyes, then rose gracefully to his feet and quietly ushered onlookers out of the room.

George continued to stare down at the dead girl as if

he couldn't quite believe she was gone. He motioned to Harlen and Dobbs, and without a word they obediently went to stand on either side of the cook.

I watched in astonishment as George approached the Chinese man and said in a flat, authoritative voice, "Chin Lee Fong, I arrest you for the murders of Lucius Arlen and Dora Clemens."

CHAPTER EIGHT

Eddie Cooper ran out of the hospital after us. I hadn't seen him in the kitchen, but of course he couldn't have missed all the commotion.

"What happened to the girl?" he asked eagerly. "Was it some kind of fit, do ya think?"

"We don't know yet, Eddie," I told him. "No one does."

"She looked awful, didn't she, miss?" the boy said, his eyes alight with excitement.

"Yes, it was awful," Robert broke in before I could answer. I noticed my colleague seemed unusually subdued. Now that I thought about it, Robert had hardly spoken a word since we found Dora collapsed on the kitchen floor. I knew him well enough to realize he was endeavoring to cover his emotions. It was clear he'd been as shaken by the poor girl's death as I had been.

Giving the lad a grumpy look, Robert added, "And you needn't look so pleased with yourself, young man.

Death is never something to be made light of."

Eddie's face instantly sobered. Mumbling apologies, he reached out to help me into the brougham. Naturally, I required no assistance, but I allowed the lad to aid me since I feel it is important for the younger generation to learn proper etiquette. If Eddie Cooper hoped to make a living driving a hack in San Francisco's better circles, possessing good manners would be an absolute essential.

As soon as Robert was seated in the carriage, Eddie leapt into the driver's seat and clicked the dappled gray into an easy trot.

"Don't say it," Robert declared, as I drew breath to speak. "There's no need for you to argue that Arlen's death was deliberate. Nor the girl's, for that matter. I agree they were both poisoned. And since we know who the murderer is, you can spare me the tiresome lectures."

"Oh? And who do you suppose that person to be?"

He gave me a sharp look. "You're being deliberately thickheaded, Sarah. You know as well as I do that Chin murdered them both. The girl came right out and accused him, for God's sake. She said he was stealing money meant to run the kitchen, and when Arlen found out, Chin slipped poison into the accountant's coffee."

It was my turn to stare. "Talk about making things up out of whole cloth! Dora said no such thing. In fact, she could hardly speak at all."

"That's right, she was dying. And people don't lie on their deathbeds. She pointed a finger directly at Chin and said he'd put poison in Arlen's coffee. You were right next to her, Sarah. You must have heard."

"Yes," I answered softly, "I must have." I tried to remember exactly what I *had* heard. When Robert started to speak again, I motioned him to be quiet while I removed the pencil and notebook from my reticule. It was important to record everything I could remember about the girl's death while the details were fresh in my mind, especially the words she spoke, and in what order. When I was finished, I studied the page thoughtfully.

"Interesting," I said at length. "Very interesting."

"What's interesting?" he demanded. "You just can't leave well enough alone, can you? You always have to orchestrate everything into a big dramatic production."

"Robert, please!" I placed the notebook back in my bag. There was no sense discussing the subject with Robert when he was in this sort of mood. Besides, I wanted time to consider matters. "Well, at least I'm to be spared the bother of convincing you the four deaths are connected," I went on, straightening my hat, which had become disarranged in my rush to the kitchen.

Robert groaned. "Not that again. I merely said Lucius Arlen and Dora Clemens's deaths were undoubtedly committed by the same person. Josiah Halsey is an entirely different matter. And how in God's name you can lump Mrs. Godfrey into this drama of yours is beyond comprehension!"

Rather than engage my cranky companion in a frustrating and probably useless argument, I rode the rest of the way to the office in silence. This seemed to suit Robert, since he made no effort to break our standoff. Unfortunately, without the distraction of my colleague's chronic obtuseness, my mind played and replayed poor little Dora's horrible death. Who would be so ruthless as to wish that kind of agony on a fellow human being?

I considered Chin Lee Fong—his total lack of social graces, his volatile temper, the chip that seemed to be perpetually affixed to his shoulder—and decided he would have a difficult time proving his innocence. There would be little public sympathy for a Chinese man accused of murdering two white people, especially when one of the victims was a young girl. As if his situation weren't dire enough, Chin made no secret of his dislike for the accountant. And of course, Dora had all but accused Chin of arguing in the kitchen with Arlen on Monday evening and of poisoning the accountant's coffee. No matter how one viewed it, matters looked extremely grim for the explosive cook.

Which did not mean for one moment I thought him guilty. Assuming Arlen's and Dora's deaths were part of a larger picture, it was possible to view the crimes from an altogether different perspective. While I could imagine Chin killing Arlen out of anger and fear—and silencing Dora if she were a witness to this act—it was impossible to imagine his motive for killing Caroline Godfrey or Josiah Halsey. As far as I knew, the cook had never met either of these victims. Certainly, he could have had no opportunity to kill Caroline, even if he'd wished to. And why, for heaven's sake, would he want to end Halsey's life?

I was still mulling this over as Eddie pulled the brougham up at Clay and Kearney streets. Over Robert's disapproving glare, I paid the boy for the morning, adding a generous tip in the bargain.

"Ya want me to wait here?" Eddie asked with his usual enthusiasm.

"No need for that, boy," Robert told him. "Go pick up some honest fares or you'll find yourself out of a job."

Eddie looked crestfallen. Repressing a smile at his eagerness, I said, "We have no more need of your services today, Eddie. I'll get word to you if something comes up. I assume a message sent to"—I read the cab company's name embossed on the side of the brougham—"Laine Carriages and Company will reach you?"

The boy hesitated, and I quickly guessed the problem. "Just to make certain there's no mistake," I said, not letting on that I'd deduced his secret, "I'll sign the note with my initials, SLW, and draw a circle around them, like this." Matching my actions to the words, I again drew out my notebook and demonstrated what I had in mind. "That way, I can make my intentions clear to you without revealing them to anyone else."

The boy smiled broadly at this strategy. Taking the paper, he tipped his hat, leapt into the driver's seat and clicked the dappled-gray mare back into noon-hour traffic.

"What was all that about?" Robert wanted to know as we entered the building. "Why couldn't you just sign your name and be done with it?"

"Because the lad can't read," I answered, stating what seemed to me patently obvious. "My initials will be a good deal easier for him to identify than my full name." Giving my hat another slight adjustment, we entered the rising room.

"I'll have to do something about that boy's sad lack of education," I added as we rose to the top floor of the building. "He's quite bright, you know. I'm sure he'll pick up his letters quickly."

My companion's only response was a grunt, which I chose to assume to be his agreement to this sensible objective.

I stopped at the tea closet before going to my office. As usual, considerable disorder greeted me: cups, saucers, plates, cookie and cake crumbs, even a soggy pile of tea leaves tossed onto the table, when the trash receptacle stood only a few inches away. It hardly mattered how often I tidied up, the closet was invariably a mess. Of late, I'd begun to suspect this continual disorder was yet one more attempt to drive me out of the firm: one, I thought in frustration, that just might work!

When I finished, I went directly to my office. There, I found a sealed envelope on my desk, my name printed in a bold masculine hand. It turned out to be an invitation from Pierce, requesting me to dine with him the following evening. Despite my vow to keep our relationship professional, I was tempted to accept. Since my talk with Octavius Sloan, I'd been consumed with curiosity about Pierce's alleged affair with Caroline. Granted, it was a long shot, but I had to know if it related in any way to her death. Finally, I took out pen and paper and accepted the invitation, then placed it in an envelope and dropped it into the box set aside for outgoing mail. That taken care of, I returned to my office and settled down to work.

As usual these days, the afternoon seemed to pass at a snail's pace. I had difficulty paying proper attention to my work, when only hours before I'd witnessed such a dreadful death. Did Lucius Arlen suffer the same horrible fate as the kitchen maid? I wondered. If so, his death dragged on a good deal longer—over twenty-four hours, according to his landlady. It must have seemed an eternity to the poor man. If only a doctor had been summoned sooner, perhaps he'd still be alive—and able to explain why he'd been so insistent on speaking to Mrs. Barlow that Monday afternoon.

I was increasingly convinced that this episode was key to understanding his murder. Had he discovered discrepancies in the hospital books and been killed to insure he told no one?

I sighed as I went back to my typewriting. There was no way around it, I told myself. I must at least try to find answers to these questions. As far as I could see, only one person could help me. I would speak to Mrs. Barlow as soon as possible.

I have good news and bad news, little sister," Samuel said that evening as we sat on our favorite bench in the garden. "The bad news is I couldn't find one lick of information about who owns that sweatshop. The good news is I happened onto something I think you'll find interesting." He lit a cigarette, relishing my curiosity. "Guess who owns the warehouse the new hospital is leasing?"

"The warehouse?" I repeated rather stupidly. "Why should it matter who owns it?"

"I'm not sure that it does. Still, I thought you might like to know that it's registered to Godfrey Shipping."

"What?"

"That's right, your new client and his brother purchased the building some fifteen years ago. They kept offices there for six or seven years until it became too small, then moved to new quarters. The place has been empty ever since. Until the hospital came along, it was considered a very costly white elephant, too large and in too much disrepair to rent, much less to sell. Leonard and Pierce must have been ecstatic when the hospital offered to take the place off their hands."

"You mean all this time the hospital board has been negotiating with the Godfrey brothers to lease the warehouse?" I shook my head. "Yet this is the first I've heard of it. Who do you suppose knows?"

"Very few people, it seems. Arlen and the board dealt with the Godfreys' property manager, not with the brothers themselves. What I find most strange is that Leonard, who was, after all, married to the board's chairwoman, never mentioned that his company owned the building."

"Caroline must have known—she was his wife."

"If she did, she never let on."

My mind whirled with possible implications. What, if anything, could this have to do with the murders? And why had the Godfreys kept their ownership of the warehouse a secret?

As if reading my thoughts, Samuel said, "I don't see how this could have anything to do with Mrs. Godfrey's death, which isn't under investigation anyway. I can envision, though, how it might have some bearing on the other deaths."

"Yes," I said, catching his meaning. "Halsey's constant ranting about the new hospital might have eventually scotched the deal, leaving the brothers sitting with their empty warehouse. They must have been delighted to see Halsey out of the way, especially after his behavior the night Caroline died."

"That makes sense, as far as it goes. But what about Arlen? Why would they want him dead?"

"I think he may have discovered some inconsistencies in the account books," I answered slowly. "The kitchen maid, Dora Clemens, clearly knew more about what happened than she told the police. If she saw the person who poisoned Arlen—"

"She'd have to be disposed of before she could talk," Samuel finished for me.

"Yes, but I don't see how either brother could have access to hospital funds."

"Ah, but they do have access, little sister. That was something else I discovered today. Leonard Godfrey is still a member of the board. He and Caroline were responsible for a large percentage of the fundraising activities. What if he figured out a way to skim off some of the profits?"

I thought of the stove and water heater Leonard donated to the hospital. In light of this generosity, it was hard to imagine him stealing hospital money.

"But why would they do such a thing?" I asked. "Surely not just to find renters for their warehouse."

Samuel ground out his cigarette. "No, they had a more serious reason than that. I came across some articles that mentioned several Godfrey ships that sank over the past two years. The loss in cargo alone was so severe that for a time the brothers were in danger of going out of business."

"But I still don't see—"

"You just said you suspected someone on the board of directors was pilfering from the hospital fund. Well, with Leonard still on the board, he and his brother might have devised a scheme to pocket donations or even pad hospital expenses. Anyway, they're suddenly back in the black. Did you know they're purchasing a new fleet of ships?"

Icy fingers gripped my heart. Good lord, I thought,

the order from Finney's! "Yes, as a matter of fact I do know about the ships." I thought for a moment. "Samuel, we've got to learn more about the Godfreys' finances, especially regarding their shipping firm. There may be a logical explanation for how they managed to revive their business after losing those ships."

Samuel smiled wryly. "You mean an explanation short of murder."

I felt a stab of guilt. Surely it wasn't that obvious? For a brother who knew me as well as Samuel, it probably was. My feelings toward Pierce were confused. Despite his supposed affair with his sister-in-law, I couldn't deny I felt an attraction for him. I wasn't proud of my feelings, but it was vital I face them honestly.

"Yes," I admitted. "It's difficult for me to picture Pierce as a murderer, but I won't let that bias my thinking. Now," I went on more briskly, "I plan to visit the Barlows tomorrow afternoon. If Margaret had a chance to speak to Arlen before his death, that may answer a number of questions." I paused until a neighbor's dog stopped barking. "Oh, and Pierce is taking me to dinner tomorrow night."

Through the soft glow of moonlight, I saw Samuel's eyebrows rise. "Really? Are you sure that's a good idea? Until we know more about the Godfreys, I don't like the idea of you being out with him alone."

"I'll be careful, Samuel. I promise."

"Hah," he snorted. "Where have I heard that before?"

"This time I mean it. We'll be out in public, and I'll make some excuse to come home early. I'll be fine, really."

Samuel looked me in the eye. "You'd better be damn careful with that man, Sarah. In fact, you'd better be bloody cautious about this whole thing. We're dealing with someone who's killed three, possibly four, people. I don't want my little sister to be victim number five!"

As fate would have it, my employer actually facilitated my plan to visit the Barlows the following afternoon. Instead of having to fabricate an excuse to leave the office, I merely had to agree to deliver a portfolio across town to one of Shepard's clients.

Hurrying downstairs, I flagged down a cabriolet, which I knew would make excellent time. I felt a momentary pang of guilt that there'd been no time to summon Eddie and his brougham, but it was imperative that Shepard's errand be completed as quickly as possible, so that I might conduct business of my own.

I was in luck. The client—a tall, stooped man who, when told I was an attorney for Shepard's firm, treated me like a freak attraction in P. T. Barnum's sideshow—was at home and I was able to turn over the papers without delay. My next stop was Rincon Hill, where I picked up Celia, who had agreed to accompany me to the Barlows.

Good fortune continued to be on my side. Arriving at the Barlow home, we found both Margaret and her mother, Adelina French, receiving guests. Using the not wholly dishonest pretext that we were concerned over Mrs. French's health, we were warmly greeted and, at their insistence, pressed into remaining for tea.

As Margaret showed us into the beautifully furnished front parlor, a black Scottish terrier bounded into the room, jumping up and barking loudly at Celia and me.

"McKenzie, down!" Margaret ordered the animal, to no avail. "I'm sorry, ladies," our hostess said, grabbing the dog's collar. "McKenzie is my husband's dog. I'm afraid the judge is the only one who can make him behave." Ringing for a maid, Margaret ordered the dog confined to another room, then turned to us with an embarrassed smile. "Perhaps it's because we weren't blessed with children, but Tobias dotes shamelessly on that dog."

Now that quiet prevailed, we settled down to enjoy a delicious assortment of cakes and finger sandwiches, as well as excellent tea. While Mrs. French spoke with enthusiasm about the new hospital, I surreptitiously studied the woman.

Adelina French certainly was attractive, I mused, thinking once again that mother and daughter could truly have passed for sisters. Tall and slender, Adelina obviously went to some pains with her appearance. This afternoon she wore a dark lavender morning dress of washed silk, fashioned with a double fishwife skirt. She'd pinned a striking diamond and amethyst broach to her bodice. Her light brown hair showed minimal strands of gray and she wore it drawn into a neat braided bun at the nape. Her skin was remarkably smooth for a woman of sixty, revealing only a few small crow's feet around quite remarkable green eyes. I decided she must have been quite a beauty in her youth. Even today, though more frail than usual, her smile was warm and convivial.

While we ate, Margaret explained that her mother's arthritis was often exacerbated by cold and foggy weather.

"We've certainly experienced more than enough of that this spring," Celia said sympathetically. "I'm sorry to hear it aggravates your condition."

"Yes," Margaret agreed, "it's caused poor Mama a great deal of discomfort."

"Don't make a fuss," Adelina put in. "I'll be right as rain in no time. The last thing I want is to become a burden to my family."

Margaret reached over and patted her mother's arm. "Don't be silly, Mama, you could never be a burden. You've done more work for the hospital than anyone I know. I couldn't get through a single day there without your help. And look at how many people have stopped by to pay their respects since your illness."

Adelina flushed and made a disparaging gesture with her hand. To the woman's credit, she never once complained about her painful knees and joints, although I noticed her grimace when she touched the lovely brooch at her throat.

"Why aren't you wearing your matching earrings, Mama?" Margaret asked, also noticing the gesture. "The earrings and brooch were a gift from my husband," she told Celia and me proudly. "He's enormously fond of Mama."

Adelina fingered her ears curiously. "You know, I think I must have left them in my room. No matter, I'll get them later."

We went on to chat about matters of little importance, at least in my opinion, and I blessed my foresight in bringing Celia with me. On occasions such as this, I freely admit that my social skills are sadly lacking. Fortunately, my dear sister-in-law more than makes up for any deficiencies on my part, even knowing the name of the young society bride Margaret and Adelina kept going on about.

When the tea things were cleared away, I was at last able to introduce the real purpose for our visit. Leaving Celia to entertain Mrs. French—another reason I wanted her along—I asked Margaret if she would show me her lovely garden.

"You must have a very talented gardener," I said with genuine admiration, taking in the vast array of colorful and naturally arranged flowers and green plants.

Margaret laughed. "Oh, no, Mama wouldn't hear of it. This yard is her doing. Not only do we have fresh flowers for the house all year round—a feat in itself, I assure you—but you should see the vegetables and fruits she manages to produce."

I looked around at azaleas just coming into bloom, rosebushes of every conceivable color, daylilies, geraniums and even a California desert willow. One side of the yard had been set aside for vegetables and herbs, many of the varieties beyond my limited ability to identify. Peaceful as I found the setting, it was time to wade into more serious waters.

"Mrs. Barlow, I noticed that neither Mr. Arlen nor Miss Clemens was mentioned during tea. You know of the kitchen maid's death yesterday, don't you?"

Margaret's face grew solemn. "Yes, Nicholas—that is, Reverend Prescott—told us." She gave an involuntary shiver and motioned toward a stone bench out of sight of the house. When we were seated, she said, "My mother knows—she was here when he gave us the news. She found it most unsettling, especially coming so soon after poor Lucius's death. In fact, she took to her room for the afternoon. I've tried not to bring it up today. I don't want to add to her distress."

"No, of course not." I paused to watch a small blue jay land on a Japanese maple across from our bench. Tilting his head, he trilled for a moment, then lifted his wings and flew away. "I wondered if you'd had an opportunity to talk to Mr. Arlen before he became ill?"

"No," she replied unhappily, "and I can't tell you how desperately I wish I had. But my husband and I had a meeting with our architect that afternoon. When I heard Lucius was ill the next morning, I considered going to his rooms. Unfortunately, my mother suffered her arthritis attack and I was obliged to bring her home from the hospital instead. If I'd known I would never have another chance—"

"You mustn't blame yourself, Mrs. Barlow," I said,

trying, despite my disappointment, to sound sympathetic. "You couldn't have known what was going to happen."

"But what if the matter he wished to discuss with me had something to do with his death? The police questioned us yesterday. They seemed to think Lucius was poisoned."

"You know they've arrested Chin Lee Fong?"

"Yes, we heard. I can't believe Mr. Chin could do such a terrible thing. I realize he can be bad-tempered, but he's not violent—not a murderer. The police must be mistaken."

"If not Chin, then who do you think killed Mr. Arlen and Dora?" I asked, watching her closely.

Again, she shook her head. "I have no idea." Tears glistened in her eyes. "I hired Chin, Miss Woolson. He's a wonderful cook and came with outstanding references. I thought—I truly thought well-prepared, nourishing food would be good for our patients." She could no longer hold back the tears and, reaching for a handkerchief, buried her face in the lacy white linen.

Awkwardly, I placed a hand on her arm. "Please, Mrs. Barlow, you can't assume responsibility for this. I didn't mean to distress you."

"It's not your fault," she sniffed. "I've tried not to let Mama see how upset I've been. And Tobias is not, well, the most sympathetic of men."

Ah, yes, I thought, another understanding husband. Aloud, I said, "You have enough on your mind with the hospital, without worrying about Mr. Arlen and Dora Clemens."

"You're right, Miss Woolson. I must not let the board down, or the women and children who are depending on us for shelter and care." She passed the handkerchief over her face a final time, then stood and straightened her gown. "Let's return to the house now, shall we? Mama and your sister-in-law will wonder what has happened to us."

We entered the French doors into the drawing room to find Judge Barlow and Reverend Prescott chatting comfortably with Mrs. French and Celia. As usual, Adelina's attention was focused on Prescott, and her cheeks had taken on a becoming flush that hadn't been there before. I had to give the minister credit; Prescott's appeal evidently knew no bounds if he could charm a woman old enough to be his mother. Reconsidering this, I realized that Adelina was probably no more than seven or eight years his senior. The minister was one of those fortunate men whose energy and good looks make them appear considerably younger than their years.

Prescott had risen to his feet as we came in, but the judge, who was holding McKenzie in his lap, merely rose a few inches and nodded his head politely.

"I trust you enjoyed your tour of the garden, Miss Woolson?" Judge Barlow said.

"I certainly did. You're an accomplished gardener, Mrs. French. I'm most impressed."

Mrs. French smiled warmly. "That is kind of you to

say, Miss Woolson. This summer I will send you vegetables for your table. We always have more than we
can eat."

"Thank you, Mrs. French," Celia told her, with
delight. "That will be a rare treat."

We chatted for several more minutes, then Celia and
I stood to take our leave. Mr. Barlow, the little terrier
still in his arms, rose, and he and his wife escorted us
to the door. Prescott started to follow but stopped when
Adelina took hold of his arm.

"Do stay and keep me company, Nicholas. Being
confined to the house is so tiresome. I long to hear all
the news."

Reverend Prescott nodded agreeably and, after
politely paying his respects to Celia and me, returned
to his chair beside Mrs. French.

When the rest of us reached the hall, I asked the
judge if he'd heard any news concerning Chin.

A frown crossed his face. "I've heard nothing, Miss
Woolson. As far as I'm concerned, they can string the
little devil up by his thumbs for what he's done. Horrible crime, just horrible! I sincerely hope he'll be pun-
ished to the full extent of the law."

His wife blanched but said nothing. Apparently, the
judge's view of the crime brooked no argument.

Thanking our hosts, we stepped outside to find it had
started to rain. As I looked up and down the street for
a carriage, I was pleasantly surprised when a hansom
cab reined up directly in front of the Barlows' house.

"Bad weather," the driver said from his elevated seat

in the rear of the vehicle. The man was dressed entirely in black, with a dark cap pulled low over his eyes so that it was impossible to see his face. "You need ride?"

Something about the way he spoke caused me to hesitate, but Celia was not as reluctant. Taking hold of my arm, she said, "Sarah, please, we're getting drenched."

The wind had picked up and indeed, Celia and I were already soaking wet. "All right," I said and, giving the driver our address, stepped gratefully into the two-passenger interior. Sitting closely together, we arranged the wool blanket we found on the seat to cover our damp skirts.

Considering the weather, we reached Rincon Hill in good time. The driver assisted Celia from the carriage, but when I started to follow, he said, "Please, missy, friend want see you."

I jerked my head up to catch my first real glimpse of the driver's face. He was Chinese!

"Mr. Li say it important," the man went on, an urgency to his voice. "Need see you right away."

Hearing that name, I paused only a moment before informing Celia there was one more errand I wished to take care of. Assuring her I would be home in time for dinner, I instructed the driver to depart before she could question my abrupt change of mind.

Looking back, I could still see her surprised face in the rain, as the driver clicked his horse down the hill toward Chinatown.

CHAPTER NINE

W hen we arrived at Sacramento Street—known to its residents as Tong Yan Gai, or Chinese Street—the driver stopped the hansom. Climbing down from his seat, he bowed politely and handed me a colorful silk scarf, indicating I should wrap it over my eyes. As I did so, I couldn't help but compare this visit with my first venture into Chinatown several months earlier. On that occasion, the two men who rudely abducted me did not bother to ask my permission before covering my eyes, stuffing a rag into my mouth, and half carrying me to meet the mysterious—and by all accounts extremely dangerous—tong lord, Li Ying.

After the scarf was in place, the driver returned to his perch at the rear of the hansom and clicked his horse forward. We traveled for some time in this manner. Aware that Chinatown was hardly more than ten square blocks, I suspect he took a circuitous route in order to disorient me further. Since there was no one in the carriage to ensure I didn't peek out from beneath the scarf, I found this a somewhat amusing precaution.

When we stopped again, the driver helped me out of the carriage and into a building. Moments later, the scarf was removed and I found myself in the same amazing room I'd originally visited during the Nob Hill affair. That first time I'd been understandably frightened. Now, the familiar Chinese objets d'art and exquisite European and American paintings and sculptures seemed to greet me as old friends. Once again this anomalous yet harmonious blend of East and West made me feel oddly at peace.

"Welcome to my home," a cultured voice said in perfect English.

I smiled to see my host, Li Ying, ensconced on his kuan moa chair, set on a raised dais. He wore a rich, dark green satin robe, exquisitely embroidered with a dragon and some Chinese characters I couldn't decipher. As always, his black hair, which showed little gray, was meticulously shaved and oiled into a neat queue reaching to his waist. He returned my smile, his smooth, unlined face regarding me with a comfortable respect that belied the fact that we'd only met on two previous occasions. Indeed, our unusual relationship still mystified me. I don't consider myself anyone's fool; I had every reason to fear and distrust the infamous tong lord. Yet from our first meeting, I'd been irresistibly drawn to the man.

"It is good of you to grace me with your presence on such short notice, Miss Woolson," he went on in that assured voice I remembered so well. "Again I apologize for requiring you to wear a blindfold. I assure you it is as much for your protection as it is for mine. If I did not follow this practice with all my guests, I fear some of my more unscrupulous enemies would not hesitate to employ, shall we say, horrifying methods to ascertain my whereabouts."

190

I blinked, trying to banish the unsettling pictures that flashed into my mind at these words. "I understand, Mr. Li. Your man was very polite and, I might add, trusting."

His smile deepened. "You have shown yourself worthy of trust, Miss Woolson." He pulled a golden cord hanging behind the dais, and an elderly manservant, wearing traditional black pants and tunic, appeared bearing a tray. Upon the tray rested the most beautiful tea service I had ever seen. The ebony teapot and tiny cups bore a hand-painted floral design at once vibrantly colorful and elegantly delicate and graceful.

"I see that you appreciate my humble tea service," he said, noticing my admiring glances.

"It's exquisite," I exclaimed, holding one of the dainty cups up to the light. The tiny flowers and interweaving vines were perfectly rendered down to the smallest detail, as if by a master artist. "I don't think I've ever seen anything so lovely."

"It was my father's, Miss Woolson, and his father's before him. It is one of the few possessions I managed to bring with me from China." He smiled. "You will allow me to pour?"

"Yes, Mr. Li, if you please."

As usual, we discussed inconsequential matters while we ate. It was only when the servant collected the tray that Li regarded me with serious contemplation.

"I requested this visit to ask your help in a matter of some importance," he said at last.

My curiosity was piqued. I was eager, albeit a bit fearful, to hear what he had in mind. "If I can be of service, Mr. Li, naturally I'll be happy to oblige."

To my surprise, he laughed. "Do not look so apprehensive, Miss Woolson. I would never ask you to do anything which went against your laws. Actually, I would like to engage your services as an attorney."

"An attorney?"

He regarded me with his customary calm. "Yes—to defend Chin Lee Fong, who, as you know, has been arrested for the murders of Mr. Lucius Arlen and Miss Dora Clemens."

My mouth fell open in astonishment. "Mr. Li, surely you realize I only recently became a practicing attorney. Moreover, I've had no experience whatsoever in criminal law."

Li inclined his head, his serene expression unwavering. "I am fully aware of your qualifications, as well as your limitations, Miss Woolson." A slight smile formed on those finely chiseled lips, and he tilted his head very slightly to the right. "I have also heard of your successful meeting with Mr. Henry Finney. Pierce Godfrey must be pleased. The new contract should save him a great deal of money."

I looked at him in astonishment. "How did you hear of that? Mr. Godfrey has gone to some effort to keep the negotiations secret."

Li's smile broadened. "You should know by now that I receive my information from many sources. Perhaps you were not aware, but I have my own shipping interests to protect. Thanks to your counsel, I expect to increase my fleet by purchasing a number of surplus down-easters. At a considerable savings, of course."

It was my turn to smile. "I'm pleased to have been of service, even if inadvertently. Your ability to amass such confidential information continues to astound me."

"Information is power, and power translates into survival, both in Chinatown and in the environs beyond Dupont Gai." His penetrating black eyes narrowed as he regarded me with frank appraisal. "You are a survivor, Miss Woolson, and like myself, you take pains to arm yourself with information. That is one of the reasons you will make a fine attorney for Chin Lee Fong."

"But a murder trial, Mr. Li. Surely you can find a more experienced lawyer to defend Mr. Chin."

"Perhaps. But even if I could convince a white attorney to take this case, his prejudice and distrust of the Chinese would work against Chin. You possess an innate sense of justice for the less fortunate, Miss Woolson. There is no doubt in my mind that you will work as tirelessly to defend Chin as you would any Caucasian."

That might be true, but a dozen reasons why I should not agree to represent the cook flashed through my mind, not the least of which were the difficulties I would face as a female attorney in an all-male courtroom.

"Personally, I don't believe Mr. Chin is guilty of either murder. But the evidence against him will be difficult to refute."

"It seems I have more faith in you than you have in yourself," Li said, unperturbed by this argument. "You are Chin's best hope—perhaps his *only* hope—of going free."

"What does he say about having a woman for an attorney?" I asked, realizing Li had not mentioned the cook's preferences in the matter.

He made a dismissive gesture with his well-manicured hand, as if the question were of no consequence. "Mr. Chin knows nothing of the American legal system. He is grateful to have such competent representation."

And that his legal expenses are to be taken care of, I thought, but did not say aloud. Sighing, I considered the wisdom of accepting a case that I had little likelihood of winning. I had to admit his argument that I might be Chin's only hope was compelling. And I couldn't deny a prickle of excitement at the opportunity to prove that women attorneys were as qualified as their male counterparts to defend a capital murder case.

"All right," I agreed. "I'll represent Mr. Chin."

Li nodded his elegant head as if he'd expected nothing less. "Excellent. I am delighted by your decision."

Unfortunately, when I visited Chin the next morning at city jail, I was disconcerted to find that the cook in no way shared Li's enthusiasm for my representation.

"Never," he ranted, when I presented myself for our first attorney-client conference. "I no want woman lawyer."

"Am I to understand that you refuse my services?"

"Yes, yes, you leave. No come back. I get *real* lawyer. Man who get me out of here."

"As you wish, Mr. Chin." Silently, I stuffed my papers back inside my briefcase. "I think you had best speak to Mr. Li about this, since he is paying for your defense."

The cook gave a little gasp at the sound of the tong leader's name, and his face blanched, but he didn't break his stony silence as I departed his cell.

Well, I had done my best, I thought, joining a queue outside waiting for an approaching horsecar. Surely even Li Ying couldn't expect me to force a client to accept my services.

Pierce Godfrey took me to the elegant Maison Doree for dinner. I'd never dined there, and I was pleased to find the cuisine more than lived up to its reputation. Despite the ambience and excellent food, I found it difficult to relax. Gazing at the handsome man seated across the table from me, I found it impossible to imagine him an embezzler, much less a murderer. Yet the main reason I had accepted his invitation was to learn if he was both those things.

Pierce spent the first part of the meal thanking me again for my help in renegotiating the Finney contract, then went on to discuss several upcoming projects he had in mind. As I listened, I dreaded the moment when I'd have to shatter this easy camaraderie by asking him some hard, and personal, questions.

To my surprise, Pierce himself opened the door to that particular avenue of conversation. When the dishes were cleared and the fruit and cheese had been served, he leaned back in his chair and said, "I hear there's been some excitement at the hospital."

"I'm afraid so. There have been two suspicious deaths in the past few days." I measured my words carefully. "Since Mrs. Godfrey's passing, do you still have any contact with the new hospital?"

"Sadly, no," he answered smoothly. "Leonard told me the news. Is it true they suspect Arlen and that maid were poisoned?"

"Yes, they do. Of course, the postmortem results aren't in yet."

He looked genuinely bewildered. "But who would want to kill an accountant and a kitchen maid? It doesn't make sense."

I studied his face over the candles, searching for any nuance that might give lie to this reasonable statement. I could detect none.

"Speaking of your brother, how is he getting along since his tragic loss?"

Pierce seemed to find nothing strange in this none-too-subtle change of subject. "He's doing better, thank you. He misses Caroline, of course, but that's to be expected."

If I was ever going to ask my question, I told myself, the time was now. "I understand you and Mrs. Godfrey were seeing each other—in a way that was rather more than brother-in-law and sister-in-law."

Pierce's fork stopped halfway between the plate and his mouth. "What did you say?"

Clearing my throat, I repeated my question, then took a quick sip of wine to cover my discomfiture.

He returned the piece of cheese, untouched, to his plate. "I knew you were outspoken, Sarah, but this goes too far."

"You haven't answered my question. Please trust me when I say I'm not asking this out of idle curiosity."

"Then what possible reason could you have?" Pierce's voice rose sharply. A couple at a nearby table gave us surprised stares, annoyed, I'm sure, by this intrusion into their quiet dinner. Lowering his voice, he went on, "I can only think that you—" Abruptly, he stopped, and through the candlelight I saw his eyes widen in sudden comprehension. "Oh, I see. You think I had something to do with Caroline's death. My, my, what a sinister imagination you have, Miss Woolson."

"If I'm mistaken about your sister-in-law, then please say so. If I'm not, then I'd appreciate an honest answer. When it comes to murder, I feel I—"

"—have the right to ask anything you damn well please." He stared at me for several moments, then took a sip of his wine. "All right, not that it's any of your business, but I admit Caroline and I saw each other—in the way you not-so-delicately implied. It sounds sordid now, but at the time I think we imagined we were in love—at least, Caroline fancied she was. For my part, well, my sister-in-law was a very attractive woman."

"She was married to your brother!" I said, unable to keep the indignation out of my voice.

"Leonard and I have always competed against one another." He flashed that maddening smile of his. "The fact that Caroline was his wife, well—"

I could hardly believe what he was saying. "Heaven help us! It was just another rivalry to you, wasn't it?" This time I didn't bother to mask my disgust. "Because she belonged to your brother merely sweetened the conquest."

He shrugged. "Men have dallied with women for less reason than that, Sarah. I'm sorry if it shocks you."

"A few minutes ago I would have said nothing could shock me anymore. Now—" I took myself in hand; nothing would be gained by succumbing to prudery, no matter how justified. "Your affair with a married woman is not the point."

"Ah, yes, back to murder. Whatever reasons you imagine I had for wishing my sister-in-law dead, you're wrong. We had a falling out about a year ago. Caroline expected more of our—friendship than I was able or willing to give. Or perhaps I'd begun to experience the revulsion I see on your face right now. Sadly, the relationship had moved beyond the amusing flirtation we initially enjoyed."

"Was your brother aware of the affair?"

He hesitated. "Not at first. Toward the end, I'm not sure. If he had suspicions, he kept them to himself."

"And now?"

Pierce's eyes met mine with a directness that was disconcerting. "I informed my brother myself, sometime after Caroline's death. I assured him that the affair had been over for some months, and naturally I accepted full responsibility for what had transpired between us."

"How did Mr. Godfrey take this—confession?"

His smile was derisive. "How do you think he took it? He was understandably upset, actually quite upset. But not particularly shocked. I rather think Leonard had some inkling of what had gone on between his wife and me, even if he chose not to speak of it."

"Which is why you finally told him yourself, isn't it?"

His eyes narrowed, and I caught a quick look of surprise. "What makes you say that?"

"There was nothing to be gained, and certainly a good deal to lose, by admitting the truth unless you were fairly certain he already knew. By making a clean breast of it, you usurped his anger and invited forgiveness. The prodigal brother makes his amends."

His lips curved into the barest hint of a mocking smile. He wouldn't admit it, of course, but I knew I had guessed the truth.

"Do I detect a hint of sarcasm, Miss Woolson?"

I sighed. Frankly, I was disappointed. Not only because of Pierce's cavalier behavior, but because he'd been less than honest with me—yet again. Moreover, despite several deliberate openings, he'd failed to disclose his joint ownership of the warehouse. What else was he holding back? I wondered.

"I'm just weary," I replied, more than ready to bring the evening to an end. "Perhaps you'd be good enough to take me home. I have an early morning."

Pierce studied my face for a long moment, then signaled the waiter and paid the check. Neither of us spoke as we entered his carriage and departed in awkward silence for Rincon Hill.

A note awaited me at home, written in a precise, slightly spiky handwriting I recognized.

Miss Woolson,
  Mr. Chin offers sincere apologies for his discourteous behavior this morning. He humbly asks that you meet with him again at your earliest convenience.

The note was unsigned, but I had no doubt who it came from. Also in the envelope was a large amount of "one color," the term the Chinese used to differentiate American dollars from their own, more colorful yuan. Counting it, I found I had been paid a retainer of five hundred dollars! Li Ying seemed determined to purchase the finest defense possible for Chin Lee Fong. A shiver ran down my spine, as I sincerely prayed I was worthy of such faith.

• • •

My second meeting with Chin took place the following day. While the cook was slightly more forthcoming, it did little to reassure me about the probable success of his case. Patiently, I took him over the details of his acrimonious relationship with Lucius Arlen.

"He was fool," Chin pronounced, as if this were the only explanation required on the subject.

"Yes, but what did he actually do to you?" I persisted.

"Oh, he do plenty. Call me chink and yellow monkey, cut pay, call me thief. He no care how patients eat."

"So you and he argued about this."

"Hah! We fight all time." Chin made this sound like something to be proud of. "He say Chinese stupid. But I get him back."

My blood turned cold. "What do you mean, you got him back?"

"I tell him to stay out of my kitchen or I fix him good."

Oh, wonderful, I thought, closing my eyes while I let this latest admission sink in. "And did Mr. Arlen stay out of your kitchen?"

"Nah, he do as he please." He grinned, and I realized with a start that this was the first time I'd seen the disagreeable man smile. "But I chase him with skillet. He run so fast!" Chin dissolved into a fit of laughter, delighting in the memory. "Not bother me again for long time."

Good Lord, I prayed. Has this man no idea how damaging this sounds? Doesn't he realize how much trouble he's in?

The remainder of the interview went much the same. When I tried to point out the danger of repeating how much he hated Arlen, Chin didn't seem to comprehend. He hadn't killed the accountant, and that should be good enough for anyone. To his mind, the fact that he'd repeatedly threatened Arlen had no bearing on his current situation.

Before I left, I made Chin promise not to discuss the case with anyone, including his jailers or any fellow prisoners. His reluctant agreement was hardly reassuring.

"No one talk to but jailers," he protested. "Why can't I tell them about son-of-bitch Arlen?"

When I'd exhausted every conceivable argument, I left the stubborn cook to stew in his own juices—pun intended.

Difficult as Chin was proving to be, he wasn't the only challenge facing me as I prepared for trial. Rumors of my new client had spread like wildfire, speedily reaching Joseph Shepard and the firm's other senior attorneys. I knew the time of reckoning had arrived when a delighted Hubert Perkins cheerfully summoned me to Shepard's office.

"What's this I hear about you accepting some tom-fool case?" my employer demanded the instant I entered the room.

"As a matter of fact, I've agreed to represent a Mr. Chin Lee Fong, who's been accused of—"

"But he's Chinese!" Joseph Shepard looked at me as if I'd taken on the devil himself as a client. "You must be out of your mind to agree to defend a—a John Chinaman!"

"The fact that he's Chinese," I said, "does not preclude his right to an appropriate legal defense."

"Yes, but—" Seemingly unable to come up with another line of attack, he fell back upon that awful noise in the back of his nasal region.

Refusing to be drawn any further into this argument—which seemed to be going nowhere in any event—I silently reached into my briefcase and pulled out the portion of Li's money that rightfully belonged to the firm. Shepard's fit ended as quickly as it had begun, and his small eyes bulged as I handed him the stack of bills.

"That is the initial retainer," I explained, careful not to mention Li's name. "I think you'll find subsequent payments from my client will be more than generous."

"But he's a cook. How can he possibly afford . . . ?"

"Evidently, he has a secondary source of income." Which was true enough, I thought, if Li were viewed in that light. "Trust me, Mr. Shepard, the firm will not suffer financially by my representation of Mr. Chin."

I could see by his aggrieved expression that he was only partially appeased by the money. While the firm was always eager to bring in lucrative new accounts, the newspapers had already gotten wind of the Chin

Lee Fong case and were blazing it across their front pages. Which left Shepard in a bind. If he fired me for accepting such an undesirable client, he would not only deprive the firm of a beneficial account, but my dismissal would merit banner headlines. Once again, I'd placed him in an indefensible position.

"Very well, Miss Woolson," he said in clipped tones, "you seemed to have left me with no choice. But, as you are completely lacking in criminal law experience, I will assign someone with more practical knowledge as lead attorney. At his discretion, he may see fit to request your assistance. Under no circumstances, however, are you to appear in a court of law as an associate of this firm."

Seeming to feel he had at least partially redeemed an impossible situation, he waved a dismissive hand and went back to the paperwork crowding his desk. Knowing Li would never agree to this arrangement, I stood my ground.

"I'm sorry, Mr. Shepard, but what you suggest is out of the question."

He looked up at me with a frown, as if only half comprehending my words. "What are you babbling on about?"

"My client will not accept another attorney. We discussed my inexperience, and he was adamant he would accept no one but me as his legal representative."

"That's ridiculous! What man in his right mind would chose a woman to represent him in a murder case? Believe me, your client will be more than grateful when he discovers that Clark, or even Jefferson, will be representing him."

I stared at him in disbelief. Clark and Jefferson had been with the firm barely a year longer than I had. Neither man had acted as lead attorney in a civil case, much less one for capital murder. In fact, I wasn't sure they'd even been part of a defense team. Joseph Shepard cared not one whit whether Chin escaped the hangman's noose, only that a woman attorney not embarrass his firm in public.

"That will not do, Mr. Shepard." I steeled myself to be fired on the spot. It was bound to come sooner or later, I thought. At least this would be a cause worthy of dismissal, not some trifling typewriting or filing error.

Shepard's fleshy face turned an ugly red. "You go too far, Miss Woolson. How dare you attempt to tell me who I may or may not assign to a case?"

"It is not I who tells you, sir, but my client. He refuses to accept anyone else. If you replace me as lead attorney, I will be forced to defend Mr. Chin on my own."

His watery eyes blazed into mine. "You wouldn't dare!"

"Actually, Mr. Shepard, I would. I am morally bound to carry out my client's wishes in this matter. It is, after all, his life that is at stake."

I don't know what kind of a response I expected, but it seemed I'd driven Joseph Shepard beyond his limits.

"Get out of my office," he yelled. "Now!"

For once our wishes coincided, and I made my way out of the room as speedily as decorum, and my pride, would allow. Once I'd closed the door behind me, I stood in the hall trying to steady my thudding heart. It seemed I was still an associate at Shepard, Shepard, McNaughton and Hall, or at least I thought I was. One could never be certain with the senior partner. He was as mercurial, and often as dense, as the fog that billowed in from San Francisco Bay.

Returning to my office, I was surprised to find Robert waiting for me. "What was that all about? I could hear you two shouting at each other from the hallway. I suppose it had to do with the Chin case."

I'd made the mistake of telling Robert about my visit with Li, as well as my commitment to defend Chin.

"I'm in no mood to hear more of your gloomy ranting about my career," I said, sinking into the chair behind my desk. "I've agreed to be Chin's lawyer and that's that."

He stared at me, astonished. "Are you telling me that Shepard went along with it?"

"I didn't leave him with much choice." I ran a hand over my forehead, surprised to find it damp with perspiration. "All this wasted energy, and I haven't even begun to develop a defense strategy."

"How can you come up with a viable defense when we both know your client is guilty?"

"Not that again, Robert," I moaned. "Please."

His face contorted into a mask of incredulity. "You are beyond belief—or comprehension. Sarah, the prosecution is going to crucify you. You say you want to see women attorneys in the courtroom. Think of what a defeat like this will do for your precious cause.

"The evidence against Chin is overwhelming," he went on when I didn't respond. "The public is already clamoring for his head on a platter." His voice was heavy with sarcasm. "A woman attorney and a Chinaman. Now there's a partnership for you!"

I opened my mouth to retort, then closed it again. Li Ying once told me it was necessary to accept reality. Well, the reality was that the evidence against my client seemed all but insurmountable. And most of San Francisco, for all its pretense of valuing diversity, regarded its Chinese population as subhuman—slightly above animals, but not by much. What Robert said was true. I was risking everything I'd worked so long and hard for to defend an unpleasant, not to mention ungrateful, man, who seemed to be as eager as the police to stick his head in a noose.

"Robert, I honestly don't think Chin is guilty of killing Arlen or Dora Clemens, although I'll grant you, his innocence is going to be next to impossible to prove. But don't you see? I have to at least try. That's the promise I made when I became an attorney."

"Oh, please, spare me those damn ethics of yours!"

"It's more than ethics. Someone has murdered four people—yes, I'm including Caroline Godfrey and Josiah Halsey, whether you agree or not—and I'm convinced that person is *not* Chin Lee Fong. No one's working very hard to find Halsey's killer, and Caroline's death was ruled a heart attack. Yet I'm certain they were poisoned by the same individual who killed Arlen and Clemens. If I stand by and do nothing while Chin is convicted of two crimes he didn't commit, the real murderer—the person who has callously taken four lives—will go free. I would never forgive myself if I protected the future of women attorneys by allowing an innocent man to hang."

"All right, Sarah, I know you mean well. Drat it all, you always mean well. But altruism is not a feasible defense in a court of law. You need cold, hard evidence to prove your client's innocence."

"I know," I said, rubbing the ridge between my eyes. "I just can't shake the feeling that I'm missing something, something I saw or heard that's important to the case. I can sense it, but I just can't put my finger on it."

"Maybe because it's not there, Sarah. Have you ever thought of that?" He looked as weary and frustrated as I felt. "You're going to let this damn case destroy your professional future. It's just too painful to watch."

I was struck by a sudden idea. "Then don't just watch, Robert: help me structure Chin's defense. You told me once that you wanted to be a trial attorney. Well, here's your chance. Join me as second chair. Or, if you'd prefer, help from behind the scenes. There's going to be more than enough work for two people."

Robert stared at me as if I'd just suggested he declare his candidacy for president.

"At least think about it," I went on. "If nothing else, it will be a wonderful learning experience."

The look on his face was so comical that for the first time that day I gave in to the impulse to laugh.

Chin Lee Fong's arraignment contained few surprises. He was officially charged with the murder of Lucius Arlen, was denied bail and had his trial set for the second week of May. Although Chin still stood accused of killing Dora Clemens, the state chose to pursue Arlen's death first, undoubtedly because they felt it was the easier of the two cases to prove.

It all boiled down to means and opportunity. The autopsies showed both the accountant and the kitchen maid had been poisoned with *Actaea alba,* or baneberry, which, I discovered from my research, resembled blueberries. Since a small bag of the deadly berries, as well as their equally lethal roots, was discovered at the rear of one of Chin's cupboards, the question of "means" was quickly resolved.

That Chin also had opportunity to administer the poison was, for all practical purposes, a nonfactor. As cook for the hospital, he had unlimited access to the kitchen and to its supplies. What could be easier, the police reasoned, than for him to slip ground baneberry root or berry into an unsuspecting victim's coffee? The prosecutor must have been delighted to find himself with such an easy case. Chin not only had the means and opportunity, he continued to declare his hatred of Arlen loud enough for the entire city to hear!

I set myself a daunting schedule. Since I lacked any of the hard evidence Robert mentioned, the only way I could see to clear Chin was to find the real killer. In order to do that, I'd need to account for Dora Clemens's whereabouts the morning of her death. Normally at work by seven o'clock, she hadn't arrived at the hospital that day until eleven. Had she really been ill, as she claimed? Or had she gone somewhere else first? To see the murderer, perhaps? To ask for blackmail money?

Then there were the Godfrey brothers, either of whom might have individually, or jointly, murdered Caroline and—on far shakier grounds—the other three victims. I'd asked Samuel to look into their finances, but so far I'd heard nothing back from him.

Lastly, I wanted to go over Arlen's account books in an effort to discover why he'd been so eager to speak to Margaret the day we'd toured the hospital. I remained convinced that whatever had him so upset that day was pivotal in identifying his murderer.

Chin's case, however overwhelming, was not my only concern. I had not forgotten my promise to Lily Mankin. Despite my best efforts, I'd been unable to locate the owner of the sweatshop where Jack Mankin died. The trail always led back to the missing Bert Corrigan and Killy Doyle, one of whom must know the identity of the mysterious landlord.

In the end, it was a chance comment Samuel made about McKenzie Properties, the listed owners of the sweatshop, that gave me the idea. To confirm my suspicions, I required the services of Eddie Cooper.

As agreed, I wrote my initials on a piece of paper,

drew a circle around them, and sent it in care of Laine Carriages. To my delight, Eddie reined up in front of my home less than an hour later, eager as ever to be "hot on the trail."

I decided to start my investigation with Lucius Arlen's account books, but before I went to the hospital, I had Eddie stop at the so-called offices of McKenzie Properties on Sansone Street. The second-hand shop was much as I remembered from my first visit: run-down, grimy, and in dire need of paint. The sign above the store was so faded it was hard to make out the words: JAKE'S USED GOODS.

I told Eddie my suspicion that this was where Corrigan and Doyle were hiding. The lad's eyes grew large as I outlined his role in my plan. Eddie would take me to the hospital, then drive back here and keep an eye on the shop in case either man turned up.

"You can count on me, miss," he said with so much enthusiasm you'd have thought I'd asked him to guard the gold at the local assayer's office.

"I have no idea how long I'll be at the hospital. So, I'll take a cab and meet you here when I'm finished."

Fifteen minutes later, he dropped me off at the refurbished warehouse, then drove off with a jaunty tip of his cap and a conspiratorial wink toward Sansone Street.

Entering the hospital, I found Margaret in the kitchen familiarizing Lily Mankin—who had graciously agreed to take over as cook during Chin's incarceration—with Chin's methods of running his domain. As

I came into the room, the two women had their heads bent over the new Sterling Range.

"This stove is a wonder," Lily exclaimed upon seeing me.

"Mrs. Mankin is going to cook her first dinner for us tonight," Margaret said, smiling at the widow. "I'm sure it will be a big success."

Lily's return smile was tinged with trepidation. "I've never tried cookin' for so many people before, Mrs. Barlow. But I'll do my best."

Assuring Lily she would return to the kitchen in time to offer assistance, Mrs. Barlow led me to her office. Several account books lay in a neat pile on her desk.

"I've been meaning to go over these ledgers," she told me. "I just haven't been able to find the time."

I picked up the first account book and thumbed through it. "Tell me, Mrs. Barlow, who authorizes hospital expenses?"

"I do, for one, and my husband, of course. In fact, there are several men on the hospital's finance committee who are approved to authorize an expenditure. I'm afraid that sounds like rather a loose arrangement, but it was to facilitate the renovation and furnishing of the hospital. By giving more than one person authority to approve cash disbursements, there was always someone available to make these decisions. Actually, it's worked quite well."

"Was Mr. Arlen empowered to pay bills on his own?"

"Oh, no. All invoices and requests are sent to my office first, or to someone on the finance committee.

Once they're properly authorized, they are sent—or perhaps I should say they *were* sent—to Mr. Arlen, who paid the bills and entered them into the account books."

She consulted her lapel watch and stood. "I'm sorry to leave you, Miss Woolson, but I'm late for an important meeting. I wish you luck with these books."

I spent the next hour going over the neatly written entries, carefully tallying each sum in my notepad. It wasn't until the third ledger that I began to sense something was wrong. Then I realized it wasn't anything I'd seen on the pages, but rather something I ought to have seen in the ledgers but didn't.

I thought back to the Godfrey dinner the night Caroline died. According to Arlen, the party brought in one hundred twenty thousand dollars, twenty percent over the target goal. Yet a number of these contributions weren't listed in the ledgers. Moreover, of the pledges that were written in, some weren't as I remembered.

For instance, I knew my parents donated five thousand dollars, but they were listed as having given only three thousand. Judge Barlow's entry was off by five thousand dollars, as were the Heblers' and the Roths'. Even my own modest contribution was recorded as less than I'd actually paid. I tried to remember other sums I'd heard called out and came up with yet more discrepancies. In fact, when I totaled the figures entered in the book for that night, they came to ninety thousand dollars, not the hundred twenty thousand Arlen claimed had been brought in. What had happened to the missing thirty thousand dollars?

With renewed determination, I went over the ledgers yet again, paying attention to the smallest details. Sure enough, I discovered more questionable entries, most of them having to do with the kitchen. There were orders for flour, sugar, salt and shortening, for instance, in amounts so large I didn't see how they could possibly be consumed. The cook had also ordered enough pots and pans to accommodate a good-sized restaurant, along with a large set of dishes and every size utensil imaginable.

Closing the books, I gathered up my notes and headed for the kitchen, pleased to find that it was now deserted. Quickly, I went through every cupboard, every inch of the pantry, every pot and pan, noting each item in my notepad. As I did, I realized they came nowhere near the numbers that supposedly had been ordered. How could Chin have hoped to get away with such an obvious deception?

Finally, I attempted to satisfy myself about something Dora had said as she lay dying. Supposedly, Arlen and the maid had been poisoned with baneberries, most likely administered in coffee to mask the taste. This coincided with at least part of Dora's statement. Yet she'd also mentioned "cookies." Had the killer also served Arlen poisoned cookies?

Once again I searched the pantry, but the coffee beans I found revealed nothing. Next, I reexamined the cupboards until I came upon a tin marked "cookies," which I'd passed over as unimportant my first time through. Prying off the lid, I was surprised to find not cookies inside, but wads of money, nearly fifty dollars. I reread my notes from Dora's death. Is this why she'd mentioned cookies? Was she trying to tell us that this tin was where Chin kept the money he stole from his kitchen allowance?

There was no time now to speculate, as I still had to question the nursing and housekeeping staff. Unfortunately, this line of inquiry went nowhere. Several nurses had seen Arlen enter the kitchen shortly before eight P.M., but not a single person could say whether Chin had been with him. In fact, no one had set eyes on the cook after dinner. Had Dora been the only one to see Chin that evening? My heart sank. If that were the case, I'd lost my only witness.

Before I gave up, I decided to explore the one area of the hospital I'd yet to visit: the basement. Descending the stairs, I found myself in a damp hall with doors leading off to either side. Making my way through the dim light, I found the first four rooms unoccupied. In the fifth room, I came upon a lone Chinese man washing linen.

"You not belong down here," he said, looking as startled to see me as I was to see him. "Go away. I busy."

Ignoring this admonition, I stepped into the room. Two washtubs sat on a wood table, while stacks of dirty sheets and other linen were piled on the floor. A clothes wringer perched on the edge of the table, and beneath it sat a pail to catch water. The rest of the room was taken up by cast-iron drying racks, some of them already covered with linen. "I'd like to ask you a few questions, if you don't mind."

Plainly, the man did mind. "I busy," he repeated, inserting a sheet into the wringer and cranking the handle.

"This won't take long, I promise. You must know that the cook, Mr. Chin Lee Fong, has been arrested for murder. Two murders, in fact. I'm acting as his attorney."

This rated a derisive look that plainly questioned Chin's sanity for hiring a woman attorney, but still he didn't speak. Frustrated, I tried a different tack.

"Mr. Li Ying has employed me to handle Mr. Chin's defense. I'd hate to have to inform him you refused to speak to me."

This so surprised the man that he barely caught his fingers before they followed the sheet through the wringer.

His dark eyes opened wide with fear. "No, no, missy, I talk. No problem."

"I'm happy to hear that, Mr. . . . ."

"Kin Tsau, missy."

I introduced myself and went on to ask if he'd seen Chin the night Arlen was poisoned. He seemed reluctant to confide in a stranger, a *fahn quai*—a white person—at that. Then, after a long pause he admitted, "I see him."

My heart leapt at these words. "What time was that?"

"After dinner. Seven o'clock maybe. He go out that night. Play cards, maybe dice. All time play. Sometimes bet on cockfights, or mahjong."

This was exciting news. If Chin left the hospital by seven o'clock—and Arlen hadn't been seen going into the kitchen until nearly eight—it would establish the cook's alibi.

"Where did Chin usually gamble, Mr. Kin?"

The laundryman mentioned several Chinatown gambling dens, none more than a seven- or eight-block walk from the hospital. I'd check them out, of course. Hopefully, someone would remember seeing Chin that night.

I had a disheartening thought. Even if I did find witnesses who'd seen him, how much weight would their testimony carry in court? It was unfair, but among the city's white population, the word of a Chinese was notoriously suspect, even when it was given under oath.

Pushing aside these misgivings, I asked, "Did you see Mr. Chin leave the hospital that evening?"

"We have cigarette in back alley before he go. He want me come with him, but I say next time maybe."

"Would you be willing to testify to that in court?"

Kin's face blanched. "No, missy. No court." Then, when I again mentioned Li Ying, he reluctantly agreed to appear for the defense.

"Chin not kill anybody," were Kin's parting words. "You make court believe he innocent."

CHAPTER TEN

I took a horsecar to the address I'd been given for Dora Clemens's boardinghouse. Regrettably, all Dora's landlady would say was that her tenant— who shared an attic room with another girl who was also "in service"—left the house around eight o'clock the morning of her death, which seemed strange since the girl was usually gone by six.

"Don't know no more about it than that," she said grumpily. "Except now I gotta find me a new tenant, and that ain't easy these days."

She was about to close the door in my face when a girl of about eighteen came up the stairs.

"This here's Chloe Goodhall," the landlady said ungraciously. "The girl what roomed with Dora. You can ask her yer questions."

A plump girl with fair hair and a pasty complexion, Chloe looked weary from her day's labors but kindly invited me upstairs.

"I still can't believe what happened to Dora, miss," she said when we reached the narrow attic room she'd shared with the kitchen maid. "And just when things was beginnin' to look so good fer her and all."

"In what way were they looking good, Chloe?" I asked, taking a seat on one of two single beds set to either side of a sloping ceiling.

"Dora never came right out and said. But she

seemed real excited that mornin'. You know, the morning she . . ."

"I understand, Chloe," I said gently. "Exactly what did she tell you?"

"Said she was goin' to work late 'cause she had to see someone first. Someone who was gonna give her a lot of money."

I stared at the girl. So, Samuel and I were right in our suspicions! Dora must have seen the person who poisoned the accountant. Who else could she have demanded money from that morning? Had she been foolish enough to threaten blackmail, I wondered, or had the killer offered it to her in exchange for her silence? Silence that needed to last no longer than it took for the poison to take effect.

"Chloe, did Dora mention who this person was?"

"No, miss, just gave me a little wink, like she couldn't say no more. She looked so happy." Tears filled the girl's eyes. "Don't seem fair, does it?"

"No, Chloe. Sometimes life doesn't seem the least bit fair."

I returned to Sansone Street to find Eddie still watching the secondhand shop. Few people had entered the store, he reported unhappily, and no one resembling Bert or Killy had come out. I told him it was probably expecting too much to hope the fugitives would show themselves so soon, and I asked the lad to drive me to the city jail.

"I don't expect to be long," I told him as I went

inside the damp, dreary building I had grown to hate. A jailer escorted me to Chin's cells, where I found the cook to be his usual disagreeable self.

"I no put in for those," he said dismissively when I read him the list of kitchen requisitions made in his name. "What I do with all those pots and pans? Have plenty."

"Could someone else have ordered them for you?"

He scoffed at this suggestion. "Who do that? No one stupid enough to order me stuff like that."

Abruptly, I changed the subject, trying to catch him off guard. "What about the cookie tin you kept in a kitchen cupboard?"

Chin's face reddened. "What cookie tin? Why you ask stupid question? I no have cookie tin."

"I think you do, Mr. Chin. I believe that's where you kept the money you held back from your weekly kitchen allowance. The money you used for gambling."

He started to deny the accusation, then shrugged. "So what? Only few dollar. No big deal."

"It wasn't your money," I pointed out. "It was given to you to run the kitchen."

His only response to this was another shrug and a refusal to discuss the matter any further.

Why, I asked myself as I left the jail and once again climbed into Eddie's cab, did my first venture inside a courtroom have to be in defense of such a fractious client?

This time I had Eddie drive me to the law firm.

There, I paid the lad for his services, requesting him to keep an occasional watch on the secondhand shop and to drive past Killy's home on California Street whenever possible. There was always the chance the men might return to the house, if only to pick up something they'd forgotten.

"I'm the man fer the job, miss," Eddie said, and with a wide grin, he clicked his horse into afternoon traffic.

As I entered the clerk's anteroom, I noticed Robert gesturing to me from his glass cubicle. Not wanting to spend any more time than necessary under Hubert Perkins's rude scrutiny, I motioned the Scot to join me in my office.

"Where have you been?" he asked the moment the door was shut. "Shepard's been in an uproar all day, ranting and raving that you're going to singlehandedly destroy his firm. I can't decide if he's more upset that you're actually trying a case in court, that you're representing a Chinaman or that the story will make every newspaper in town."

"Let's face it, Robert: he'd find fault with anyone I chose to represent." Wearily, I sat behind my desk. "Actually, I've been working on the case all morning."

"Did you find out anything useful?"

"I don't know," I answered honestly. Keeping it brief, I described the discrepancies I'd found in Arlen's account books, as well as my conversation with Kin Tsau in the laundry room. I finished by recounting Dora's comment to her roommate, Chloe, the morning of her death, that someone was going to give her a great deal of money.

"I think she saw who poisoned Arlen and tried to profit by it. Poor, foolish girl. When she threatened blackmail, the killer used the same poison on her he'd used on Arlen."

"Hmm," he said, noncommittally. "Where do you find these baneberries, anyway?"

"According to the books I've consulted, they grow all over Oregon and California, especially in the forests along the coast."

"So, what you're saying is that anyone could obtain them." He shook his head. "That leaves a pretty open field."

"Yes and no. While it's true all three poisons—and I'm including the foxglove, or digitalis, used on Mrs. Godfrey, the jimsonweed that killed Halsey, as well as the baneberry given to Arlen and the maid—grow wild, the killer had to know what he was looking for in order to pick the right plant. Then, of course, he'd have to know how to use it."

"Sarah, Chin hasn't been accused of killing Mrs. Godfrey and Halsey," Robert said in a tone one might use on an obtuse child. "You have enough to do absolving your client of Arlen's and Dora Clemens's deaths without taking on issues that have nothing to do with his case."

"I know how you feel about this, Robert, but I'm more than ever convinced all four murders were committed by the same person. My only chance of freeing

Chin is to identify that person—which means I have to examine the crimes as a whole."

Robert rolled his eyes but thankfully didn't subject me to the same old wearisome arguments.

"All right, Sarah. But even supposing you're right, I just don't see how you're going to find a person who had not only the motive but also the means and opportunity to kill all four victims. It's impossible."

"I prefer to look upon it as a challenge," I replied, refusing to let him discourage me. "I'll start at the beginning, working through each murder until I find someone who benefited from all four deaths. Now, who had reason to kill Caroline Godfrey?"

"Assuming she was murdered," he said, then at my look, sighed heavily. "All right, all right, I'll play your little game, for all the good it's going to do you." He appeared to give my question serious thought. "The most likely candidate, of course, is Caroline's husband, especially if he found out about her affair with his brother. But why wouldn't he have taken his revenge on Pierce as well? I know I would have."

"I'm sure you would," I said dryly. "Taking it a step further, Leonard also had a motive for killing Halsey. If the so-called minister had succeeded in discrediting the new hospital, he and Pierce would have been left with an empty, unrented warehouse."

"That seems a pretty weak excuse for murdering someone, even a man as irritating as Halsey."

"On its own, yes. But don't forget the ships they lost over the past two years, along with valuable cargo.

Samuel said they were forced nearly out of business. How did they manage to survive their losses? Not only survive, but prosper!"

Robert looked at me incredulously. "Good Lord, woman, what are you suggesting? You think Leonard Godfrey used his wife's position as head of the board to pilfer money from the new hospital?"

"I agree it's hard to believe, but the fact remains that thirty thousand dollars is missing from the pledge dinner Caroline held the night of her death. Whoever took it must have had access to those funds. When Arlen discovered the money was missing, he had to be silenced. As did Dora when she attempted to blackmail Arlen's murderer."

Robert gave me a pointed look. "If you insist on placing Leonard Godfrey on your list of suspects, you're going to have to include his brother, you know. After all, you only have Pierce's word for how his relationship with Caroline ended. What if *she* was the one to break it off, not he? He doesn't strike me as a man who's accustomed to being rejected. Maybe he lost control and killed her."

When I didn't reply, he went on, "If it is Pierce, then Leonard's motives for killing Halsey, Arlen and Dora apply equally to him."

Much as I hated hearing this, I knew it was true. I had to remain objective, no matter how it affected me personally.

"You're right, Robert," I replied. "Both brothers must be considered." Afraid my face might reveal more than I wished, I kept it lowered as I continued down my list of possible suspects. "I suppose Margaret Barlow had a motive to kill Mrs. Godfrey, since she took over Caroline's leadership of the new hospital. It did increase her status in San Francisco society."

Robert added, "More important, it gave her unlimited access to hospital funds. The question is, did Margaret Barlow need the money?"

"That's a good question. I asked Samuel to look into everyone's finances. He learned that the Barlows lost money in the crash of 'seventy-nine."

"Half of San Francisco lost money in that debacle," said Robert, dismissing this as being of little importance.

"Yes, but not everybody spends as lavishly as the Barlows or is building an estate in Menlo Park. That sort of project must require an enormous outlay of cash. Because of Papa, I know approximately how much Judge Barlow makes sitting on the bench. It isn't enough to support their extravagant lifestyle."

"If what you say is true, then I grant you Mrs. Barlow had a motive. But what about opportunity? Didn't you say she and the judge met with their architect in Menlo Park late that afternoon? Did anyone check this out, by the way?"

"Yes, one of George Lewis's men did. According to him, the Barlows were with their architect until six o'clock that evening."

"Which rules them out. Menlo Park's a three-hour carriage drive from the city. There's no way they could have returned to the hospital by eight o'clock that evening."

"I know. But I'm still troubled by how they manage to live in such a grand style."

"Oh, for heaven's sake. I've never met a woman with such a suspicious mind." He raked broad fingers through his already disordered hair, making it stand on end. "Maybe they have an independent income of some kind. There's only so much Samuel can find out poring over old newspapers."

"You'd be surprised at the information he can dig up," I said, coming to my brother's defense.

Robert shifted in his chair, recrossing his long legs. "What about this Prescott fellow? What do you know about him?"

"Very little. But I don't see how he could be involved. He only arrived from back east a few weeks ago."

"Yes, but he was at the Godfrey house the night Caroline died."

"So were thirty other people, Robert. What possible reason could Prescott have for killing a woman he'd never met before?" I sighed. "Just to be on the safe side, though, I asked Samuel to check into his past. Prescott seems to have a fine reputation as a minister, dependable and popular with his congregations. The only thing that bothers me is that he's changed parishes a dozen times over the past twenty-five years, which seems rather a lot. But since Samuel couldn't find any suspicious reason for the frequent moves, we dropped the matter. Prescott is an unlikely suspect."

Robert gave me a sardonic smile, which never failed to raise my hackles. "What?" I demanded.

"Come on, Sarah, be honest. That's a pitiful list of suspects and you know it. Have you considered the possibility that you can't find a likely scapegoat because the real murderer is already in custody? For once, use your mind instead of your imagination and examine the facts."

He fiddled with his cravat, which was already askew, leaving it even more crooked. "Caroline Godfrey had an existing heart condition and it killed her. As for Halsey, maybe he ingested jimsonweed as part of some sort of a bizarre religious observance. Or one of his enemies finally decided they'd had enough of him. All I know is that when you keep trying to fit a square peg into a round hole, at some point you have to admit it just doesn't fit."

Really, this was too much! "Why is it so hard for you to give me a little help, for a change, instead of constantly coming up with arguments for why I'm wrong?"

"You mean help you to ruin your career before it's even started? Damn it all, Sarah, I *am* trying to help you. You're just too stubborn to see it."

He rose from his chair, placed both hands on my desk and looked me squarely in the eye. "I humored you while you went through your pathetic list of suspects. But even you have to admit it ended in a blind alley. Sarah, listen to me—*please.*" He half choked out this last word, so unfamiliar was it on his tongue. "Your insistence on defending Chin is professional suicide."

"I have to do what I feel is right!"

He took his hands from my desk so suddenly it set the rickety affair shaking. "And you consider this right? Defending a murderer? Think what you've been through, woman, to toss it all away for this churlish, lying cook."

"You sound like every newspaper in town. Chin has a right to a fair trial. I can't believe you would deny him that."

"Don't be thickheaded. Of course I wouldn't deny Chin his constitutional rights. I just don't want to see you go down with a sinking ship. You can't win this case!"

Mirrored on his broad, sunburned face, I saw anger, frustration, disappointment and, beneath it all, fear that I was destroying my chance for a career in the law.

Sighing, I said softly, "I'm sorry you feel that way, Robert. I truly would have appreciated having you by my side, sitting as second chair at Chin's trial."

He stood very still; his eyes hadn't left mine for a second. "I'm sorry, too, Sarah. There's a time when I'd have been the last person in the world to say this, but I think you would have made a gifted attorney—even if you are a woman."

I almost smiled at this backdoor compliment; I never expected Robert Campbell to make such a startling admission. My only regret was that it was under such circumstances.

"You've made your choice, Robert," I told him, determined not to let him see my disappointment. Arranging the papers spread before me, I bent to my work. "If you'll excuse me, I have a great deal to do before the trial begins."

He opened his mouth as if to speak, then closed it. With a curt nod of his head, he turned and left the room.

To say that I was nervous the first day of Chin's trial would be a gross understatement. Whether we care to admit it or not, much of what transpires in a courtroom—especially during a murder trial—can be termed theater of high drama. Without devaluing the significance of solid evidence, the manner in which that evidence is presented is often of greater import. The jury is composed of mere men, after all, susceptible to all the imperfections of our species. In an effort to sway the jury, lawyers on both sides of the aisle have been known to blur the line between justice and showmanship until it becomes all but indistinguishable.

I'd arrived early, hoping for a few minutes to collect my thoughts. Although I was alone, I felt surrounded by the spirits of all the men and women who had given testimony in this courtroom over the years—tense, worried people, some brave enough to tell the truth, others willing to lie in an effort to hide dark secrets and private sins. This chamber had seen it all: every conceivable transgression and outrage, lives devastated, defendants condemned to prison or even death. This last thought caused me to shiver. Today I would begin the fight for Chin Lee Fong's life.

The courtroom looked no different this morning than it had during the two days of jury selection. Because the fog outside had yet to dissipate, little light showed through the tall windows lining one wall of the dark-paneled room. The judge's bench loomed before me in daunting majesty, its towering size making me feel small and insignificant. The knot forming in my stomach tightened, hardly an auspicious beginning to what the city's newspapers touted as the trial of the year.

My footsteps echoed as I walked between rows of empty benches. Choosing my wardrobe for the trial had been akin to balancing on a tightrope. If I dressed too severely, I might insult the all-male jury by appearing too masculine. Too many flounces and frills, on the other hand, and I risked being character-ized as frivolous. In the end, I'd selected a fitted, two-piece navy blue suit with a very small bustle. To soften its tailored lines, I wore a hand-laced cream-colored shirtwaist, my small gold timepiece pinned to the bodice. I arranged my thick hair in a neat bun at the nape of my neck and wore a small but stylish hat Celia had found in a millinery shop on Market Street. As I took my seat at the defense table, I felt I had achieved a professional appearance without sacri-ficing my femininity.

I pulled open my briefcase and spread an assortment of papers out on the table, as well as a volume of legal lore I'd borrowed from Papa's library for ready reference. The pile seemed pathetically small, I reflected, considering that a man's life hung in the balance.

Robert possessed no more experience in a courtroom than I did. Still, it would have been heartening to have him beside me acting as second chair. But of course he wasn't here; I would have to face the enemy on my own.

Papa would have been delighted to join me at the defense table. Because he was a judge, however, he could not. He'd done the next best thing, though, spending hours with me going over courtroom protocol and procedure. He warned me of tactics I might expect from the prosecutor, how best to question witnesses, which questions to avoid, which ones to ask. A good defense attorney, he told me, must be prepared to lose a minor skirmish here and there in order to save his big guns for more critical battles. "All things come round to him who will but wait," he quoted from Longfellow.

For the hundredth time I went over my notes, asking myself if I'd done everything possible to prepare for Chin's defense. The sad fact was that I had still found no way to prove his innocence. The best I could do was try to establish that Chin's bark was worse than his bite. For all the cook's angry posturing, he'd never been known to strike anyone, much less try to kill. His reputation as a gambler was well known, but he rarely pilfered more than a few dollars to further that passion. Samuel and I had located half a dozen witnesses willing to testify they'd seen Chin at various gambling dens at the time he was supposed to be poisoning Arlen. But they were Chinese. I had no illusions about their ability to convince a jury of white men.

Then there was the matter of public opinion. While the prosecution's case was circumstantial, the public had already decided Chin's guilt. There'd even been talk of a lynching, requiring additional jail guards for protection.

Ironically, although Chin was being tried for the murder of Lucius Arlen, what most incensed the populace were much publicized rumors that he had also killed a white girl. The papers had a field day portraying Dora as a defenseless young beauty, cowering at the feet of a crazed Chinaman. The accompanying cartoons pictured Chin as a slant-eyed devil, complete with pitchfork and forked tail!

The chamber began to fill. I knew that most people had come out of curiosity, not only to see a woman attorney but to catch a glimpse of the "yellow-skinned devil" (the name with which Chin had been christened by local newspapers) pictured on every front page in town.

Fifteen minutes later the room was crowded to overflowing, and latecomers were being turned away at the door. I was pleased and touched to see my mother, Celia and Samuel seated not many rows behind me. Papa was presiding at a civil trial this morning and, much to his disappointment, could not be here to support me.

Although her husband was a judge, this was one of the few times Mama had entered a courtroom; almost certainly it was Celia's first time to witness a trial. It was considered not quite proper for a lady of society to be seen in such a place, which made their presence here this morning all the more poignant.

They gave me encouraging smiles, which I returned, even though I felt anything but confident. I could see no sign of the Barlows, then remembered that Mrs. Barlow was to be called as a prosecution witness and therefore was banned from the chamber until after her testimony. At the rear of the courtroom, I spied two Chinese men, and I wondered if they'd been sent by Li Ying. I also saw an associate from Shepard's law firm. No need to wonder what he was doing here; his sour expression said it all. He'd been sent by Shepard to make daily reports on my inability to handle the situation.

Across the aisle, Miles Dormer—a senior assistant district attorney—and his assistant took their seats at the prosecution table. Both men glanced in my direction, Dormer with a polite nod, his junior with a smile so smug I wanted to reach over and wipe it off his face.

Miles Dormer was a tall, slender man in his mid forties, with aspirations, Papa had informed me, to become district attorney. The successful conclusion of this case would prove a big step in that direction. He wore an expensive-looking black frock coat, dark gray trousers and a stiffly starched white wing collar with a perfectly knotted silver-gray cravat. Handsome in a self-important sort of way, he had brown hair just beginning to turn gray, high cheekbones and deep-set hazel eyes, which appeared as if they missed nothing.

Dormer's assistant looked to be several years younger. He affected an absurd-looking walrus mustache, which he kept absentmindedly twirling with his fingers.

A loud murmur broke out behind me, and I saw Chin being led into the courtroom. Despite his circumstances, the cook's face bore its usual truculent expression. To my dismay, he glanced around the crowded courtroom as if the spectators had gathered here to pay him homage rather than to see him convicted of first-degree murder.

But it was his garb that made me groan. In my zeal to make Chin appear as dissimilar as possible from his pictures in the newspapers, I'd insisted he wear a Western-style suit and shoes. I now realized my mistake. Instead of making Chin appear more normal, he looked ludicrous, like a Chinese man dressed for a costume party.

I had no time to lament my unfortunate lapse of judgment. As soon as Chin had been led to the defense table, the Honorable William Carlton was announced and strode with authority to the bench.

As the clerk of the court called out the particulars of the case, I studied Carlton. If anything, Papa had been overly generous when describing the man. In his mid fifties, the judge's face looked as if it had been carved in granite, his dark eyes sharp and disapproving, wholly humorless as they looked out from beneath thick spectacles to take in his courtroom. For a moment his eyes rested on me and I sucked in my breath. This man resents my presence in his courtroom, I thought, the knot in my stomach tightening. Was it possible that in the face of such blatant antipathy Judge Carlton could be impartial—either to me or my client?

He banged his gavel to bring the courtroom to order, and Dormer stood to deliver his opening statement. Smiling confidently, he introduced himself and his assistant, Leighton Pruit, then went on to lay the foundation for the state's case against Chin. Even to my ears, each piece of evidence seemed like a fresh nail being hammered into my client's coffin. When Dormer finished, he glanced at me as if to apologize for the utter hopelessness of my cause, then with a slight bow to the jury, returned to his seat.

"Miss Woolson," the judge said, his deep voice just short of mocking, "We're ready for your opening statement."

I tried to stand, but for an awful moment my body refused to move. I felt as if I were stuck to the chair. There were footsteps to my left, and I was stunned when Robert slipped into the seat beside me. I just had time to give him a questioning look when Judge Carlton growled,

"If this is your assistant, Miss Woolson, he is late."

"I apologize, Your Honor." To my relief, I found my

limbs once again functioning normally. "This is Mr. Robert Campbell."

Before Judge Carlton could find further reason to chastise me, I stood and faced the jury box. Twelve pairs of male eyes fastened on me with expressions ranging from outright disdain to boorish curiosity. Gathering strength from Robert's smile, I cleared my throat.

"Your Honor, gentlemen of the jury," I began. "I am Sarah Woolson. My associate, Robert Campbell, and I will be representing Mr. Chin Lee Fong against these outrageous charges. We've listened to Mr. Dormer describe Mr. Lucius Arlen's tragic death by *Actaea alba,* or baneberry poisoning. Yet the prosecution cannot produce a single witness who saw Mr. Chin in Mr. Arlen's company the night the poison was supposedly administered." I paused, pleased to note that the jury was carefully attending my words.

"While it is true that baneberries were discovered in a cupboard in Mr. Chin's kitchen, Mr. Dormer cannot prove who put them there. Keep in mind that anyone in the hospital had access to the kitchen. The prosecution has also made much of the animosity that existed between Mr. Chin and Mr. Arlen. It cannot be disputed that both men made what could be construed as threatening remarks during the heat of these disagreements, but we mean to show that neither man took the comments seriously."

Purposefully, I eyed each juror in turn. "Please remember, gentlemen, the prosecution has the burden to prove beyond any possible doubt that my client is guilty. The lack of evidence, which you will note over the coming days, will more than create that doubt in your minds. You will be left with no alternative but to find Mr. Chin not guilty. Thank you!"

Silence filled the courtroom as I returned to my chair. Most of the jurors were still watching me, but it was difficult to tell from their expressions if it was with favor or disapproval. At least they'd listened attentively to my opening statement, I thought, as a buzz of whispers started in the gallery. Only time would tell if I would be able to prove my assertions.

Dormer called his first witness, Lucius Arlen's landlady. The buxom woman looked anxiously around the crowded courtroom as she took the stand. In a small voice, she described the last hours of the accountant's life and how she had finally summoned a doctor. By then, she said, Mr. Arlen was claiming he had been poisoned.

I stood to cross-examine her. "Did Mr. Arlen say who he suspected of poisoning him?"

The woman shook her head. "No," she admitted. "He never said who he thought done it."

"Thank you, madam. That will be all."

The doctor who had attended Arlen took the stand next. He recalled the man's symptoms, then admitted that he, too, heard Arlen claim to be poisoned. Under cross-examination, I managed to get the doctor to admit that Arlen had not named his poisoner to him, either.

The state's third witness was the policeman who'd been called to the death scene. Appearing to enjoy himself, he described in lurid details what he'd witnessed upon his arrival. His testimony elicited gasps from several spectators and necessitated the removal of one lady silly enough to faint. I found nothing in his testimony to contest, and the man was duly excused.

At noon, Judge Carlton adjourned the court until one-thirty. Armed guards escorted Chin back to his cell, and Robert and I were able to exit by a rear door.

"What are you doing here, Robert?" I asked when we reached the street. Around the corner, I could hear newspaper reporters questioning those who had been inside the courtroom, and I was glad we'd left by a back door. "You said you wanted nothing to do with this case."

"Damn it all, Sarah, I couldn't leave you to muck this up on your own. You were as helpless in there as a mouse in a roomful of cats."

"Don't be ridiculous," I retorted. "I resent the implication that I'm incapable of trying a case on my own."

"That's not what I meant, and you know it." Spotting a reporter heading in our direction, he took hold of my arm and hurried me away from the courthouse. "Don't tell me you missed the way Carlton glared at you. It's clear he resents having a female attorney in his courtroom. I'm sure he'll do everything short of prejudicial error to see that you don't appear before him again."

I started to object, then held my tongue. After all, how could I contradict something that was so patently true?

We found a quiet hotel restaurant nearby and ordered a light lunch. While we waited to be served, I asked Robert if Joseph Shepard knew he was here.

"No, but I saw his spy in the courtroom, so I'm sure he'll hear of it soon enough." He looked around to make sure we couldn't be overheard. "Tell me, what strategy have you devised for the trial?"

I felt a familiar wave of panic at this question; it was, after all, the same question I'd been asking myself every day since Li Ying requested I take Chin's case. How painful it would be to admit that, after all my bold words, I'd failed to uncover the real murderer. And the discovery of that villain remained my lone hope of freeing my client.

"If only we could find out where Dora Clemens went the morning of her death, I'm sure we'd be able to identify the killer," I said, evading his question. "I've asked Leonard and Pierce Godfrey's neighbors, but no one remembers seeing a girl of her description that morning."

"No one is likely to remember even if they did see her. She'd be just one more maid on her way to work."

"Dora had distinctive red hair," I said, eyeing Robert's riotous orange mane. "She'd be hard to miss."

"I suppose," he mumbled, unwilling to concede that

hair color could be of any great importance. "But you still haven't told me your defense strategy."

Aware of how woefully inadequate it sounded, I described the witnesses who were willing to testify that Chin was at a gambling den the night Arlen was poisoned.

"A fat lot of good they'll do you." Robert gave a dismissive snort. "No one is going to believe a Chinaman."

Again, I found it impossible to argue. I already knew the futility of placing Chin's gambling cronies on the stand. But what other option did I have? I endeavored to keep my voice calm as I said,

"We only have another day or two at the most before we'll be called upon to put on our defense. We must find some way to cast doubt on the prosecution's case by then."

He fell quiet as our soup arrived, then said, "I did manage to learn something. Of course I have no idea how much good it will do us."

I felt a surge of hope. "What is it, Robert?"

"Leonard Godfrey took out a substantial life insurance policy on his wife less than a year before she died. Because her death was ruled from natural causes, he'll receive a sizeable sum."

"Good heavens, how did you get this information?" I hardly recognized this husky whisper as my own voice.

"I know someone who works at his insurance company. But please, this is to go no further. My friend could lose his job."

"Yes, of course." I lifted a spoonful of soup to my mouth, not because I was hungry, but to give myself time to think. Both Godfrey brothers remained on my short list of suspects, but I'd been unable to come up with anything tangible that might point to their guilt. Perhaps this information would open a new door. I was willing, nay, desperate, to grasp at any straw. Much as I hated to lose Robert during the afternoon's session, Leonard Godfrey would once again have to be investigated.

After lunch, I dispatched my colleague on his reluctant way and returned to the courtroom. As I took my seat next to Chin at the defense table, I was pleased to note that my brother Charles had joined my family in the gallery behind me. He gave me a quick smile as Judge Carlton called the room to order. Dormer stood and called the city's coroner, Dr. Levi L. Dorr, to the stand.

A tall man in his late forties, Dorr patiently went over the results of Arlen's autopsy. Reiterating death by means of baneberry poison, he explained how the amount of toxins found in Arlen's body, along with his height and weight, had been used to determine when the poison had likely been administered. Since nothing would be gained by cross-examining this witness, I allowed him to be excused.

Now that they had covered the scientific aspects of Arlen's death, the state began to lay its foundation for motive and opportunity. Dormer's next four witnesses attested to Arlen's successful career as an accountant, his dedication to his work, as well as his abstemious and laudable character. I cross-examined each witness, but accomplished little for our case.

Before Dormer could call his next witness, Judge Carlton announced court would be adjourned until the following morning. I turned to give Chin words of encouragement, but he had already risen, without a word to me, and was being led back to his jail cell.

Determined not to allow my client's discourteous behavior to dampen my efforts to set him free, I started gathering up papers when a commotion broke out at the rear of the chamber, and Eddie Cooper fairly flew into me.

"I found him, miss, I found him!" he cried, as a clerk tried to grab him by the collar.

Informing the dubious clerk that Eddie was one of my assistants, I took my briefcase and hurriedly led the boy out the same back door Robert and I had used during the noon recess.

"Now, who did you find?" I said once we were outside.

"Killy Doyle," he said breathlessly. "You know, the gent who run off with that Corrigan fellow. He came outta the shop on Sansone. First time I seen hide or hair of either of them blokes."

A wave of guilt washed through me. With all the pressure of preparing for Chin's trial, I'd completely forgotten Lily Mankin and her lawsuit. I was astonished to realize that although I had let the widow down,

Eddie had adhered to his promise, faithfully keeping watch over the shop.

"Eddie, you're a remarkable lad," I told him. "Far better than I deserve. Please, tell me everything you saw."

The boy beamed. "Well, Doyle walked around fer a while, like he wasn't goin' no place special. Then he met up with another gent, a proper gentleman an' all. The two of 'em talked fer a minute, then caught a hack to that house on California Street, you know, where Doyle lives."

He tugged me toward his brougham parked across the street. "Come on, miss, hurry! Maybe they're still there."

When I was seated in the carriage, Eddie urged his horse into a quick trot. Indignant shouts and expletives from other drivers followed us as he dodged in and out of traffic with little regard for life or limb. By the time we turned onto California Street, my heart was lodged in my throat and my knuckles were white from grasping the seat. Eddie parked a safe distance from Killy's house, then hopped down from his perch and joined me inside the cab.

"How long ago did they go into the house?" I asked as we kept our eyes fastened on Doyle's front door.

"Maybe an hour. Soon as they went inside, I come straight to the courthouse."

"You've done very well, Eddie," I said, meaning every word. "Hopefully, they're still inside."

The sun had set over the Bay and night was rapidly

approaching when Doyle's door finally opened. The unpleasant housekeeper Robert and I had encountered on our first visit stepped out and, under the pretext of shaking a blanket, looked suspiciously up and down the street. Satisfied no one was watching, she went back inside, and a moment later two men hurried out and started walking briskly in our direction.

I recognized Killy Doyle as the younger of the two figures. The second man took a moment longer to identify. Perhaps it was because my mind balked at the information my eyes were transmitting to it. In truth I had to blink twice before I could truly grasp who I was seeing.

Although the older man wore a long dark overcoat and a hat pulled low over his face, there was no mistaking the self-assured demeanor or the familiar tilt of that proud head.

Both Eddie and I instinctively ducked down as the two men hurried past our carriage, but I raised my head just far enough to make certain I had not mistaken him.

I had not. As impossible as it seemed, the man walking with Killy Doyle was none other than Judge Tobias Barlow.

CHAPTER ELEVEN

I arrived home eager to tell Samuel what I had seen. To my frustration, Edis informed me that my brother had gone out earlier and was not expected back until the following evening. Mama and Celia were at home, but I was not yet ready to tell them my news. Papa would have to be informed first, a task I frankly dreaded. It would have to be done, of course, but I'd counted on talking it over with Samuel first.

As it turned out, my brother had left me a note, presumably an update on the information he'd been able to glean from newspaper files and other sources that he vigilantly guarded from what he termed my "prying nose." Waiting until I had reached the privacy of my bedroom, I eagerly slit open the envelope. I was disappointed to find only a single piece of paper inside.

He'd found precious little new information, Samuel admitted in his untidy scrawl. But while he'd been digging up information on everyone involved in the case, he'd learned that Adelina and Nigel French had been married some twenty-eight years earlier. Given that Margaret French Barlow had passed her fortieth birthday, he considered the discovery puzzling enough to pass along. Oh, and he'd been unable to find any record of Margaret Barlow's birth. Was I certain she'd been born in San Francisco?

He went on to write that he'd found no skeletons in the Godfrey brothers' closets, apart from the ones we'd already unearthed. According to newspaper files, Margaret Barlow and Adelina French had led lives as pure as the driven snow. He was still looking into Judge Barlow's past but doubted he'd find any scandal there, either. He was waiting for his sources back east to send him more information about Reverend Prescott and would let me know as soon as it arrived.

I read the note through twice, then decided that the disparity between the Frenches' marriage and Margaret's birth could have little, if anything, to do with my case. Still, the circumstances were peculiar. It was possible, of course, that Margaret had been born before the couple legalized their union. But if that were so, surely I would have heard rumors of it years ago. Society has a very long memory for such indiscretions.

As I changed for dinner, I wished Samuel was here so I could inform him how far off the mark he was about Judge Barlow's scandal-free life. I especially longed to ask his advice on how to tell Papa that his best friend might not be the man he supposed him to be. Waiting until he returned tomorrow night seemed like an eternity.

Mama and Celia smiled at me as I entered the courtroom the next morning. I noticed they had taken seats closer to the defense table today, and I found their presence comforting. Instead of Samuel, who, of course, was out of town, I was delighted to find my brother Charles seated next to them. I felt a glow of reassurance; their support went a long way toward bracing me for the upcoming ordeal.

The two Chinese men I was sure had been sent by Li Ying occupied the same seats at the rear of the room, while Shepard's scout sat grumpily across the aisle.

Robert was already ensconced at the defense table. He wore the same suit as the day before—which could have benefited from the use of a flatiron—and as usual his thick red hair was tousled, his cravat askew and the papers on the table before him in disarray. For all that, I was delighted to see him. By now I was fairly bursting to tell someone about finally finding Killy Doyle—and in the company of Judge Tobias Barlow, of all people!

Before I could get out a word, Robert said solemnly, "You're not going to like this, Sarah, but Pierce Godfrey was seen at the hospital the night Arlen was poisoned."

I stared at him, mouth agape. "Are you sure?" was all I could manage.

"Of course I'm sure. I wouldn't tell you if I weren't. It was pure luck that I stumbled upon a nurse who saw them together in Arlen's office a little after seven o'clock."

I was still struggling to make sense of this revelation when Chin arrived at our table wearing, I was relieved to note, a Mandarin jacket and loose-fitting black pants. His hair was shaved and neatly braided into a long queue. The one discordant note was the pair of

247

heavy brown boots on his feet. Oh, well, I consoled myself, they were unlikely to be noticed beneath the table.

The prosecution called George Lewis as its first witness of the morning. For a change, the policeman's unruly hair lay neatly combed back from his high forehead, and his uniform was carefully pressed. As if aware his testimony was going to be damaging to my client's case, he avoided looking in my direction.

George soberly answered each of Dormer's questions, but added little that was not specifically asked of him. The gist of his story was that he'd been summoned to Arlen's boardinghouse, where he'd found the victim lying in his bed close to death. George had dispatched one of his men to summon a doctor, but it had been too late. He concluded by verifying that Lucius Arlen had indeed insisted to the end that he'd been poisoned.

George's testimony was no more than I'd expected. Dormer's next line of questioning went straight for the jugular. Looking pointedly at the jury, the prosecutor asked Lewis to recount Chin's behavior during his police interrogation.

"Mr. Chin was surly and uncooperative," George said.

"Did he mention his feelings toward the victim?"

"Yes, sir. He made no bones about how much he hated Mr. Arlen."

"Did the defendant demonstrate any remorse over Mr. Arlen's painful death?"

"No, sir."

"Well, did he at least comment upon it?"

"Yes, sir. He, er—" George face turned pink, as if he wasn't quite sure what to say.

"He what, Mr. Lewis?" Dormer prodded. "Please answer the question."

Looking embarrassed, George blurted, "He said it was no more than the filthy bastard deserved."

A shocked murmur swept through the courtroom.

"I'll thank you to watch your language, Sergeant Lewis," Judge Carlton warned him severely. "This is a court of law, not a saloon."

"Yes, Your Honor," George answered meekly. His boyishly handsome face had by now turned the color of a boiled lobster.

"Mr. Lewis," Dormer continued, watching the jury's outraged response to Chin's statement with ill-concealed delight. "Will you please tell the court what you discovered in Mr. Chin's kitchen?"

George described finding the baneberry roots and berries hidden at the back of one of Chin's cupboards. When Lewis finished, the prosecutor looked pointedly in my direction, then declared he had no more questions for this witness.

Rising to my feet, I smiled at George. "You say that Mr. Chin acknowledged his animosity toward Mr. Arlen. Did he indicate this dislike was so intense he wished to kill him?"

George blinked at this blunt question. "No, Miss Sar—I mean, no ma'am."

"Did you ask the defendant if he poisoned Mr. Arlen?"

"Yes, ma'am."

"And what was his response?"

"He laughed. Said he wouldn't waste perfectly good poison on such a fool."

Noise filled the gallery, which Judge Carlton subdued with his gavel.

"So, Mr. Chin denied any responsibility for Mr. Arlen's death."

"Yes, ma'am."

"Very good. Now, about the baneberries you discovered in the hospital kitchen. Isn't it true, Mr. Lewis, that the door to this room is never locked? Indeed, that it isn't even equipped with a lock?"

"That's right, ma'am, there's no lock on that door."

"Then it is perfectly possible that anyone could have placed those berries in the kitchen cupboard, isn't that right?"

George looked doubtful. "Yes, I suppose it is, but—"

"Thank you, Mr. Lewis," I said, cutting him off. "I have no further questions for this witness, Your Honor."

Miles Dormer was instantly on his feet. "Mr. Lewis, did you or your men attempt to ascertain whether anyone else hid the baneberries in the kitchen?"

"Yes, sir, we did. No one reported seeing anything suspicious. We were told that Mr. Chin spends most of his time in the kitchen, so it would have been hard for anyone to hide something there without his seeing them."

"Thank you, Mr. Lewis. One last question, if you please. In your experience, how common is it for a murder suspect to willingly admit his guilt?"

For the first time, George smiled. "It's not at all common, sir. In fact, most of them never do."

"Thank you, Mr. Lewis." Dormer smiled conspiratorially at the jury. "I have no further questions."

The prosecution called an elderly gentleman, reportedly an expert on poisonous plants, as their next witness. He testified that baneberry could be found in most wooded areas along the Pacific Coast. He also described in lurid detail the excruciating pain Arlen must have suffered during his prolonged and violent death. Not surprisingly, this testimony elicited outcries from several women seated behind me in the gallery. Since there seemed little to be gained by cross-examination, I allowed the man to be excused.

Banging his gavel, Judge Carlton tersely announced the noon recess. As I watched the jury leave the room, I was dismayed to see several men nod approvingly to Dormer. With just the right hint of solemnity, the prosecutor returned their nods, then, with a sympathetic smile in my direction, exited the courtroom.

I'd hoped to discuss Judge Barlow and Killy Doyle with Robert over luncheon. Before I could broach the subject, he announced he was meeting a colleague and would rejoin me for the afternoon session. Without waiting for a response, he strode out the side door we'd been using to avoid reporters and was gone.

I started to follow when I felt a hand on my shoulder. Turning, I found my father.

"Papa, this is a surprise," I said with delight.

"One of my cases was canceled this morning, so I thought I'd drop in and see how you're doing." His face sobered. "Looks like you're having a rough time of it."

I nodded grimly. "Let's get out of here before the reporters find us."

We lunched at the same small restaurant Robert and I had discovered the day before. Once we'd placed our order, I told him about Pierce's alleged encounter with Arlen the night he was poisoned.

"I just wish I knew why they met," I finished.

"Yes, so do I," he said thoughtfully. "An extraordinary coincidence, isn't it?"

"If it *is* a coincidence. Pierce is the last person I'd have expected to meet with Arlen. He acted as if he hardly knew the accountant."

"You never know, do you?" Papa studied me curiously, and I guessed he was wondering just how friendly I'd become with the younger Godfrey brother. "Do you know any reason why Mr. Godfrey might want to see Arlen dead?"

I had to stop myself from flinching at this. "No, Papa. I have no more cause to suspect him than anyone else involved in this affair. Actually, less than some."

I waited until the waiter served our antipasto, then said, "I don't think it will be long before Dormer winds up the prosecution's case, and I still haven't come up with a viable defense. At least, not one strong enough to convince an all-white jury of a Chinaman's innocence. My best hope is to try to draw things out until the weekend, but even if I somehow manage that, it hardly solves my problem. Unless we're blessed with a miracle, Papa, I haven't a chance of winning this case and saving Mr. Chin."

Papa pursed his lips but said nothing. Reaching into my briefcase, I pulled out Samuel's note and handed it to him. "What do you make of this?"

Papa scanned the message. "There's no mystery here, my girl. Actually, Margaret Barlow was born in New Jersey, not San Francisco. At the time, I believe her mother was married to a man named Radley, a chemist, as I recall. After Radley died, Adelina took Margaret and moved to San Francisco. I think the child was about eleven or twelve. Evidently Mrs. French was quite a beauty in her day, because she had no trouble catching Nigel French's eye. They were married within the year, and Mr. French adopted Margaret. I believe he was quite fond of the girl."

"Oh," I said, somewhat deflated. I never seriously supposed the matter of Margaret's birth had anything to do with the murders, but I was at a point where I was willing—nay, eager—to grasp at any clue, no matter how tenuous.

I hesitated, wishing again that I could speak to Samuel before I broke my news to Papa. Yet what was to be gained by putting it off? There was never going to be a good time to break my father's heart. Before I lost my nerve, I blurted, "Speaking of Judge Barlow—"

I went on to tell him about spotting Judge Barlow with Killy Doyle the previous afternoon.

Papa didn't immediately make the connection. "Killy Doyle? Isn't he the man you're hoping will lead you to the owner of the sweatshop that burned?"

"Yes," I said, then watched him as the significance of this slowly sank in.

His face paled. "Sarah, are you suggesting Tobias Barlow has something to with that sweatshop?"

"Actually, I think he may be the owner."

"Why? Because you saw him walking with Doyle? It was probably nothing more than a chance meeting."

"No, Papa, it was a good deal more than that. It was obvious they weren't strangers. Remember, Doyle regularly visited the sweatshop to check that production was up to schedule. He has to report back to someone. My guess is that someone is Judge Barlow."

I paused, as a plethora of expressions crossed my father's face. I hated myself for having to plunge the knife in even deeper. "That's not all. According to city records, McKenzie Properties is the official title holder, not only of the sweatshop that caught fire but of a dozen similar properties. Of course it's just a fictitious company set up to shelter the real owner, but Judge Barlow owns a little terrier named—"

"McKenzie," he said in voice so flat I hardly recognized it as my father's.

At that moment, the waiter brought our meal, but my father—who dearly loves his food—hardly seemed to notice. He stared out the window, but I doubt he saw anything but his friend's face. Perhaps he was searching for clues he had missed, signs he had failed to notice.

"I'm not surprised he would choose that name," he said at last, absently pushing aside his meal. "Tobias dotes on that dog. And of course owning those sweatshops would explain how he and Margaret have been able to live beyond their means all these years." His face seemed to crumple, as the full implications of Tobias Barlow's secret life began to sink in. "Lord, what a fool I am, Sarah. I've been in the Barlow home hundreds of times; I've seen the furniture, the paintings and statues, that ridiculously expensive tapestry they bought in France. I guess I just didn't want to know how he managed it."

"Owning sweatshops isn't illegal," I pointed out, trying to lessen the blow.

"No, but the way the owners treat their workers is immoral, if not downright criminal. I suppose you realize they regularly hire children as young as six or seven years old, working them twelve to fourteen hours a day. The pay is shameful and the working conditions are wretched. I'm sure Tobias isn't the only city official to be lured by easy money, but fair or not, judges are expected to rise above such temptations." He ran a hand over his forehead, then looked at me with weary eyes. "So, my girl, what now?"

"Before I can file suit on Mrs. Mankin's behalf, I first need to confirm my suspicions."

"Yes, I suppose you do," Papa said heavily. Then, after a pause, he went on quietly, "I'll look into it for you, Sarah. As a judge I have connections you don't have. Perhaps I can find your answer. And mine, too." He sighed. "Tobias is—*was*—my best friend. I have to know if our relationship all these years has been based on a lie."

"All right, Papa. I appreciate that." Privately, I hoped whatever he found would ease the pain of what must surely seem like a cruel betrayal. "I already have more on my plate than I can possibly eat." I looked down at my untouched lunch and gave an ironic little laugh. "Literally, it seems."

"What are your plans?" Papa asked.

"I'll start by interviewing the nurse who claims to have seen Pierce with Mr. Arlen at the hospital that night. Perhaps she knows more than she was willing to tell Robert. For instance, what the two men were talking about in Arlen's office."

"You think she might have 'overheard' part of their conversation?"

"I sincerely hope so."

Robert returned to the courtroom that afternoon looking grim.

"I didn't want to get your hopes up earlier, in case nothing came of it," he said quietly, "but I lunched with an old friend from Edinburgh. As it happens, he spent several years in New Jersey, where he occasionally attended a church where Nicholas Prescott served as minister."

I leaned forward. "What did your friend say about him? From the look on your face, it wasn't good."

"Oh, Prescott was an effective enough preacher, and his services were always packed. But his reputation with the ladies—" He paused, always uncomfortable discussing delicate subjects. "Let's just say he had no problem finding willing companions. And," he went on as I started to speak, "after Prescott took over the church, weekly contributions began to decline. A great fuss was raised over it; even the police were called in to investigate. Unfortunately, nothing was ever proved. It may be just a coincidence, but my friend found it interesting that Prescott moved to Chicago shortly after the incident."

"What happened to the weekly collections after he left?"

"Back to pre-Prescott days."

"Oh, my," I said, realizing how inadequate this sounded under the circumstances. I remembered Samuel's report that Prescott frequently changed parishes. I was beginning to understand why these moves might have been necessary. It seemed I would have to rethink my opinion of the charismatic minister.

Before I could question Robert further, Chin was brought to the defense table. For some reason, he looked even more bad-tempered than usual.

"What's wrong?" I asked, as he muttered under his breath in Chinese.

"Bah!" he snapped. "Food here awful. Like eating slop for pigs. I tell them, but they no listen. Just laugh. Bastards! All filthy bastards!"

"Shh, Chin, please," I warned him, unhappy to see several nearby spectators regarding my client with unease.

"Didn't you learn anything this morning?" Robert told him in a harsh whisper. "You can't go around calling everyone you don't like a filthy bastard."

Chin opened his mouth to say something as Judge Carlton entered the court but quickly fell silent when Robert poked him hard in the ribs with his elbow. We all stood and the judge brought the afternoon session to order.

Dormer called several hospital nurses to the stand to describe arguments they'd witnessed between Arlen and Chin. Thinking the women might react better to a man, I asked Robert, as second chair, to conduct the cross-examinations. The testimony of one of the young women in particular was especially damaging. With wide, frightened eyes, she told of a particularly rancorous fight in which Arlen vowed to see Chin thrown out on his ear. According to the nurse, my acerbic client yelled back that he would see the accountant in his coffin before he'd permit any such thing. I noticed several jurors directing accusing glances at Chin, who sat, still disgruntled, by my side.

Although Robert used care when he cross-examined

the last young woman—who tended toward hysterics—he was unable to shake her testimony in any significant way. Fearful that further questioning would be perceived as badgering by the already sympathetic jurors, he allowed the girl to return to her seat.

Mr. Richard Palen was next called to the stand. A stout man of middle age, Palen had slightly protruding teeth that gave him a noticeable lisp when he spoke. Dormer quickly established that Palen had been Chin's employer at a popular restaurant on Market Street.

"Can you tell us why Mr. Chin left your establishment, Mr. Palen?" Dormer asked.

Palen smiled with natural good humor. "Chin was a good enough cook, but he had a foul temper. We had to let him go when he threatened to poison Shaw, our pastry chef."

This created an uproar in the courtroom, and it was several minutes before Judge Carlton could restore order.

"My, my, Mr. Palen," Dormer said in mock horror. "Why do you suppose Mr. Chin would say such a thing?"

"There were bad feelings between the two cooks," Palen answered. "At one point, Chin warned Shaw to watch what he ate because he knew more than one way to poison a rat."

Again, there were exclamations of surprise, but before Judge Carlton was forced to intercede, Dormer announced that he had finished with the witness.

Chin tugged my arm as I stood to cross-examine the

witness. "Ask what that pig Shaw do to me."

I gave a little nod, then turned to the witness. "Mr. Palen, do you know the reason for the chef's animosity?"

"Sure, it was over a gambling debt. Chin claimed Shaw owed him a hundred dollars." Palen smiled. "Shaw got back at him by putting a tarantula in Chin's boot. That was when Chin warned him to watch what he ate."

I glanced at the jury, pleased to see several jurors nodding their heads as if in sympathy with my client. There probably wasn't a man among them who hadn't had someone welsh on a gambling debt at one time or another.

"To the best of your knowledge, did Mr. Chin carry through on his threat?" I asked.

"Naw. Chin was always making threats; it was nothing but talk. When their fighting started bothering the customers, though, we had to fire them both."

"I see. So you never feared that Mr. Chin might actually take Mr. Shaw's life."

His dark eyes twinkled as if I'd made a good joke. "No, ma'am. Never."

"Thank you, Mr. Palen. That will be all."

Dormer started to rise from his chair to reexamine his witness, then thought better of it. Instead, he called another employee of the same restaurant, who gave more or less the same testimony as his predecessor. When it was my turn to cross-examine, I spent only a few minutes reestablishing that no one took Chin's threats seriously, then allowed the witness to be excused.

The moment Palen stood down from the stand, Judge Carlton abruptly adjourned court for the day.

"Finally," I said to Robert, hurriedly placing my papers in my briefcase. "There's something I've been trying to tell you all day."

As we left the courtroom, I told Robert about seeing Judge Barlow with Killy Doyle the day before, as well as Papa's disclosures about Margaret Barlow being the child of her mother's first husband. I was disappointed by my colleague's response.

"What in God's name does that have to do with anything?" was his clipped reply. "The way you bounce about from one suspect to another makes me dizzy— and gets you nowhere, by the way. Only one thing matters, Sarah: who was in the kitchen with Arlen the night he was poisoned?"

"Oh, for heaven's sake," I exclaimed. "That's exactly what we're going to try to find out."

Ignoring his protests, I signaled to a passing hansom. "Do hurry, Robert. We want to catch this nurse of yours before she goes off duty for the day."

We found the nurse in question, Emily Harbetter, assisting the midwife in a difficult delivery. We were met at the door to the maternity ward by Lily Mankin, who was bustling about delivering fresh water, clean cloths and various other supplies in a remarkably efficient manner. Robert paled at the sight and sounds of the women grouped around the expectant mother and hastily departed for the kitchen, claiming he wanted to find a cup of coffee.

As I had never before witnessed a woman giving birth, I must confess I was tempted to join him, especially when the poor young mother-to-be began screaming most alarmingly. I'm pleased to report that I quickly banished this cowardly impulse and, bracing myself, boldly advanced into the ward.

"I know what the poor soul's goin' through," Lily said, nodding sympathetically toward the woman's bed. "It's gonna be all right, though. The baby's head is finally showin'. Mark my words, the babe will soon be out and testin' its lungs for all to hear."

Barely five minutes later, Lily was proven right as a healthy baby girl made her very vocal entrance into the world. Not long afterward, Miss Harbetter, Robert and I sat in the kitchen drinking fresh coffee brewed by Lily, before she discreetly left us to talk.

Miss Harbetter, a gray-haired, hardy-looking woman in her mid fifties was, I discovered, the head nurse. Her intelligent brown eyes and no-nonsense manner announced that she did not suffer fools easily. On his earlier visit, she'd informed Robert that she had served with Florence Nightingale during the Crimean War, which, I thought, explained her outspoken air and self-confidence.

"Why didn't you tell the police about seeing Mr. Pierce Godfrey that evening, Miss Harbetter?" I asked.

"The police," she said dismissively. "Pack of fools!

Tried to tell them what I saw, but they were so sure they had their killer, they wouldn't listen. Just kept asking if Chin had been in the kitchen with Arlen. Since I was upstairs sorting supplies, I couldn't answer that one way or the other. It was while I was working in the linen room that I saw Mr. Godfrey go into Mr. Arlen's office."

"You're certain it was Pierce Godfrey?" Robert asked.

"Of course I'm sure." She sounded offended that he would doubt her word. "He was here the day the hospital opened. Caused a ruckus with the nurses, I'll tell you. You'd think they'd never seen a man before— fawning all over him like silly schoolgirls."

Eager to get back to that fatal Monday night, I asked, "Did you happen to hear what Mr. Godfrey and Mr. Arlen were discussing in the accountant's office?" At her injured look, I quickly added, "I'm not suggesting you would eavesdrop, Miss Harbetter. I just thought perhaps you might have overheard something in passing."

"I'm not blessed with ears that can hear through closed doors," she replied shortly. She seemed to think of something and added, "You might ask Mrs. Barlow. She was here that night. Maybe she knows what Arlen and Godfrey were talking about."

Robert and I stared at her.

"Mrs. Barlow was here that evening?" I asked her. "Are you quite sure?"

Again, I received what I was coming to regard as *the*

look. "Of course I'm sure. Saw her just as she was going into the kitchen. After that, who knows where she went?"

"What time did you see her?" Robert inquired.

She considered this. "It must have been fifteen or twenty minutes after seven. I remember because I'd just gone downstairs to fix Mrs. Hall's seven-thirty medicine."

"Did you happen to speak to Mrs. Barlow?" I pressed.

"Only saw her for a second before I went into the ward." She looked at each of us in turn. "Why are you asking all these questions, anyway? It isn't unusual for Mrs. Barlow to be here some evenings. You act as if my seeing her that night is somehow important."

"Yes, Miss Harbetter," I told her. "It may be very important indeed."

Robert and I spent the next hour going over Arlen's office. Everything was neat and well organized, yet we found nothing to indicate why the accountant met with Pierce that night. We went through Arlen's files and even examined a dozen or so accounting books arranged on a shelf behind his desk, along with an address book and a small silver salver filled with business cards.

While Robert inspected the address book, I glanced through the cards. Most were from the contractors, plumbers and painters engaged in renovating the warehouse. There were also cards from various board members and one printed with the name Matthew Grady, of the First National Gold Bank of San Francisco. Someone, I presumed Arlen, had penned the initials "PG" on the card, along with the notation "Tues. 3:30." Not very helpful, I thought in frustration. If Arlen and Pierce really did meet that night, the accountant hadn't seen fit to keep a written record of what transpired.

On impulse, I placed the business cards inside my briefcase before we finally gave up the search. At least, I thought, I wouldn't go home empty-handed.

That evening, Papa, Samuel, Robert and I gathered in my father's study in yet another attempt to formulate a defense strategy. I brought my brother up to date on our latest findings, then said, "This afternoon Robert and I questioned the nurse who saw Pierce Godfrey at the hospital the night Arlen was poisoned. She claims she also saw Mrs. Barlow there that evening. She seems certain of her story, although I question how the Barlows could have returned from Menlo Park so early."

"They were never in Menlo Park," Papa said quietly.

"What?" Samuel and I said simultaneously.

It was obvious Papa took no pleasure in this revelation. "We assumed the Barlows were meeting their architect, Harold Peterson, in Menlo Park, because that's the location of their new home. If you remember, the police report stated they left the architect's office shortly after six o'clock. What the report failed to mention is that Peterson's office is here, in the city."

"Oh my," I said, considering how this news changed

things. "I was sure the Barlows had an alibi for that evening. Now—"

"Now we have to reexamine their movements that night," Papa put in.

My heart went out to my father. The discovery of his best friend's secret life seemed to have aged him overnight. "Oh, Papa, I'm so sorry."

"No need to apologize, Sarah. Tobias knew what he was doing when he got into the sweatshop business. Once the news becomes public it will destroy his career, of course. But that was a risk he accepted when he chose to exploit children and poor immigrants with no other means to support their families."

"So," Samuel asked, "where do we go from here?"

"Now that we know there's no good reason the Barlows couldn't have been at the hospital that evening, it seems to me we have five main suspects: Leonard and Pierce Godfrey, Reverend Prescott and, of course, Margaret and Tobias Barlow. Each of them, either individually or working together, had motive and probably opportunity to kill all four victims.

"Yes," I continued before I was interrupted, "I'm including Caroline Godfrey and Josiah Halsey with Arlen and Dora Clemens. It's the only theory that makes any sense. Burying our heads in the sand will only insure that the killer goes free."

This prompted a lively discussion that went on for the next half hour. Who knows when it might have ended, if Edis hadn't brought in a fresh pot of coffee.

"Please!" I interjected, as Papa poured hot coffee

into our cups. "This is getting us nowhere. We have five primary suspects. You can debate all night whether or not the crimes are connected, but the fact remains that these five people are all we have to work with. The prosecution may rest its case as early as tomorrow afternoon. After that, I'm going to have to stand up in front of the jury and present my defense. We must come up with a plan."

"I've spent days trying to dig up dirt on these so-called suspects of yours," Samuel said, looking bleak. "It hasn't gotten us very far."

"I agree, Sarah," put in Robert testily. "As usual, you've bitten off more than you can chew. I warned you not to take this case in the first place, but you were too obstinate to listen. Now you're paying the price for being so confounded stubborn."

"Calm down, everyone," Papa admonished, silencing Robert with a look. "Recriminations aren't going to help. We're here to decide how best to construct Chin's defense. Sarah's right; she's the one who's going to be in the line of fire. For her sake, we must stop arguing and settle on a strategy."

"Sorry, little sister," Samuel said quietly. "All right, what course do you propose to follow?"

I had been considering this question while the men squabbled amongst themselves. I had finally reached the conclusion that the only logical option was to launch a three-pronged attack.

"First, we must ascertain why Pierce Godfrey met with Lucius Arlen at the hospital that night," I began, ticking each action off on a finger. "Second, we have to determine if Margaret Barlow was also at the hospital during this critical time period, or if Nurse Harbetter was somehow mistaken. Third, we should question the suspects' neighbors to learn if anyone saw Dora Clemens the morning of her death. There can be little doubt she left her boardinghouse at eight o'clock to meet with the killer. According to her friend, she fully expected this person to give her a large amount of money."

"Instead, she was murdered," Samuel put in. "Blackmail is a dangerous game."

Papa nodded thoughtfully. "Sarah's right, you know. If we could trace Dora's movements that morning, they might well lead us to the killer."

"It won't be easy," I said, pleased that he agreed with my strategy. "I've already spoken to the Godfreys' neighbors, but they deny seeing a girl fitting Dora's description that morning."

"What made you start with the Godfreys?" Samuel asked curiously.

"It's obvious she wants to clear her friend Pierce Godfrey of suspicion," said Robert, an acerbic edge to his voice. "Lately they seem to have become very—close."

"Oh, for heaven's sake, Robert!" I exclaimed. "I'm weary of your innuendos. A man's life is at stake. If you can't add anything constructive to the discussion, then keep silent."

Robert's face colored. He started to retort, then

noticed my father and brother watching him and instead lowered his head to his coffee.

"Just because no one remembers seeing the girl doesn't mean she didn't visit the Godfreys that morning," Papa pointed out. "It's too bad we can't talk to their servants."

"You know, I think we can," Samuel said, his handsome face breaking into a sudden grin. "As it happens, both Godfrey brothers belong to the Bohemian Club. Since I'm also a member, I'd say that provides me with a good enough excuse to pay them a social call. Especially when I know they're not home," he added with a wink. "If I play my cards right, I should be able to wheedle some information out of the servants."

"That's a wonderful idea, Samuel," I exclaimed, then looked at my father. Allowing Papa to use his connections in city government to obtain information was one thing. Asking him to go to his old friend's home and question his servants behind Barlow's back was quite another. At this point, however, I couldn't let niceties stand in the way of saving my client.

"Papa, would you consider trying the same ruse at the Barlow house? Their servants know you so well after all these years. They might feel more comfortable talking to you than to Samuel or me."

My father leaned back in his chair and closed his eyes. After a few moments, he opened them again and reluctantly nodded his head. "I suppose I can, if I must."

"Thank you, Papa. I wouldn't ask if it weren't so

important." I turned to Robert. "I'd like you to visit the hospital again tomorrow morning and try to verify Nurse Harbetter's story about seeing Mrs. Barlow. Better yet, see if you can find anyone who saw Margaret in the kitchen with Arlen that evening."

"Again? Oh, all right," he agreed without much enthusiasm. "But that still leaves us with why Pierce Godfrey met with Lucius Arlen that night."

"I'll take care of that," I said.

Robert's eyebrows rose. "And just how do you plan to pull off that little maneuver?"

"We're running out of time," I said, getting to my feet. It was well after midnight, time we were in bed. Tomorrow would be a busy day for us all.

"The quickest way to obtain information is to go straight to the source," I added matter-of-factly. "After court tomorrow, I'll pay Mr. Godfrey a visit and ask him."

CHAPTER TWELVE

As it happened, Pierce saved me a trip to his office that afternoon. I was surprised—and yes, I admit, pleased—to see him enter the courtroom and take a seat in the gallery several rows behind Mama and Celia. Catching my eye, he rose and started toward the defense table. Beside me, Robert gave a little groan, but I paid him no mind.

"You've been having a rough time of it, I hear,"

Pierce said, after he and Robert exchanged more or less polite greetings. "The press has been merciless." His face creased in a smile. "Although I seem to recall someone once telling me not to believe everything I read in the newspapers."

"I only wish more people would heed that advice." I paused, then said impulsively, "Have lunch with me this afternoon, Pierce, and I'll bring you up to date on what's really been going on."

His answering smile sent unwelcome warmth to my cheeks. "Nothing would please me more, Sarah. Until then?"

I nodded, not trusting myself to speak. The man was a philanderer, an adulterer, a liar—if only by omission—and God only knew what else. He was also beguiling, considerate and incredibly handsome. A lethal combination, against which—God help me!—even I did not appear to be totally immune.

"Have you any idea how pathetic you behave whenever that man is around?" Robert remarked, after Pierce returned to his seat. "It's disgusting!"

"Don't be ridiculous." Despite this spirited response, I secretly feared Robert might not be too far off in his assessment, a fact that did not please me one iota. Still, it was no business of his how I behaved toward my friends. "Jealousy does not become you."

"Jealousy!" he exclaimed, his sunburned face turning crimson. "Of what, you irritating, egotistical woman? If you think I give a damn who you make yourself a fool over, you're even more—"

Fortunately, the Scot—his *r*'s rolling along in excellent form—was cut off as Chin was ushered to the defense table. He wore his customary dark tunic and trousers, his hair fashioned into a long queue. Ignoring the packed gallery as if it was beneath his notice, he nodded sourly and took his seat between us.

Dormer stood and called Ah Kwung, a cross-looking Chinese man, to the stand. This caused an immediate stir in the courtroom. Citizens of Chinatown rarely gave evidence in the white man's courtroom; in some instances they were forbidden by law to testify altogether.

As the witness walked to the front of the courtroom, Chin half rose from his seat and began shouting at Ah in a furious torrent of Chinese.

"Silence!" the judge commanded, banging his gavel with authority. "If you cannot restrain your client, Miss Woolson, I will have him removed from the courtroom."

Ignoring the judge, Chin continued his harangue, all the while shaking his fist at Ah as if eager to engage him in mortal combat. It took the combined efforts of Robert and myself to force our client back into his seat.

Fixing Chin with an equally baleful scowl, Ah Kwung acknowledged that he had known the defendant since they'd arrived in San Francisco some fifteen years ago. He went on to portray Chin as a liar and a thief, a man as likely to stab you in the back as to say hello.

Upon cross-examination, I established that Ah and

Chin were old enemies who had once fought over the affections of the same young woman. In the end, the girl had wisely chosen another man altogether, but Ah and Chin's animosity had grown and festered with the years. I glanced toward the jury and decided that at best I had merely nullified Ah's testimony. But I was growing weary of engaging in a solely defensive battle. In three days I had done nothing to cast doubt on my client's guilt!

Dormer next called upon a succession of hospital board members who had observed the last fight between Chin and Arlen that fatal Monday afternoon. Robert and I took turns cross-examining these witnesses. We did our best to neutralize their testimony, but as they were basically describing what I, too, had witnessed, our efforts were less than spectacular.

After the third board member was excused, Judge Carlton called the noon recess and the courtroom quickly cleared. Pierce and I exited through the side door that Robert and I now used exclusively to avoid reporters.

As I professed to have little appetite, we chose a small French patisserie located across the street from the courthouse. After we'd been served coffee and an assortment of pastries, Pierce regarded me speculatively.

"All right, Sarah, to what do I owe this honor? I don't for one moment believe you suggested we have lunch together because you've missed my company."

I had already made up my mind that professionalism—and honesty—was my best approach. "I have a difficult question to ask, Pierce. Actually, three difficult questions."

"That sounds intriguing. What do you want to know?"

"First, why have you and your brother kept your ownership of the warehouse on Battery Street a secret?"

He looked surprised. "That's a strange thing to ask. Why on earth do you care?"

"I understand the building stood vacant for more than eight years. You must have been pleased when the hospital board showed an interest in leasing it."

His face lit with sudden comprehension. "So that's it. You think Leonard and I were so desperate to rent that old place, we killed three people to clinch the deal."

Put like that, the notion sounded ludicrous. Still, I pressed on. "We're engaged in a murder trial, Pierce. We have to investigate every possibility."

"Of course you do," he answered in mock solemnity. "No matter how preposterous they seem."

"Be that as it may, I would still like to know why you chose to keep your ownership of the warehouse a secret."

"Oh, for God's sake, Sarah, think about it! My brother's wife led the group in charge of renting the new hospital facility. How would it have looked if they'd known her husband owned the warehouse they wished to lease?" He held up a hand. "Before you raise a din about nepotism and unfair business tactics, know that neither Leonard nor I had anything to do with the lease negotiations. They were handled exclusively by our representative." He reached into his pocket and pulled out a card. "If you doubt my word, you can check with him yourself."

He sipped his coffee, still angry, but apparently satisfied he had won the first round. "What's your second question? You said there were three."

"I understand you've lost several ships over the past two years, and this has led your company into grave financial difficulties. Yet, as we both know, you've recently put in an order for six new vessels."

For a long moment he said nothing as his dark eyes bored unflinchingly into mine. "Let me see if I've got this right. Because we were in danger of losing our company, Leonard and I decided to resort to whatever means necessary—including murder, evidently—to lease our warehouse." His sober expression turned to one of wry amusement. "Do you know how much money the hospital pays us for renting the warehouse, Sarah?"

"No, but I—"

"Allow me to enlighten you. In one year, the income we receive from the hospital is enough to run Godfrey Shipping for about three months—if we're lucky. Believe me, nothing is left over from the lease money to buy one new ship, much less a small fleet."

I felt my face grow warm at his condescending tone. "Then how were you able to turn things around so expeditiously?"

"For a start, all our ships—including their cargoes—are generously insured. Then there's a little thing called a bank loan. Surely you've heard of those, Sarah?"

"You must have good friends in the financial community to obtain a bank loan for a company facing bankruptcy," I replied, ignoring his sarcasm.

"I have my share." He swallowed more coffee. "Not that it's any of your business, but we obtained the loan from the First National Gold Bank of San Francisco, authorized, I might add, by Matthew Grady himself."

Matthew Grady. The name rang a bell. Of course, I thought, making the connection. Grady was the name embossed on one of the cards I'd taken from Lucius Arlen's office. I was surprised I hadn't recognized it at once. Grady was one of the city's most influential bankers. Pierce might be lying, but why fabricate a story Samuel could verify in five minutes?

"Question number three?" he went on coolly.

I steeled myself. "Why did you meet with Lucius Arlen at the hospital the night he was poisoned?"

His lips curled in a mocking smile. "Well, well, you are well informed. Have you taken to having me followed? I wouldn't put it past you."

"You were seen by a nurse in Arlen's office," I told him, controlling my temper with difficulty.

"I see." He drummed long fingers on the table. "All right, Sarah. Since you seem so eager to pry into my affairs, Lucius Arlen brokered the loan application

276

between Godfrey Shipping and the bank. He has acted on our behalf on and off for the past several years, especially when we wished to keep a low profile. Let's just say Leonard and I preferred our dealings with the bank to remain private."

"Yes, I can see why you would." I studied his face but could detect no sign of duplicity. But then Pierce Godfrey was a master at masking his emotions. "Can you prove that was why you met with Arlen that night?"

"No, of course I can't prove it. I just told you we didn't want our competitors—or the confounded newspapers—getting wind of the loan. I met with Arlen that night to finalize the details of our agreement with the bank."

By now he appeared thoroughly annoyed and was probably as repulsed as I was at the thought of food. Still, we went through the motions of eating, although we barely spoke a word to each other and made little dent in the excellent pastries set before us.

It was a wretched lunch. I'd obtained the information I'd come for, yet I felt dispirited and strangely empty as I returned alone to the courtroom.

Taking my seat at the defense table, I ignored Robert's inquisitive looks and glanced around the gallery, not surprised when I saw no sign of Pierce. After our little tête-à-tête, I doubted our paths would cross again anytime soon. I did spy Adelina French and Reverend Prescott seated across the aisle from my family, and I was delighted to see Samuel making his way to sit with Mama and Celia. They both smiled and gave me a wave.

A moment later, an unusually sober-looking Chin was escorted to our table. He silently took his usual seat between Robert and me. When I asked him a question about this afternoon's session, he merely shook his head, as if he cared little about the outcome of the proceedings. Lord, give me patience, I prayed, wondering yet again if any novice defense attorney had ever been cursed with a more fractious client!

That afternoon, yet more witnesses testified to the acrimonious relationship between Chin and Lucius Arlen. They were followed by an accountant who had been hired by the police to examine the hospital's accounts. He described several discrepancies he'd found in the books, all of them illicit items entered in Mr. Chin's name.

Under cross-examination, the accountant reluctantly agreed it was possible the items could have been entered by someone else, without the cook's knowledge. It was a hollow victory. The jurors' expressions left little doubt they considered this explanation improbable. Strangely, not one word had been said about the thousands of dollars missing from the hospital fund, just Chin's bogus orders for his kitchen. I debated raising this subject with the witness, then decided to let the matter rest, at least for now.

An expectant murmur filled the courtroom when Margaret Barlow was called to the stand. Every eye in the gallery followed her progress down the center aisle as she walked, head held high, to the front of the room. Mrs. Barlow looked elegant in a forest-green taffeta gown, with a long cuirass bodice. The front of her skirt was trimmed with pleated flounces, while the back was equipped with a particularly large bustle, an accessory that forced her to sit uncomfortably straight and well forward in the witness chair. On her carefully styled hair she wore a small green velvet hat, tilted becomingly to one side of her face.

Because of her place in San Francisco society—as well as her husband's position as superior court judge for the county of San Francisco—Dormer treated Mrs. Barlow with considerably more deference than he'd shown previous witnesses. With embarrassing obsequiousness, he asked her to describe the fights she had witnessed between Chin and the accountant, especially the row they'd had the day Arlen was presumed to have been poisoned.

With an uncomfortable glance in my direction, Margaret depicted Chin's mercurial temperament, then related the brawl he'd had with Mr. Arlen while she'd been conducting a tour of the hospital. She described how anxious the accountant had been to speak to her after the fight, saying she'd had to put him off because of a previous appointment. In the end, she'd agreed to meet with Mr. Arlen the following morning.

"Did you have any idea what was upsetting Mr. Arlen?" Dormer asked.

"From his manner, I presumed it had something to do with the hospital's accounts. He was adamant he would discuss the matter with no one but me."

"Since Mr. Arlen had just accused Mr. Chin of being a thief, do you think it reasonable to assume he had discovered some spurious entries made in Mr. Chin's name?"

"Objection," I called out. "The witness cannot speculate on what was bothering Mr. Arlen, or what, if anything, he'd found in the books."

"Sustained," Judge Carlton agreed.

"My apologies," Dormer said with a smug smile, and thanking his witness, he returned to his seat.

Before I stood to cross-examine, Carlton looked at his timepiece and declared that, as the hour was growing late, it was time to adjourn for the day. If I wished, I could conduct my cross-examination of Mrs. Barlow on Monday.

"Have you any more witnesses to present, Mr. Dormer?" he asked the prosecuting attorney.

"No, sir," Dormer informed him, looking serenely confident that he had already presented far more evidence than was necessary to prove the defendant's guilt.

The judge turned to me, saying in a clipped voice, "When you have concluded your cross-examination of this witness, Miss Woolson, I expect you to be prepared to open the defense's case. Is that understood?"

"Yes, sir," I answered, keeping my tone civil. "We'll be ready."

"You'd better be," came his ill-mannered reply. His skeptical expression proclaimed his grave doubt that I was capable of any such feat. With a dismissive shake of his head, Judge Carlton banged his gavel. "Court is adjourned."

A s we had arranged the night before, Papa, Samuel, Robert and I met at our house that night to discuss last-minute strategies for Chin's defense. Robert and I brought my father up to date on the day's court session, after which Samuel related visiting the Godfrey house that morning. As planned, he'd chosen a time when neither brother was present, and in their absence he'd been able to question half a dozen servants. No one remembered seeing Dora Clemens the morning of her death.

"What about you, Papa?" I asked, praying he had something more substantial to report.

Papa didn't answer for several moments. His face was gray and somber, his lips drawn into a tight thin line.

"Papa? Are you all right?" Samuel asked.

"No, Samuel, I'm not. At the moment, I hardly feel I shall ever be all right again. According to one of the Barlows' maids, Dora Clemens visited the judge's house the morning of her death."

It took Samuel, Robert and me a moment to absorb this bombshell. I was the first to recover my wits.

"Whom did she ask to see?"

"No one seems to know. The servants were preparing for a dinner party that night, and the household was in some disorder. The maid I spoke to hadn't actually let Miss Clemens into the house, but she remembered seeing a girl of Dora's description entering the morning room. I questioned a footman and several other maids, but no one else remembered seeing her."

"What if the maid is mistaken?" Robert wanted to know.

"I only wish she were," was Papa's quiet reply. "But she described Dora's hat and coat—the same costume Sarah said she was wearing when she arrived at the hospital. And the girl's bright red hair was unmistakable."

"Well, then," Samuel said. "It looks as if we just narrowed the field down to three suspects: Judge Barlow, his wife and Reverend Prescott."

We sat silently for several minutes, each of us lost in our own thoughts.

"Sarah had lunch with Pierce Godfrey on Friday," Robert announced, breaking the silence. "Although so far she hasn't seen fit to tell me what they talked about."

"Don't be overdramatic, Robert." Ignoring his sputtered protests, I related my conversation with Pierce the previous afternoon, including his explanation for why he had met with Lucius Arlen that fatal Monday night.

"Likely story," Robert grumbled when I'd finished.

"Actually, it is." I reached inside my briefcase and pulled out the business cards I'd taken from Arlen's office. "Pierce said Arlen dealt directly with Matthew

Grady, the president of the Gold Bank. I found this card behind the accountant's desk. It's embossed with Grady's name and position at the bank, and it bears the handwritten notations 'PG' and 'Tues. 3:30.'" I handed it to my father.

"I suppose the initials could stand for Pierce Godfrey," Papa commented, examining the card. "There's only one way to know for sure. I'll arrange to meet with Grady tomorrow. He won't be free to discuss details of the meeting, of course—assuming it took place as young Godfrey claims—but at least we'll know one way or the other."

We spent some time going over the pros and cons concerning the guilt of each suspect, but we kept coming back to Margaret Barlow. We all agreed she had motive; once Margaret took Caroline Godfrey's place as chairwoman of the board, it would have been simplicity itself for her to embezzle money from the hospital fund. When Reverend Halsey became a threat to the project—and consequently to her pilfering—he, too, had to be eliminated. Arlen's insistence on speaking to no one but Margaret the day of our tour also pointed to her culpability. And if Dora Clemens witnessed Margaret poisoning Arlen's coffee, it would explain her reason for visiting the Barlows' house the morning of her death—to demand blackmail!

Mrs. Barlow also possessed the means to commit the crimes. Margaret's biological father had been a chemist—very likely, the "dear friend" she admitted helping as a young girl. What better way to learn about

283

medicines—and poisons—than from a chemist? Then there was the proficient manner in which she'd treated my facial lacerations after I was hit by Bert Corrigan's rock.

As for opportunity, well, Margaret had as much chance to poison the four victims as any of our other suspects. She was at Caroline Godfrey's house the night of the charity dinner, and she was seen at the hospital the night Arlen was poisoned. Most damaging, of course, was Dora Clemens's visit to Margaret's home that morning.

Taken as a whole, the evidence against Margaret was compelling. Still, I found it difficult to cast her in the role of murderer.

"What about Judge Barlow?" I asked, feeling obliged to play devil's advocate. "The fact that he owns a string of sweatshops confirms his greed. And it will require a great deal of money to build their lavish home in Menlo Park."

"Good points, Sarah," Samuel agreed. "Except that Tobias wasn't seen at the hospital the night Arlen was poisoned. His wife was."

Papa stirred. "I've known Tobias for years, and I doubt he'd know a poisonous plant if one were thrust in his face."

"Perhaps not, but there are any number of books on the subject," I replied. "Anyone who puts his mind to it can easily learn. I did. And we don't know for a fact he wasn't at the hospital that night, only that no one saw him there."

"You're both forgetting Prescott," Robert remarked. "I wouldn't call his reputation exactly sterling."

This set off yet another round of discussion, which got us nowhere. When all was said and done, Margaret Barlow remained our primary suspect. I didn't like it, but my job was to defend my client, and that meant utilizing every means at my disposal. Somehow I had to offer the jury an alternative theory for how Lucius Arlen met his death, hopefully creating enough uncertainty in their minds that they would return a verdict of not guilty.

I didn't deceive myself; there was little likelihood this strategy would succeed. After all, I'd be asking the jury to chose between a belligerent Chinese cook and a respected society matron. Yet I had little choice. Margaret Barlow represented my best, perhaps my only, hope of clearing my client. In all good conscience, I could not allow my respect, and genuine affection, for the woman to deter me from my duty.

As I took my seat at the defense table on Monday morning, Robert met my somber gaze with one of his own. "Are you ready?" he asked.

"Yes, I'm ready," I told him with resolve. "I take no pleasure in what I must do, but I'm prepared to see it through to the end."

Although Mama and Celia were, as far as I knew, unaware of our defense strategy, they both bore grim expressions. As each of them caught my eye, they made a gallant effort to smile encouragingly. I wasn't fooled for one moment. Even they knew the bleakness of our position.

I turned toward the front of the room as Chin was led to our table. This morning, I sensed a new tension to his body as he took his usual seat. Even he seemed to appreciate that today was different: this morning his life hung in the balance. I leaned over to whisper words of encouragement, but he shook his head.

"Those men," he said, nodding toward the jury. "They no believe you. Think Chinaman guilty no matter what you say."

"That remains to be seen," I told him with a confidence I was a long way from feeling. "I can promise you one thing: we won't give up without a fight."

The clerk recalled Mrs. Tobias Barlow to the stand, and again the courtroom buzzed with anticipation. Today, Mrs. Barlow wore a dark gray gown with far less bustle than the dress she'd worn the previous Friday. Evidently, the expediencies of the courtroom—and her comfort on the witness stand—had won out over fashion.

"Good morning, Mrs. Barlow." I said, rising to begin my cross-examination. I repressed a stab of guilt as she responded with an innocent, even trusting, smile. "Regarding your testimony last Friday afternoon, were you able to meet with Mr. Arlen the day after you and Judge Barlow consulted with your architect?"

Margaret's gaze dropped to her lap. "No, Miss Woolson. Mr. Arlen did not come to the hospital the next morning. He'd seemed so upset the previous day that I considered visiting him at his rooms, but my mother was ill and I was reluctant to leave her. I thought I might see him at your parents' dinner party that evening, but of course he was too ill to attend."

"So, Mr. Arlen never had an opportunity to tell you the cause of his concern."

"No, he didn't. And I will regret it for the rest of my life. If only I had—"

"Perhaps you would be so kind as to relate your reasons for hiring Mr. Chin for the position of hospital chef?"

She looked startled at this abrupt change of subject but obligingly listed Chin's references, including his employment as cook for some of San Francisco's finer restaurants. As she did, I noticed several jurors raise questioning eyebrows, as if they found it difficult to picture the truculent cook actually working in such establishments. Mrs. Barlow admitted that although Chin's temper was notorious, no one took it seriously.

"Then you weren't overly alarmed when Mr. Arlen and Mr. Chin threatened each other that afternoon?" I asked.

"It was unsettling, of course. But it never occurred to me that Mr. Chin might actually harm Mr. Arlen. They were always bickering. It meant nothing."

"I'm pleased to hear you say so, Mrs. Barlow." I made a pretense of examining my notes. "Now, I believe you stated that you and your husband met with your architect at his Kearney Street office that afternoon. Would you please tell the court what time you concluded your business?"

Once again, she looked taken aback. "Let me see. As I recall, the judge and I left sometime after six."

"And where did you go from there?"

At this, her green eyes grew wide. "I don't understand. What can that have to do with Mr. Arlen's death?"

"I agree," Dormer said, rising to his feet. "Your Honor, where Judge and Mrs. Barlow went after their appointment is none of Miss Woolson's business."

"I concur, Mr. Dormer. Is there a purpose behind these questions, counselor?" Judge Carlton asked, embellishing the word counselor with sarcastic emphasis.

"Yes, Your Honor, there is. If you'll be patient—"

"I have little patience when it comes to wasting the court's time, Miss Woolson," he interrupted sourly. "Please come to the point—if there is one."

"Yes, sir." I turned back to Margaret. "Mrs. Barlow, please tell us where you went after leaving your architect's office that evening."

"Why, I went home, of course."

"And Judge Barlow? Did he return home with you?"

"No. After dropping me off, I believe he went on to his club."

"I see. And what did you do after you arrived home?"

"Your Honor, objection!" Dormer called out in an aggrieved tone. "This line of questioning is inexcusable!"

"What do you have to say for yourself, madam?" the

judge demanded, subjecting me to a withering glare.

"I assure Your Honor that Mrs. Barlow's actions that evening are pertinent to my client's case. If you'll allow me a few more questions, I promise it will become clear."

"I'll give you five more minutes," the judge spat. "Not one second longer. Now, get on with it."

"I went to my boudoir," Margaret said, no longer bothering to hide her anger at what must have seemed a cruel betrayal of our friendship.

"Did anyone see you? Your mother, or your maid, perhaps?"

She took a deep breath. "No, I saw no one. I rested in my room until dinner was served around eight-thirty."

Out of the corner of my eye, I noticed Dormer beginning to stand. Before he could object, I hurried on.

"As it happens, someone did see you that night, Mrs. Barlow—actually the head nurse at the Women and Children's Hospital. You were observed going into the hospital kitchen around seven-thirty, the time the police believe Lucius Arlen was poisoned. It has also come to my attention that you are well versed in herbal medicines and that you had good reason to wish Mr. Arlen dead."

The courtroom sat in stunned silence, then suddenly erupted with noise. I heard a woman cry out and realized Mrs. French was on her feet. Beside her, Reverend Prescott was regarding me with incredulity, then growing anger.

Carlton banged his gavel but seemed unable to restore order. Angrily, he called for a brief recess, warning there were to be no further outbursts when court resumed.

I had just returned to the defense table when a shrill voice called out, "How could you do that to my daughter? You are trying to destroy her!"

Adelina French was standing behind me, so distraught she was shaking. Her beautiful eyes were filled with tears. "I never thought you capable of such cruelty!"

Adelina's outcry had drawn the attention of several reporters. An irate Reverend Prescott was also approaching us.

I took the agitated woman's arm. "Please, Mrs. French, allow me to buy you a cup of coffee. It would be best if we discussed this privately."

As I led Mrs. French out of the courtroom, I noticed Reverend Prescott being waylaid by the members of the press. Hurrying outside, I took Margaret's mother to the same patisserie across the street where Pierce and I had lunched the previous Friday, and I hastily ordered coffee and pastries. To my dismay, Adelina continued to cry into a lace handkerchief.

"I don't see why you brought me here," she said, dabbing at her eyes. "There is nothing you can say that can undo the damage you inflicted in that courtroom."

"I'm sorry, Mrs. French, truly I am." I felt like a perfect villain. "I know I've caused you and your daughter a great deal of pain. Please, try to understand: my first duty is to my client—and his life is at stake."

We stopped speaking as the waiter delivered our coffee and pastries. I had ordered the food for Mrs. French's sake, but I had to admit it looked tempting, especially as I had not taken time for breakfast that morning.

"What if your client isn't innocent?" Adelina asked when the waiter left. "Have you thought of that? If he is guilty—as everyone but you believes—then a good, honest woman's reputation will have been ruined for no reason whatsoever."

I understood her distress. She was a mother, and I was destroying her child. If the situation were reversed, I knew I would feel the same anger and helplessness.

"I'm simply searching for the truth, Mrs. French."

"No! That's a lie! All you care about is saving the life of that wretched Chinaman. But why you've chosen my daughter as your scapegoat, I will never understand or forgive. The very idea of Margaret murdering someone is ludicrous. She can hardly bear to kill a fly. And she wouldn't know baneberry or jimsonweed if they were served to her on a platter."

"Please, Mrs. French," I said, aware we were beginning to annoy other patrons. Looking around, my companion noticed the unwelcomed attention we were receiving and self-consciously reached for her coffee cup. I noticed her hands were shaking as she lifted it to her lips.

"It's rather strong," she said with a little grimace.

Adding more cream and sugar, she took another sip, then returned the cup to its saucer. "Please, Miss Woolson, I beg you to cease this terrible attack on my daughter. It is entirely without foundation. What possible reason could Margaret have for killing Mr. Arlen?"

"Whoever poisoned him did it for money and to save themselves from exposure. When I went over the books, I found the same discrepancies Mr. Arlen must have discovered. Believe me, they were far more serious than the paltry entries made in my client's name. Thousands of dollars are missing from the hospital fund, none of which could have been stolen by Mr. Chin, since he had no access to the books."

"I don't believe you! This is the first time I've heard of missing money. Besides, my daughter has no need to steal. The judge has provided her with a fine home, servants, even a new country residence. Margaret lacks for nothing." She lifted her chin in a defiant challenge. "I would like to see these so-called discrepancies for myself—if they actually exist."

I silently bent down to where I had placed my briefcase beside my chair, searching until I found the entries I'd copied from Arlen's ledgers. Straightening, I handed her the documents, then took a sip of my own coffee. Adelina was right, it was strong. While she scanned the papers, I added sugar and cream to my cup, then succumbed to an apple dumpling, which was every bit as delicious as it appeared.

Shaking her head, Adelina handed back the papers.

"I have no head for figures, but if, as you say, funds are missing, Margaret cannot possibly have taken them. You do not truly know her, Miss Woolson, or you would appreciate that her honesty is beyond reproach."

"Mrs. French," I said, washing down the last of my apple dumpling with more coffee. "I'm an attorney, bound by the rules of my profession to do everything possible to save my client. I know the murderer isn't Mr. Chin, and I sincerely hope it isn't Margaret. If she truly is innocent, I promise to do everything in my power to restore her good name."

"By then it will be too late! Her reputation will be ruined. There will always be doubts, whispers behind her back, cruel gossip." She looked at me pleadingly. "If it's a matter of money, Miss Woolson, I am well able to—"

"No, Mrs. French, it's not a matter of money." I knew she was too distressed to realize she had just offered me an illegal bribe. "As I said, it's about finding the truth." I glanced at my timepiece. "Oh my, I didn't realize it was so late. I have to get back to court."

I picked up my briefcase and, looking again into those sad green eyes, added, "I'm sorry, Mrs. French. Believe me it was never my intention to hurt you—or Margaret."

I paid the bill and was walking out the door when I bumped headlong into Reverend Prescott.

"Oh, it's you," he said, favoring me with a sour look. "I'm trying to find Mrs. French."

"We had coffee," I said and motioned to the table I had just vacated. When I would have passed by him through the door, he blocked my way.

"You were very hard on Margaret, Miss Woolson. I can think of no excuse for bullying her in that manner."

"I realize it seems cruel, Reverend Prescott, but I must do what I feel is best for my client."

I was taken aback when the minister's normally pleasant face twisted into something far more menacing. "You would destroy Mrs. French's daughter because of a—a worthless Chinaman? What kind of a person are you, Miss Woolson, that you could stoop so low?"

I felt my hackles rise at this blatant display of prejudice. "I understand your distress, Reverend Prescott, but that's no excuse for you to—"

Suddenly, he moved closer, and I retreated several steps back into the pastry shop. "I'm warning you, Miss Woolson," he said, his compelling eyes dark with fury. "I will not stand by and allow you to badger Mrs. Barlow. Margaret is the only family Mrs. French has left. I won't see her destroyed by a stupid, callous woman who fancies herself an attorney."

With that, he pushed by me to join Adelina, who sat weeping at the table. I watched as he put a consoling hand on her shoulder and whispered something in her ear, then I turned and hurried from the shop.

As I crossed the street, I wondered if ensuring that justice was served would always entail enraging and, in some instances, injuring the innocent. Then I realized true blame must lie with individuals who choose to break the law. Their actions inevitably affect their family and friends. If Margaret did turn out to be the killer, she was the one responsible for her mother's pain and suffering, not my efforts to defend my client.

It wasn't until I stepped inside the courthouse that it hit me. I'd been so distracted by Adelina's distress, the significance of our conversation had not occurred to me until that moment. Now the answers I'd been struggling to find struck me like a physical blow. And, heaven help us, what a blow it was!

Ignoring the bustle of people around me, I sank onto a bench inside the domed entry hall. Leaning back my head, I closed my eyes and shuffled facts, ideas, assumptions around in my mind, adding the bits I'd just discovered to others I'd previously discarded as unimportant. I forced myself to think objectively, to concentrate on the details of the four murders as I now knew them to be. No matter how I looked at it, I continued to come up with the same answer. But, dear Lord, could it possibly be true?

Try as I might, I could detect no holes in my theory. An explanation for such appalling wickedness—yes, that remained to be revealed, if never to be completely understood. But the motive, means and opportunity all fit neatly into place. This time, I was confident there could be no mistake.

CHAPTER THIRTEEN

"W here the devil have you been?" Robert demanded, as I took my seat beside him at the defense table. "You tore out of here so fast I didn't have time to ask where you're going with this cross-examination. I know we agreed to target Margaret Barlow, but this is no way to get her to confess, if that's what you're trying to do."

Before I could answer him, Chin arrived, silently taking his usual seat at our table. If anything, his expression looked even more grim than it had earlier that morning. I wondered if he could already feel the noose tightening around his neck. I was tempted to share my discovery with him, then reminded myself there was a wide chasm between knowing the truth and proving it in a court of law. It was far too premature to tell anyone, even Robert, until I was certain I could prove my suspicions.

I took a long sip of water from one of the glasses the bailiff regularly placed on our table, then rose as Margaret Barlow was called back to the stand. Out of the corner of my eye, I saw Adelina French and Reverend Prescott taking their seats in the gallery. Adelina's red eyes stood out against her pale face, and she leaned heavily on Prescott's arm. Several rows behind them, Pierce Godfrey sat with his brother, Leonard. Catching my eye, Pierce surprised me by smiling. After our less than cordial lunch the previous afternoon, I hadn't expected pleasantries from a man I'd all but accused of being a murderer. But this was hardly the time to speculate on the eccentricities of the male mind.

As I put down my water glass, I spied Papa, Samuel and Charles entering the courtroom. My father gave me a encouraging wink, as he and my brothers took seats by Mama and Celia, but he couldn't totally mask his concern. More than anyone else, Papa recognized the hopelessness of our cause. He would never come right out and say it, but I knew he felt I had little, if any, chance of winning Chin's case.

"Miss Woolson?" Judge Carlton said impatiently. "The court is waiting."

"I'm sorry, Your Honor," I answered, and turned to face Mrs. Barlow.

Further delay was pointless, I told myself. Even if I had hours to come up with a strategy, it wouldn't change the fact that I lacked one shred of evidence to prove my theory. That being the case, there was only one possible course open to me. For Chin's sake I prayed it would work!

Margaret watched me warily from the witness stand, no doubt terrified of what I might say. I smiled in an attempt to put her at ease but was not wholly surprised when she didn't return the gesture. Plainly, Margaret Barlow no longer considered me a friend.

"Your Honor, I have no further questions for this witness," I announced, shocking my second chair as much as assistant district attorney Dormer and the judge. "I would, however, like to reserve the right to call Mrs. Barlow back at some future point in the trial."

Judge Carlton eyed me suspiciously. "Very well, Miss Woolson, you may reserve that right." He turned to Dormer. "Does the prosecution wish to call any more witnesses?"

Dormer was clearly baffled. "No, Your Honor. The prosecution rests its case."

"Miss Woolson, are you prepared to present your defense?" he queried, regarding me doubtfully over his thick spectacles.

"I am, Your Honor," I answered, displaying what I hoped was an air of confidence. "The defense calls as its first witness Mr. Kin Tsau."

"What in the name of all that's holy are you up to?" Robert whispered, as I walked over to glance at my notes.

"If all goes well, you'll know soon enough," I told him, refusing to be drawn into further conversation. I had noticed a dull ache developing between my eyes, and I took another long drink of water. Strange, it seemed to be growing uncomfortably stuffy in the usually chilly courtroom. Now, of all times, I could not allow nerves to get the better of me!

An anxious Kin Tsau took the stand and was sworn in. After attesting to his occupation as laundryman for the new Women and Children's Hospital, he obediently related his conversation with the cook the night Lucius Arlen had been poisoned. I was pleased when he went out of his way to emphasize the fact that Chin had left the hospital by seven o'clock.

I watched the jurors while Kin spoke, dismayed, if not surprised, to read distrust, skepticism and even outright amusement on their faces. I was certain not one of them believed a word of the laundryman's account.

When Dormer rose to conduct his cross-examination, it was all too obvious he shared the jury's opinion of my witness. With the court's permission, I'd asked the tong leader, Li Ying, to provide an interpreter to avoid misunderstandings by either side. Even this precaution was not enough to prevent Dormer from twisting Kin's words into pretzels.

With discouraging ease, he proceeded to inflict the same fate on my next four witnesses. These were the Chinese men Samuel and I had found in Chin's favorite gambling dens. One after another they testified the cook was with them at the time Arlen was supposedly being poisoned. One after another, Dormer distorted their words until the poor men were no longer sure what they'd seen.

So rapidly did Dormer dispatch my unfortunate witnesses, their combined testimony lasted barely more than an hour. The fact that he seemed to be having such a good time doing it fueled my anger, as well as my escalating headache. Every time one of his disparaging comments brought a titter from the spectators, he would dart a smile at the jury as if to say, What can you expect when your opponent puts imbeciles like this on the stand?

It was no more than I'd expected, but it rankled

nonetheless. I'd called upon these men hoping their honest stories would spark even a tiny glimmer of conscience within the twelve jurors. I had failed. Now I had no choice but to play my last and most perilous card. I refused to be deterred by the fact that I could be sanctioned—or even disbarred—for such behavior by the recently formed San Francisco Bar Association.

Before calling my next witness, I went back to the table for more water, only to find my glass empty.

"Here, drink mine," Robert said, handing me his glass. He examined me warily. "Sarah, are you ill? You look flushed."

"Don't be silly, Robert, I'm fine." Turning back to the judge, I said, "The defense calls upon Mr. Harold Peterson."

The Barlow's architect, a pale, pencil-thin man of about forty, looked uneasily about the courtroom as he took the stand. Speaking in short, clipped sentences, Mr. Peterson described his meeting with the Barlows on the Monday afternoon in question. He had spent about two hours with the couple, he testified, going over plans for their new country home. To the best of his recollection, they had left his office just before six o'clock. Mr. Peterson explained that he'd had an appointment with another client at six, so Dormer had little hope of shaking his testimony. After one or two attempts, the prosecutor excused Peterson without further cross-examination.

Again, I returned to the table for another drink of water from my glass—which the bailiff had by now kindly refilled. When I turned back to call my next witness, I suddenly lost my balance and would have fallen if Robert hadn't bolted forward to give me a helping hand. By now, concern was written all over his broad, open face. Hastily pulling myself together, I ordered my second chair back to his seat, lest the prosecution think I'd imbibed during the recess.

Baffled by my unexpected dizzy spell, I took care to plant my feet firmly on the floor as I called Miss Emily Harbetter as my next witness.

Nurse Harbetter—neatly attired in a dark blue muslin gown, a small, matching straw hat perched atop her graying hair—entered the courtroom and took her place on the stand. Unhampered by a cumbersome bustle, she was able to sit bolt upright in the chair, gazing at the spectators much like a school headmistress might examine her pupils.

Succinctly, the head nurse told of seeing Pierce Godfrey enter Mr. Arlen's office around seven o'clock the night the accountant was poisoned. She went on to describe how she had observed Mrs. Margaret Barlow entering the hospital kitchen some fifteen to twenty minutes later. Not surprisingly, this was greeted by exclamations from the spectators, as well as incredulous looks from the judge and both prosecutors.

Miles Dormer did his utmost to shake Nurse Harbetter's testimony, but about all he obtained was her reluctant admission that she'd seen little more than Mrs. Barlow's profile as she'd entered the kitchen that Monday night. On all other points, the head nurse not only proved Dormer's equal—deflecting those questions she obviously considered mindless—but once or twice using his own words to make him out a fool. These instances elicited so much laughter from the gallery—and even worse, the jury—that a very pink-faced Dormer could hardly get Nurse Harbetter off the stand quickly enough.

"So far so good," I told Robert, as I returned to my seat for yet another drink of water. Where in the world had this insatiable thirst come from? I wondered. And why did the room seem to be growing warmer by the minute?

Using a handkerchief to dab at the perspiration on my forehead, I started to call out my next witness, when the room unexpectedly tilted to one side. Holding fast to the edge of the table, I closed my eyes to stem a sudden rise of bile in my throat. When I opened my eyes again, Robert was trying to assist me into my chair.

"Robert, let go!" I told him under my breath, as the room finally righted itself. "It was just a momentary dizziness. I'm fine now."

Ignoring the fear on my colleague's face, I requested that Mrs. Tobias Barlow be called back to the stand.

Oddly, the murmurs of expectation that filled the room seemed to be coming to me from a great distance. Stranger still, I found it necessary to blink several times before Margaret came into clear focus as she entered the courtroom. I watched Judge Barlow sit forward in his seat as his wife walked toward the witness chair. Even Pierce and Leonard Godfrey's interests seemed to have been piqued. A few rows ahead of them, a pale Adelina French leaned closer to Reverend Prescott. He patted her hand as if in reassurance, then whispered something in her ear which seemed to ease her perturbation.

My family were all regarding me apprehensively. Indeed, Mama looked so upset I feared she might actually order the judge to stop the trial while she saw to her daughter's well-being. I gave her a confident smile, or at least I think I did. To be honest, everything seemed a bit fuzzy. I had the odd sensation I was seeing the room through someone else's eyes.

Very deliberately, I turned to face my witness. "Mrs. Barlow, you told the court earlier that you went directly home after your meeting with Mr. Peterson. Is that correct?"

"It is," she responded guardedly.

"Yet Nurse Harbetter testified she saw you enter the hospital kitchen that very evening. Would you please tell us how you managed to be in two places at the same time?"

Mrs. Barlow's eyes flew open in surprise. "But I didn't! I wasn't at the hospital that night. It isn't true!"

"Isn't it, Mrs. Barlow? Miss Harbetter was a nurse in the Crimean War. She's an intelligent, trained observer. Why would she lie about seeing you if it weren't true?"

"I don't know why she would say such a thing. I have the utmost respect for Miss Harbetter. I cannot imagine why she would make up such a story."

"My point exactly. Do you know what I believe, Mrs. Barlow? I believe you walked into the hospital kitchen that night to keep the meeting you'd arranged with Mr. Arlen earlier that day. While you waited for him to arrive, you brewed a pot of fresh coffee to mask the taste of the poisonous baneberry roots and berries you planned to slip into his cup."

"Objection!" Dormer cried out. "This is outrageous! Miss Woolson is attacking the witness."

Judge Carlton looked sharply at me, then at the prosecuting attorney. For the first time since the trial began, I saw a flicker of interest—and doubt—cross his granite-hard face.

"I will allow Miss Woolson to continue, Mr. Dormer," he pronounced. "At least for another question or two."

"Thank you, Your Honor," I said. I placed a hand over the right side of my face. That was peculiar—my voice had begun to echo in my ears. Perhaps Robert was right, I thought. I did feel slightly off color. Just a few more questions, I promised myself, and the entire matter would be settled one way or the other. Then I could go home, lie down in my bed, and place a cold cloth on my pounding forehead.

Once again the spectators were murmuring in the gallery, and I saw Robert lean forward in his seat, his face creased with worry. I tried to give him a reassuring nod, but my head felt as if it were made of lead; it simply did not want to move. Robert must have caught the startled expression on my face, because he rose suddenly from his chair. I finally managed a weak shake of my head, and he unwillingly sank back into the seat.

A soft cry from the witness stand tore my attention back to Margaret Barlow. The tears she'd been fighting to hold back were coursing down her paper-white face. I had to finish this now, I told myself. I had to keep applying pressure.

"While you waited for Mr. Arlen, you hid some baneberry in one of Mr. Chin's cupboards," I said. "You knew the police would find the poison when they searched the kitchen, didn't you, Mrs. Barlow?".

"No," Margaret cried, looking desperately around the room for support. Her eyes fastened pleadingly upon her husband. He started to get to his feet, then, at a warning look from Judge Carlton, sank angrily back down again.

"Your real father was a chemist, wasn't he, Mrs. Barlow? You gained your knowledge of poisonous herbs from him—an adoring father introducing his only child to the wonders, and dangers, of nature."

By now, Margaret was weeping so hard I doubt she heard a fraction of what I was saying. Still, I kept up my attack, ruthlessly spewing out accusations. Behind me, I heard the rush of newspaper reporters pushing their way to the front of the courtroom. From the corner of my eye I saw Dormer stand and protest, but for some reason I couldn't make out his words. Indeed, my own voice was almost unrecognizable. It was as if I were listening to someone else standing at the front of the courtroom pretending to be me.

"You used that knowledge to collect the plants you needed to poison Caroline Godfrey, Josiah Halsey, Lucius Arlen and Dora Clemens," I pressed on. "You deliberately ended the lives of four human beings—causing them to suffer a horrible, agonizing death."

From a great distance, I heard a woman scream. With enormous effort, I managed to turn my head toward the gallery. There, I saw Adelina French on her feet. Or was it Margaret? I couldn't tell—the two women were so alike.

"You're a devil!" Adelina screamed at me, her green eyes blazing.

Beside her, Reverend Prescott's expression was one of pure malevolence. In my dazed state, I could have sworn I was looking into the face of the devil himself.

"Stop torturing my daughter!" Adelina shrieked. "She has done nothing wrong."

Again the room seemed to tilt, and I felt my stomach lurch. I closed my eyes and gulped in deep breaths of air, willing myself to concentrate solely on Margaret's mother. As if through a fog, I saw my own mother's lips moving as she stared at me, her face frozen in fear. Beside her, Celia looked equally distressed. I saw Charles rise to his feet and, followed by Samuel, hurry toward the side aisle. Robert, too, was coming toward me. Even Chin was staring at me as if I'd taken leave of my senses.

"You're right, Mrs. French," I doggedly persisted. "Your daughter has done nothing wrong. It's you who is the monster. You murdered four people because you thought it was the only way to—" Dizzily, I pointed more or less in Prescott's direction "—to keep the love of the man you adore."

Prescott dropped his grip on Adelina's arm as if it had suddenly caught fire. "That's a lie," he shouted. "There's not a word of truth to any of this." He appealed to the judge. "For God's sake, stop her!"

Robert, his hand on my arm for support, pressed a glass of water to my lips. I swallowed greedily. "Sarah, you're ill," he implored. "You must sit down!"

"Almost through," I told him. "Another minute."

"Can't you see this woman is mad?" Adelina cried, her face twisted with hate. "She has no idea what she's saying."

"Oh, but I do. You're the master gardener, Mrs. French—you said yourself Margaret can't tell a flower from a weed. You learned—you learned all about poisonous plants from your first husband, the chemist. You make potions—and creams. Margaret used one on me when I was hit in—in the face by a rock. It worked—it worked very well."

Behind me, someone was pounding what sounded like a hammer, causing blinding pain to shoot through my head.

"You poisoned Caroline Godfrey so—so Margaret would be named head of the hospital board—giving you access to fundraising money. Josiah Halsey threatened your scheme, so you killed him. Arlen—Arlen discovered your embezzling and you poisoned his coffee—then hid baneberry in Chin's cupboard.

"Dora—poor Dora Clemens," I stumbled on, realizing my words were becoming slurred and disjointed, "saw you poison Arlen. Came to your house—demanded blackmail money. You killed her, too. It was you, not Margaret, Nurse Harbetter saw—saw going in—into the kitchen. You and Margaret—so alike—easy to confuse."

Oh, lord, I wished whoever was pounding that hammer would stop! There was so much confusion—so much noise. People were on their feet pressing forward, shouting. Flash powder exploded as reporters recorded the scene for tomorrow's papers. Through a confused haze, I saw Pierce leave his seat, his face grim and white. Then I lost sight of him as I attempted to block out the din, to press on.

"You murdered four people because—because of your obsession with Nicholas Prescott—an evil, corrupt man—who—who uses his—his clerical collar to cheat and steal—to debauch innocent young women."

"No! No! It's all lies!" Prescott yelled. "Why doesn't somebody stop her?" Adelina was reaching for him through her tears. He pushed her away so roughly, she stumbled against the bench and nearly fell to the floor. "I swear Adelina French means nothing to me. I had no part in this."

An uncomprehending expression crossed Adelina's lovely face. "Nicholas, this is no time for levity." Her tone was that of an exasperated but loving parent, admonishing an ill-behaved child. Then her voice rose, growing shrill as she fought to be heard over the court-room clamor. "You know you love me as much as I love you. You've told me so a thousand times. Look at all I've done for you."

"Get away from me, old woman. Why would I ever care for an ancient relic like you?"

Prescott continued to back away from her, forcing those sitting behind him on the bench to hastily vacate their seats. Adelina followed, clutching at him with frantic fingers.

"Nicholas—my darling, you're distraught," she screamed. "You can't mean that. Wait!"

"For God's sake, shut your mouth!" Grabbing her by the shoulders, he gave her a violent shake. "Listen to me, Adelina. You've done nothing for me. Absolutely nothing!"

I watched in fuzzy focus as Adelina's expression turned to shock, then profound hurt. Fresh tears filled her eyes. "But my darling, I've done *everything* for you. I killed my husband so we could be together. Then, when you told me to take my daughter and move West to avoid suspicion, I did as you asked. I even forgave you for all the years you made me wait before you finally came for me."

"Damn it all, woman, be still!" he hissed, giving her another shake. By now, Adelina and Prescott were surrounded by reporters. "Don't say one more word!"

Adelina seemed not to hear him. "You needed money to build a new church, and I found a way to obtain it for you. I stole from the hospital fund, I even sold jewelry that fool Tobias gave me so I'd keep his nasty secret about the sweatshops. I removed the people who would have stopped you from fulfilling your destiny. I did it all for you, my dearest, for your ministry. You've been chosen as God's emissary, Nicholas. No one must be permitted to stand in your way."

Distantly, I heard Prescott's continuing protests, the incessant, awful hammering, the cacophony of voices, the press of reporters, the blinding blaze of their flash powder. The room was spinning out of control, capturing me in a dizzying vortex. Then suddenly everything stopped, as the floor flew up and struck me in the face.

Robert was beside me, calling out my name. Then Pierce knelt by my other side. I thought I saw Charles and Samuel's faces floating disjointedly above me, but they kept fading in and out of my vision.

I tried to suck air into my lungs, but my chest muscles refused to function properly. I'd seen this before, I thought hazily. Someone else had been sick like this—but who?

Then the memory of Dora Clemens's body, writhing in agony, came crashing back to me. I'd been poisoned! Somehow, Adelina French must have slipped poison into my coffee.

"Poison," I gasped, fighting to speak.

"What is it, Sarah?" Robert asked, leaning his ear close to my mouth. "What are you trying to tell us?"

"Adelina—poisoned me. It must be—poison must be in her reticule."

I felt my brother's fingers pressing against my wrist, then everything went blessedly black.

The room I awoke in was not my own. Two figures sat by my bedside, but several moments passed before I recognized them as my parents. I tried to speak, but my mouth felt as if it were filled with cotton.

"Shh, darling, don't try to talk," Mama said, reaching over to kiss my cheek.

"You need to rest, my girl," Papa told me, his voice strangely tight.

Comforting hands adjusted my covers as I closed my eyes and drifted off to sleep. When next I awoke, I found my mother and Samuel holding vigil by my bed.

"It's about time, sleepyhead," my brother joked, looking pleased to see me awake.

"Sarah, darling, how do you feel?" Mama asked.

Again I tried to speak, but no words came out. Seeing me struggle, Mama held a glass of water to my parched lips. Gratefully, I took a small sip, but when I tried to drink more, she took the glass away.

"Charles says you are to have only a few small sips at a time. I'll let you have more in a few minutes. Now, how is your head?"

I tried lifting up from the pillow and was jolted by a stab of pain. "Where am I?" I managed, sinking back onto my pillow.

"At the new Women and Children's Hospital, my

dear," Mama answered. "They even gave you a private room."

"The board members insisted you be brought here," Samuel explained. "They maintain that without you they might have been forced to close the hospital. It turns out that Adelina and her lover boy managed to steal over fifty thousand dollars from the fund. No wonder Lucius Arlen was so concerned about the budget."

"Where are they?" I managed to croak. "Adelina and Prescott."

"In jail, I'm happy to say." He grinned. "You must have broken at least twenty rules of protocol in that courtroom. If you hadn't fainted dead away, I think Judge Carlton would have tossed you into a cell with those two and thrown away the key."

"I hardly remember any of it," I murmured.

Tears sprang into Mama's eyes. "You were deathly ill, darling. We could have lost you—we almost *did* lose you. Don't you ever, ever do that to us again!"

I was overcome by an intense sense of guilt at having caused my family such pain. Looking more closely at my mother, I detected new worry lines around her eyes and mouth. I had done that, I thought. I was responsible for each and every one of those lines.

Undoubtedly guessing what was on my mind, Samuel shook his head at Mama and went back to his story.

"When you collapsed, little sister, Adelina and Prescott made a run for it. The court was in such chaos

312

they probably would have made it, too, if two Chinamen hadn't bounded out of nowhere to grab hold of them."

I tried to ask another question, but he held up a hand. "No more questions, Sarah. Just listen. You're supposed to be saving your voice."

He sat back in his chair and crossed one perfectly creased trouser leg over the other. "On the judge's order, one of the bailiffs grabbed Adelina's reticule, and lo and behold, there was the poison she'd used on you. Turns out it was jimsonweed, the same stuff she'd used on Halsey. Once Charles knew what you'd been given, he started treating you immediately." Samuel's handsome face grew solemn. "Even so, it was nip and tuck. You gave us all one hell of a scare, little sister."

I tried to say something, but my eyes had become heavy weights. I don't remember falling back to sleep, but when I again awoke, it was to find Robert sitting by my bedside. Lily Mankin was also there, placing a cool cloth on my forehead.

I tried to swallow, but couldn't quite manage enough saliva to do the job. Lily noticed my discomfort and brought a glass of water to my lips.

"Just a bit now," she cautioned, helping me raise my head.

"I keep falling asleep," I said hoarsely. "What—what day is it?"

"It's Thursday afternoon," Lily told me. "You've been sleepin' the better part of three days. And lookin' better for it, too." She smiled, and I saw tears welling in her eyes. "And thank the good Lord for that. The children and me—well, you're like family, miss. We couldn't bear to lose you."

Lily wiped her eyes and gave us a bright smile. "I'll leave you to talk, then. But I'll be back soon enough with supper. Real food tonight, mind you. Cook insisted on cookin' you somethin' special, you savin' his life an' all."

I looked questioningly at Robert after she left. "Cook?"

"Yes, believe it or not, Chin's back in the kitchen, as churlish and bossy as ever. The hospital board said that after all he'd been through, the least they could do was offer him his old job. Providing, of course, that he promised not to pocket another penny from his kitchen allowance."

"How is—Margaret?" I managed.

"No one knows. She's been in seclusion since her mother and Prescott were arrested. It must be hard for the poor woman. Her world has more or less come crashing down around her head."

"Yes," I said hoarsely. My deepest regret was the anguish I'd put poor Margaret through on the stand. It had been a necessary ploy to trick her mother into confessing, yet I doubted she would ever fully forgive me. I couldn't blame her; given the circumstances, I would probably feel the same deep hurt and sense of betrayal. "And Judge Barlow?"

"Humph. Adelina's little courtroom announcement made the front page of every newspaper in town, side by side with his mother-in-law's alleged murders. Of course sweatshops aren't illegal, but it looks damn bad when a prominent judge turns out to own an entire string of the places. It looks especially bad when one of them burns to the ground and, because of his negligence, kills five people in the process."

"Has Adelina—" I was forced to stop for another sip of water. "Has she admitted killing Caroline and Halsey, then?"

"She isn't admitting anything. Ever since her incarceration, she's been blaming her late lamented love for everything. She says Prescott put her under some sort of diabolical spell." Robert chuckled. "A little late, I'd say, but probably the best she could come up with after all the mouth-wagging she subjected us to in court. I'm guessing that will be her defense." He grunted derisively. "As Shakespeare so aptly put it: 'There is nothing more dangerous than a woman scorned.'"

"Do you think the jury will buy it?"

"I try never to second-guess a jury, but there's a lot of evidence against her. To begin with, the police found a box of nitroglycerine pills in her bedroom. The theory is that she ground up some of these tablets and dropped them into Caroline's soup the night of the charity dinner. You said the soup course had already been served when you entered the dining room. Well, Adelina must have gotten there first and carried out the dirty deed before there were any witnesses. Her pills, together with the nitroglycerine Charles administered during her attack, were more than enough to provide a fatal dose."

"And Halsey?"

"So far they've found nothing to connect Adelina to his murder except a damn good motive—the fact that he was trying his best to close down the source of her ill-gotten gains. And, of course, there's the jimsonweed they found in her reticule. They're searching for anyone who might have seen Halsey and her together that Sunday. My guess is, Adelina somehow convinced Halsey to meet with her, then managed to slip the poison into his coffee. Just as she did into yours."

I lay for several minutes thinking about how close I had come to dying. I, who prided myself on being such a shrewd judge of character, had been taken in by a sweet face and grandmotherly manner.

"I should have seen it sooner," I said, feeling terrible that my blindness might have resulted in two unnecessary deaths. "Lucius Arlen and Dora Clemens might still be alive if I'd put it together sooner. The day Margaret showed me Adelina's garden and told me how knowledgeable she was with herbs and plants, I should have seen a connection. But Mrs. French seemed so gentle and loving, it never occurred to me she might be a vicious killer."

"Don't start, Sarah. You figured it out sooner than anyone else, including San Francisco's finest."

"You know, if Adelina hadn't mentioned jimsonweed while we drank our coffee the last day of the trial, I'm not sure I ever would have suspected her. Remember,

Robert, the police deliberately withheld the name of the poison that killed Halsey."

"That's right, I'd forgotten! We knew because Charles was privy to Halsey's autopsy report. But there was no way Mrs. French could have named that poison unless she'd given it to him herself."

"It struck me as strange that the morning after we toured the hospital, Adelina suffered an arthritic attack—a spell that just happened to prevent Margaret from visiting Arlen at his rooms. But at the time I thought it was just a coincidence."

Robert's mouth twisted into an ironic smile. "Adelina must have been madder than hell when she realized she'd misjudged the amount of poison she'd given Arlen. That must have been a hard day and a half for her while he lingered on. She certainly didn't make the same mistake with poor Dora. Or with you."

"No, she didn't," I said, flooded by memories of the poor maid's death and how close I had come to sharing the same fate. "Thank God she's finally behind bars."

"I agree." His eyes grew serious. "But I've a bone to pick with you, Sarah Woolson. If you ever expect me to join you in another courtroom, I want your solemn word you'll warn me—in advance—what bombshells you plan to pull out of that overimaginative mind of yours."

"I'm sorry, Robert, but there wasn't time—"

"Then you *make* time, Sarah. You take me aside and tell me what the hell you're up to."

"Even when I've just been poisoned and—"

"Here we go," Lily interrupted, coming into my room bearing a covered tray. By now, the widow had grown so large with child she was forced to hold her burden straight out in front of her. Chin bustled in closely behind her carrying another tray, which he set in front of Robert.

"You eat, too," he told the Scot, as Lily delivered my own tray to the bed.

"Oh my!" Lily exclaimed as Robert and I lifted the lids off our plates. Turning a little green, she clapped a hand to her mouth and ran quickly from the room.

I didn't blame her. Curled around the circumference of my plate was a shiny black creature that looked for all the world like a snake. Inside the circle this created were white rice and several other strange-looking globs of food I couldn't identify. Robert's plate was similarly arranged.

Chin beamed at our startled expressions. "You not get food like this before, I say. Fresh eel, just kill myself." He pointed to a pile of deeply browned morsels. "Deep fry grasshopper. Very good." Finally, he pointed to an unappetizing mass of something I couldn't begin to describe. "Fungus," he told us with a broad grin. "Chinese call it cloud ears. And this bean curd. It sit on bed of seaweed. You try, you like."

He stood there watching us, pride written all over his usually ill-tempered face. Robert and I looked at each other, not quite sure what to do. Not wishing to hurt his feelings, I tried a bit of white rice and found it had been steamed to perfection.

I will be forever grateful that Chin's duties called him back to the kitchen before I was forced to sample anything else on my plate. In fact, he was hardly out of sight before Robert scooped the contents of both plates into one of my empty pillowcases and threw it under the bed.

"I'll take it with me when I leave," he said, making a face. "I suppose the fellow means well, but my God, have you ever seen anything so disgusting?"

There was movement from the doorway and Charles entered carrying his medical bag. "Well, you look a good deal livelier today, Sarah. How do you feel?"

I shot Robert a look, then smiled at my brother. "Other than a sore throat and a dry mouth, I'm fine. It seems I owe you my life."

"I think, my dear Sarah, you owe your life to the fact that you didn't finish all the coffee Mrs. French managed to poison. Thankfully, the restaurant was slow to wash their dishes that morning, and we were able to analyze what was left in your cup. Mrs. French gave you enough jimsonweed to kill an elephant."

I felt the blood drain from my face. "Oh," I said rather inadequately.

Charles smiled. "Now, my dear sister, I have a little surprise for you. It seems you have a visitor. A most unusual visitor."

I was considerably taken aback when Charles ushered Li Ying into my room. The tong lord bowed deeply, then placed a large package at the foot of my bed.

"I am pleased to note your remarkable recovery, Miss Woolson," he said, favoring me with a warm smile. He turned politely to Robert and executed a slightly less pronounced bow. "Mr. Campbell, it is an honor to see you again."

"What brings you here, Mr. Li?" Robert asked warily.

To my delight—and to Robert's consternation—Li burst out laughing. "Please, Mr. Campbell. Unlike the infamous Trojan Horse, I have not come here under false pretenses. The sole purpose of my visit is to pay my humble respects to a brave and exceedingly noble young woman."

Turning to my brother, he said, "You must be most proud of your sister, Mr. Woolson. She possesses the heart of a lion and the courage of ten dragons."

"Perhaps she would be better off with a few less dragons, Mr. Li," Charles answered with a wry smile. "She tends to be a bit foolhardy at times."

"Ah, but did not the Greek philosopher Plutarch say, 'If all men were just, there would be no need of courage'? It is gratifying to find someone willing to champion those who would otherwise receive little justice in this world."

Robert gave a little grunt, but at a look from me, kept silent.

"I must, however, offer you my sincere apologies," Li went on more soberly. "It is I who inadvertently put your life in danger when I requested you represent Mr. Chin. Please believe me when I say I had no idea it would prove such a perilous undertaking. I shall not soon forget what you have done, Miss Woolson." He again bowed deeply, then was gone as quickly and silently as ever.

"That man gives me the creeps," Robert said. "I have the feeling he knows more about me than I know about myself."

"He probably does," I said, using my foot to nudge Li's package closer. "Let's see what he brought."

Robert and Charles watched as I opened the box, which was beautifully wrapped in delicate, hand-painted rice paper. When I pulled off the top of the box, I could only stare in shock at what lay inside.

"Well, what is it?" Robert demanded.

With the utmost care I lifted out—one exquisite piece at a time—the magnificent tea service I'd admired on my last visit to Li Yin's home.

"My God!" Charles exclaimed. "It's exquisite. The set must be worth a fortune."

"Its worth can't be measured in money," I whispered. Tears filled my eyes as I held one of the diminutive teacups in my hands. "It belonged to Li's father."

No one spoke for several moments, all of us dumb-struck at the incalculable value of such a gift.

Robert broke the spell. Examining the various pieces, he said, "There's something stuck inside the tea kettle."

He was right; a white envelope lay nearly hidden beneath the delicately curved rim of the vessel. Care-fully I pulled it out and cut open the flap.

My breath caught in my throat. Inside the envelope was the thickest stack of money I had ever seen in my life!

CHAPTER FOURTEEN

Sarah Jacqueline Mankin entered the world one week after I was discharged from the hospital. According to Lily, little Jackie was already living up to her late father's and her godmother's names, with Jack's bright, quick blue eyes and my inquisitive, impatient nature. I wasn't sure I entirely agreed with this assessment, but I was far too besotted with my godchild to care what anyone said.

As I stood with Robert in the church the day of her christening, holding our godchild between us, I was filled with a remarkable feeling of peace. The infant, who had been loudly protesting all the folderol, suddenly stopped crying to study her godparents with bright-eyed curiosity and then, wonder of wonders, a little smile. Robert says this is fanciful, that a four-week-old baby is incapable of recognizing anyone and certainly is too immature to smile. But I know what I saw—and I am not given to whimsy. I recalled the words of the old nursery rhyme—Thursday's child has far to go. Well, little Sarah Jacqueline Mankin had been born on a Thursday, and I've no doubt whatsoever that she is destined to go very far indeed!

It pleases me to report that her mother has come a considerable distance herself. Emily Harbetter confided to me that, in time, she was sure Lily would become a skilled and dedicated nurse.

"She has intelligence and a cheery nature," the head nurse pronounced. "Most importantly, she possesses an innate love for people. A little love goes a long way when you're trying to help someone heal."

I remembered Lily's kind ministrations when I was in the hospital. "Speaking from my own experience," I told Nurse Harbetter, "I heartily concur."

After exhaustive soul-searching, I decided that I, too, was ready to spread my wings and fly. The day after little Jackie's christening, I crossed Kearney Street, took the familiar rising room to the sixth floor, and opened the solid oak doors of Shepard, Shepard, McNaughton and Hall for the last time. I had chosen a morning when Robert would be out of the office. He was not pleased with my decision to leave; in fact, he had done everything possible to change my mind. I held firm to my resolution. In my heart I knew it was time to set off on my own.

Stopping first at my office, I packed what few personal items I had collected over the past nine months, then looked around, surprised to feel a twinge of nostalgia. I had expected to experience nothing but relief in putting Shepard's firm behind me. But this had been my first office in my first legal practice; even I couldn't pretend this counted for nothing.

One thing I would not miss was the abominable

Caligraph machine, still perched, like the instrument of torture it was, on the side of my desk. I paused to wonder who had taken over its care and feeding since I'd been in the hospital, then had to smile. It was true. Ever since the typebar machine had invaded my sanctuary, I'd regarded it as a living, hateful adversary I'd have to tame, or die myself in the attempt. With some humor I could finally admit that, although I hadn't actually expired from the effort, the machine had never been in slightest danger of being tamed!

At eleven o'clock precisely, I entered Joseph Shepard's office. Although I had won my first court case—a murder trial, at that—I did not expect a gracious greeting from my employer. Nor was I disappointed. In Shepard's opinion, I had once again shamed the firm beyond redemption. Chin's trial, with its dramatic and frenzied climax—involving as it did the cream of San Francisco society—had made the front page of every newspaper in the state, perhaps even the nation. Suffice it to say, Joseph Shepard's manner toward me that morning fell considerably short of enthusiastic.

"You have done it again, Miss Woolson," he growled. "You have made not only yourself, but my firm, a subject of derision and scorn."

"May I remind you, sir, that we won our case?" I commented, realizing even as I said it the effort would be futile.

"If that is your idea of a successful conclusion," he retorted, "I pray I will not be around to see you fail."

"This must be your lucky day then, Mr. Shepard, because your prayer has been answered." I removed a signed sheet from my briefcase and placed it before him. "I have come to tender my resignation."

It was difficult not to laugh aloud at his expression. It was as if he couldn't make up his mind whether to jump for joy or have me examined for mental incompetence.

He regarded me with suspicion. "No attorney in his right mind would voluntarily leave the most prestigious law firm in San Francisco. Especially a female. You realize there isn't another legal office in this city that will have you." A new thought came to him. "Don't tell me you've finally come to your senses and are prepared to assume a woman's rightful role as wife and mother?"

"You may set your mind at ease, Mr. Shepard, I have come to no such conclusion. On the contrary, I have decided to establish my own practice."

"You have what?" His beady eyes appeared in danger of popping off his pudgy face. "Is this some kind of joke? Your own practice? Such an idea is—is patently impossible! No one will consult with a woman. You'll have no clients!"

I regarded him serenely. "I believe that is my problem, Mr. Shepard, not your. Oh, I almost forgot." Reaching into my briefcase, I brought out an envelope. "Here is the firm's portion of Mr. Chin's final payment. Since you did not see fit to assist me financially during his defense, I have deducted expenses incurred during the trial. I've included a detailed account of these costs."

His mouth opened in astonishment as he peered inside the envelope. But when he again looked up to me, I saw his wariness had returned.

"You are new to the legal profession, Miss Woolson. Please understand that you must leave behind any clients you may have served during your months with us."

He referred, of course, to one of the firm's most affluent clients, a young widow I had successfully represented in connection with the Nob Hill murders.

"I shall make no attempt to contact any of my prior clients," I told him. "On the other hand, if they should seek my services on their own account, I will, at my discretion, decide whether or not I care to represent them."

"You can't do that. It's unethical. It's dishonest. I'll have you disbarred!"

He began that irritating noise at the back of his nose. Realizing that, blessedly, I would never be forced to listen to one of his childish fits of pique again, I smiled.

"That is a preposterous threat, and you know it. As long as I do nothing to persuade my former clients to leave your firm, you have no say over whom I represent."

I gathered up my briefcase. "Despite our disagreements, Mr. Shepard, I've decided not to hold your petty, mean-spirited and prejudiced opinions against you. I shall endeavor, therefore, to keep my true feelings about your firm to myself."

With an amazingly light heart, I wished him a good day, closed the door on his outraged sputtering and departed Shepard, Shepard, McNaughton and Hall for the last time.

P ierce Godfrey paid a surprise visit to my house that evening. He had visited me in the hospital, but this was the first time I'd seen him since my release. As was frequently his habit, he wore a frock coat that perfectly matched his midnight-blue eyes, while his dark tan trousers emphasized a narrow waist and long, powerful limbs. His chiseled features and long black hair—pulled back into a horsetail at his nape—once again put me in mind of a pirate standing at the helm of his ship, setting off on a voyage of adventure and ill-gotten riches.

As it turned out, this guess was uncannily close to the truth. As we sat on the back parlor sofa enjoying cups of brandy-laced coffee—the lights of the city twinkling below us like so many fireflies—he informed me he would be leaving the following day to set up a shipping office in Hong Kong. His brother, Leonard, planned to hire someone to take over the San Francisco operation, at least while Pierce was in the Orient.

"I know your low opinion of me, Sarah," he said, flashing that irresistible smile of his. "But I couldn't leave without saying goodbye and thanking you for all you've done for my company."

His eyes softened, and his entire persona seemed to alter with that one small change. Suddenly his gaze was far too intimate for my liking. To my annoyance, he seemed to read my thoughts.

"Is my being here making you nervous, Sarah?" His dark blue eyes were twinkling now, as if at some private joke. I decided I didn't like them any better this way than when they were overly familiar.

"Is there something on your mind, Pierce?" I asked, shifting my weight to put more distance between us.

"There's always something on my mind when I'm around you, Sarah," he said, his tone sending unwelcome shivers down my spine. "More often than not, those thoughts have nothing whatsoever to do with business."

I tried to move even farther away from him but found my back pressed against the sofa arm. This did nothing to lessen my uneasiness. "Pierce, if there's something you want to say, for heaven's sake say it."

With no warning he took my hand, smiling when I jumped in surprise. "All right, Sarah, right to the point, then. I've come here tonight to ask you to marry me."

My mouth fell open and I was too shocked to close it.

"I can't guarantee you the safety and stability you're accustomed to," he went on. "On the other hand, I can promise that our life will be a great adventure."

"You can't be serious," I finally managed. "I'm far too outspoken and opinionated—we'd be fighting all the time."

"Good," he said, not in the least put off by this possibility. "We'll never be bored."

"Pierce, think about it. We both want different things from life. You love the sea and I love the law. I'll admit I've grown fond of you, but it just wouldn't work."

He looked at me for a long moment, and I was afraid my words had hurt him. Being new to this proposal business, I'd gone about it all wrong. Belatedly, I realized I should have been more sensitive in my response.

To my consternation, he began to chuckle, and I was furious to see the twinkle back in his eyes.

Jumping off the sofa, I exclaimed, "What are you playing at, Pierce? If you meant that proposal as some kind of joke, it wasn't funny."

To my surprise, he reached for my hand and pulled me back down beside him. He whispered in my ear, "I meant every word I said, Sarah. I can't think of another woman I'd rather have as my wife. I'm only laughing because I was so sure that's what you'd say. You're so refreshingly straightforward. That's one of the things I love most about you."

His eyes never left mine as he slowly leaned over and kissed me on the lips. To my surprise, I found myself kissing him back. It was a heady, surprisingly enjoyable sensation. I admit I felt rather sorry when it came to an end.

Smiling, Pierce poured another healthy dollop of brandy into our cups, then held his up for a toast.

"To you, Sarah Woolson, and your brilliant career as

an attorney. May you have countless more victories to celebrate."

I clinked my cup on his. "And to our continued friendship, Pierce Godfrey. No matter where your life of adventure leads you."

Robert kindly helped me move into my new office. It had taken me nearly a month, but I'd finally found two rooms that, although smaller than I would have wished, would serve the purpose. They were located above a lady's millinery shop on Sutter and Montgomery streets, an excellent part of town for a new attorney to set up private practice. Best of all, thanks to Li Ying's generous gift, I was able to afford the rent, at least for the first six months. If I had not attracted a modest clientele by then, well, I would cross that bridge when I came to it.

Actually, I'd won my first case before I'd even opened the door to my new office. Shortly after I was released from the hospital, I filed suit against Judge Barlow on behalf of Lily Mankin and the families of the other victims who had lost their lives in the sweatshop fire.

It came as no great surprise when Judge Barlow showed no desire to air his dirty linen in public. He was already under considerable fire from the press, not to mention the judicial system. Eager to salvage what little he could of his tarnished reputation, he sold off all his sweatshops and begged to settle our lawsuit out of court. My clients received a generous recompense for the loss of their loved ones. It was hardly a fortune, but it would pay the rent, put food on the table and ensure an adequate education for those children who wished to pursue their learning.

Lily Mankin now had sufficient funds to move out of the hospital and into a flat of her own, but in the end she chose to remain where she was. Not only did her three older children love their new home, but Lily was assured of continuous child care, enabling her to pursue her training as a nurse.

While Robert applauded my win over Judge Barlow, the victory had not been enough to persuade the attorney to leave Shepard's firm and become my law partner. Stubbornly, he insisted he had no desire to keep me company in poverty and starvation.

"It's not that I doubt your ability," he assured me, slightly out of breath from rearranging my new (well, new to me, at least, since all my office furniture was secondhand) cherry wood file cabinet for the third time. "I just don't think this city is ready for a female lawyer. You live at home with your parents, so if you fail you'll still have a roof over your head. I don't have that luxury." He stood back and ran an arm over his forehead. "I hope you're satisfied with that cabinet where it is now, Sarah, because I'm not moving it again."

Eddie, who was also assisting in my move into my new office, looked at the Scot in surprise. "Why'dja wanna say a thing like that, Mr. Campbell? Miss Woolson could never fail. She can do anythin' she sets her mind to."

The young cabbie was perched on the edge of the

heavy, almost matching cherry wood desk, which had, to Robert's immense relief, required only two location changes before meeting with my approval.

"Thank you, Eddie," I said, trying not to let him see my amusement. Being looked up to as a demigod, even by a fifteen-year-old boy, was a new experience for me. "I have no intention of failing. That's a terrible attitude, Robert."

"It's reality, Sarah. San Francisco is filling up with lawyers faster than you can say 'jurisprudence.' Every arriving boat and train spews out another bushel of them. How can you hope to compete with that?"

"Cream always rises to the top, Robert," I replied, placing a vase of cut flowers on a cherry wood table opposite my desk. As I stepped back to judge the effect, I added, "I shall compete by offering exceptional service for a reasonable fee."

That elicited a loud guffaw from my former colleague. "As I said, living in your parents' home has its advantage."

I started to retort, when I heard footsteps running up the flight of stairs from the street. A moment later, a young boy about Eddie's age came bursting into my office. He slid to a stop when he saw me and, looking a bit pink in the face, quickly scooped his cap off his tousled hair.

"Is there something I can do for you?" I asked, regarding him questioningly.

The boy's eyes went to Eddie, then to Robert, and finally back to me. "I, ah, I come to see you, miss."

"To see me?" I repeated in surprise.

Eddie slid off my desk. "This here's Archie, miss, a pal of mine from the cab company. I told him you was just the person to help him."

Eddie was eyeing me with such faith, I decided being a demigod had a downside. "I'll do my best, Archie. What seems to be the problem?"

Archie's expression was one of fear mixed with hope. "It's this way, miss. I had this gent in my cab yesterday. Today he comes back sayin' he left his wallet on the seat and that I must of took it. Says he's gonna go to the police. But I didn't take it, miss. I swear I didn't."

Robert, who'd remained silent since Archie's entrance, chuckled and moved toward the door.

"I think you've just been handed your first cup of cream, Sarah," he said. "Be sure you give exceptional service. Oh, and don't spend your reasonable fee all in one place."

His laughter echoed all the way down the stairs to the street.

HISTORICAL NOTE

After receiving several inquiries regarding the role of the San Francisco Coroner's Office in the early 1880s, I decided a brief history of this noble, if not always pleasant, institution would not come amiss.

It is a matter of record that the San Francisco Coroner's Office came into being in 1850. While it is true that not all coroners in the state are physicians, I'm proud to boast that since 1857, starting with J. M. McNulty, M.D., San Francisco has solely selected medical doctors for this position. In fact, Levi L. Dorr, M.D.—the coroner who appears in this narrative— served in that office from 1878 to 1882.

As early as 1830, chemical analysis could detect most mineral compounds during an autopsy, although not organic poisons. By 1851, however, Jean Servais Stas, a Belgian chemist, discovered a process for extracting alkaloid poisons from postmortem tissue. Since then, the science of detecting poisonous sub- stances in victims thought to have met with foul play has steadily improved.

I am pleased to add that since its humble beginning in 1850, the San Francisco Coroner's Office has become a forerunner for such systems throughout the state of California, if not the country.

Yours sincerely,
Sarah Woolson

Center Point Publishing
600 Brooks Road ● PO Box 1
Thorndike ME 04986-0001 USA

(207) 568-3717

US & Canada:
1 800 929-9108

```
FIC                    Large Print
Tal
 M


The  Russian  Hill  murders.



          SPENCER COUNTY PUBLIC LIBRARY
          210 WALNUT
          ROCKPORT, IN  47635-1398




                                    DEMCO
```